SECRETS OF SUNSHINE

BENJAMIN R. NYSSE

www.ten16press.com - Waukesha, WI

For information, please contact:

www.ten16press.com
Waukesha, WI

Edited by Lauren Blue
Cover art by Amy Kleinhans
Back cover photo compliments of Pewaukee School District

For Rose of Sheboygan,
whose stories continue to inspire us all.

The Secrets of Sunshine - Abby Whitworth

They are hiding in the cracks
Between the walls. On paths
Blanketed with pine straw
So soft, I can wander seemingly
Unnoticed, as I sneak up
On feelings too quick for thoughts.

The new moon breeds a darkness
So complete, each star
Defines itself, hiding worlds unknown
Like the whispers he speaks in my ear
While we lie together alone.

Now, new lines emerge
To contain our lives
On grassy fields bound
By rules beyond my control.
He flows smoothly, cutting,
Jumping, like a deer in the woods
Dodging trees, darting
Into the unknown.

The secrets of sunshine
Are hidden from me.
Kept safe in the knowledge
That if he is with me,
I know all I need to know.
The morning water, clear
In its stillness,
Lets me see the truth
Hidden beneath the calming ripples.

CHAPTER 1

Abby hunkered in her room, comfy in her own bed at six thirty in the morning, scanning a poem she had written the night before. Ever since she had to compose a few poems for English class her first semester of college, it had taken hold of her. She wrote to process what she was going through. She wrote to let herself dream. She wrote to bring herself home. But now that she was home, wrapped in the forest of her dreams, sitting in her own room filled with pictures of the lake and her friends, she couldn't escape the idea that something was missing.

Looking for Craig

I feel like I've lost something.
Maybe not lost, I just can't
Find what I'm looking for.
You know that feeling
When you lose your keys
Or can't find that one
Piece of paper you need?
That's the feeling. Lost for now,
But I know it's here, somewhere.
If I keep looking,

Turning over every pillow,
Straightening every cushion,
Putting everything in its place,
Then, I will find what
I need more than anything.
Then, I will find you.

Abby liked the poem, but it didn't seem finished. It probably wouldn't be until Craig came to the resort the following week. For now, despite being home and safe in her favorite place in all the world, the burden of her daily schedule was descending upon her. There was so much to do, and Claire was arriving that afternoon. Abby clutched a postcard Craig had sent her from Chicago that she kept tucked under her pillow. He had gone to help Claire move her things into storage the weekend after Abby left school. She read it over again.

Hey Abby, I'm sitting here having lunch down by the river in Chicago thinking of you as the water slowly runs by. I can't wait to come up north. It's going to be a great summer. Miss you. Love you,
   Craig

Abby stood up from her bed and went to her desk to stick the card to her memory board, right next to the leaves pressed in wax paper that Craig had given her before she left for the summer. On one of the leaves, the words "I Choose Her" were written. As she read that promise each morning, Abby felt confident and sure about where she and Craig had worked their way back to over the past few weeks. However, it was time to get to work, and her list was long. She wanted to have time to show Claire around when she arrived. Excited by the prospect of a new visitor, Abby went out to the kitchen.

"Abby, you have to get over to the office and meet your dad. You're already running late. I have to get to work. Vacation hasn't started for some of us," her mother snapped.

Rolling her eyes, Abby grabbed a piece of toast. "Ok, Mom. I'll see you later. I'm off to work too." She said the last sentence as sharply as she could. Abby knew her mother still had a week and a half of school left, but her work was just beginning. She hoped her mother would break out of her dismal mood when school finally let out for the summer.

As Claire pulled into the resort in the late afternoon, the lot was half full, and after a trip around the entire parking lot, she found the driveway to Abby's home. The world was in full bloom. The smell of pine trees filled the air, and the flowers all seemed to stand straight on this sunny day. There was a freshness to the place that Claire suspected would be there, and that suspicion was now confirmed in vivid colors. She parked her new VW Jetta, which she had received for college graduation, next to a large building near Abby's house. The irony of her willingness to accept some of the perks of her parents' wealth in the midst of her rebellion was not totally lost on her. The car made up for the fact that her graduation had barely been celebrated, unlike the year before when the family had a big party for Sarah.

No one was at the house, so she texted Abby. Almost immediately, Abby texted back that she would be over in a minute and Claire could let herself in. The exterior of the house was dark wood in a log cabin style. Nothing like this had ever been a part of Claire's world, especially not over the last four years living in Chicago. Walking to the door, Claire felt the gravel under her feet, and a pebble smarted her arch as it wormed its way into her flip flop. 'Might not be the best choice,' she thought, looking down at her feet. She went back to her car to get a different pair of shoes before entering the house.

Going in through the only door she could find, Claire walked down the hallway past the laundry room and two bedrooms. When she came to the great room, she was drawn to the floor-to-ceiling windows at the back of the house. Outside, a deck with a great view of the lake spread out before her. Claire went onto the deck, took out her camera, and snapped a few pictures, standing for a while just watching the lake sparkle in the sunlight. Some trees seemed to sway in the wind while others held their ground. The leaves were a vibrant green and punctuated by pine needles. Claire heard squeals of children through the woods to the right of the deck, and she assumed that was the direction of the resort. At this point, despite circling the parking lot, she was a bit turned around. Craig had told her a little about the place when he helped her move her stuff into the storage unit in Chicago, but really, she had no idea what the resort was all about. The only resorts Claire had ever visited were in Colorado, Florida, or Mexico. All of those places had a fakeness that was not hard to decipher. This place was real. Abby had sent pictures, but that was nothing like being immersed in it. Claire had learned well that immersion was the only real way to know about anything. When she went back into the house, she noticed the simple grandeur of the place: the stone fireplace with pictures of the family on the mantel, other pictures of the lake hanging throughout, and a staircase going to a lofted area with rooms behind it. There was a homey feel, and the room was straightened up, but not spit-shined clean. Claire liked that she could see how Abby's family really lived. Jackets draped over the backs of the dining room chairs, and a pair of very dirty boots sat by the door to the deck. This home had personality, unlike her own home in Hartland.

Claire waited only a few minutes until Abby arrived. She was wearing cut-off jean shorts and a "Wood Lake" T-shirt, and her hair was tied back with a bandana.

She ran right up to Claire and gave her a big hug, saying, "Hey there! How are you? How was the drive?" Abby was thrilled to have another person to talk with other than her parents and sister, Taylor, who was growing more annoying by the day. At least she was still in school, for now.

"It was fine. No problem finding the place." Claire was happy to see Abby in her element. There was a different air to her. She was relaxed yet energized.

"Did you do something different with your hair?" Abby asked, touching Claire's hair. It was cut short and dyed an orange-like red.

"Why yes, I did," Claire said with a little pose.

"It looks great." Abby giggled. "Let me show you around."

"That would be nice. I'm kinda lost already." Claire looked around the room. "You have a lovely home though."

"Thank you."

After Claire changed her shoes, Abby took her out by the deck and then down to the lake. She wanted to put the resort in the best light, and she enjoyed showing it off. "I might have to do some things along the way if you don't mind."

"No, not a problem. We could do the tour later if you like. Maybe when you're off work?" Claire looked out towards the lake, already seeing places where she would like to take pictures. But then, she heard Abby snicker. "What?" Claire innocently asked.

Abby smiled knowingly. "When I'm off work. That's funny."

Claire could not think of anything she said that was funny, so she replied, "Really? Why?"

Abby stopped walking and turned to face Claire. "Claire. I've only been home for a few days, but there is one thing you will learn quickly around here. I'm not off work until the work is done. And that is rarely." Claire nodded her head as Abby continued, "Come on. There's lots to see."

They walked through the woods along the lake, emerging by the beach and the main green space in front of the lodge. Claire could barely keep up as Abby talked about everything from the trees that were native to the area to the myriad of things to do in and around town for both guests and her family. A smile poured over Abby's face as she worked through her list of events and activities. Finally, they stopped as Abby began to straighten up some of the beach toys and sporting equipment out of habit. She didn't really need to do it, but it was there, and she preferred things to be in order. Claire helped her, and they made quick work of it. After they were done tidying up, Abby explained the different boating and water activities. There were two jet skis, a speedboat for skiing, a pontoon, and canoes. She told Claire that she would take people out on tours once or twice a day to take pictures and show them the lake. Even though Abby was not entirely comfortable in front of large groups, she could talk about the lake forever. They also had a boat launch for people who brought their own boats. Sometimes, if people were up early, she would take them fishing, although, she explained, she would rather go alone.

Claire listened intently, then looked out over the lake again. Only a few boats were out, but none were moving fast. They looked like fishing boats. "I would love to go around the lake on a picture tour," she said.

"Oh. I'll take you myself. It will be better than going with the group. No time schedule. We can go tomorrow on my boat. It's faster than taking the pontoon."

"That would be great!" Claire thought again about the new side of Abby she was witnessing. She felt that Abby was letting her in on a secret side of herself that she reserved for those who were close to her. The only other time Claire had seen her like this was when they stayed up late the first night Abby came to visit her house at Thanksgiving, but even then, she seemed reserved. Claire was on Abby's turf now.

Abby grabbed Claire's hand. "It's a date." Gently tugging, she continued, "Let's go up and see Frank. He's been waiting to meet you. My dad might be at the lodge too."

"Ok. Let's go." Claire could already tell that the life of the resort was exactly what she would need to get herself refocused and ready for graduate school in the fall. What she assumed were the easy rhythms of resort life would be a welcome relief from the hectic schedule of classes, art shows, and meetings with advisors that had filled the last few months.

The lodge deck was fabulous. Large and high off the ground, it was the perfect place for both a celebration and for reading a book in the late afternoon. However, from the sound of things, Claire didn't think there would be a lot of downtime to relax.

When Claire entered the lodge, she was struck by the stereotypic nature of the place. There was no attempt to run from the Northwoods. Instead, the lodge embraced the cliché: a large wood structure with trophy deer heads on the walls and a floor-to-ceiling stone fireplace. The bar was empty in the mid-afternoon, as well as the dining room. Abby explained that dinner service did not begin until five and it lasted until seven. Aside from a few kids in the game room upstairs, there was no one in the place, but smells filled Claire's nose. There was certainly activity in the kitchen.

Abby took Claire back towards the kitchen to meet Frank. Having people meet Frank was always exciting for Abby because she held him in the highest regard, and so far, anyone she felt was worth introducing to him, he had liked. She loved his approval. When they went into the kitchen, Abby called out and Frank emerged from the cooler.

"Hey, girl. Who do we have here?" He set down the packages he was carrying, picked up a towel, and walked towards them, wiping off his hands.

Abby turned and said, "This is Claire, Craig's sister. She's the artist."

"Oh, an artist you say. Ever done anything with food?" Frank asked. He was older than Claire imagined he would be, but there was an intensity about him that captured her immediately.

Claire smiled. "Why yes, I have. I can make some mean desserts."

His eyes twinkled as he broke into a smile. "Well, that's great! All I can make is pie."

"You can do more than that," Abby said jokingly.

"Not well. Want to make some desserts this summer?" Frank asked, finally reaching out and offering a hand to Claire, which she took in both of hers, gripping tightly.

"That would be fun, sir. Anytime." Claire loved the idea of a new challenge. She could tell she was going to like Frank. He had an inviting energy.

He let go of Claire's hand. "Call me Frank."

Nodding, Claire said, "Ok, Frank."

"Have you met John yet?" Frank asked with a serious tone.

"We spoke on the phone, but not in person."

"Sounds good." Returning to his cheerier demeanor, Frank continued, "Well, unless you girls are going to help, you best be moving on. I have to get prep done." He went back to his make table and sat down on a stool.

Abby spoke first. "I want to finish our tour and then we'll come back to help out. Is that ok?"

"Sure thing, girls."

They turned to leave, and just before they got to the door, Frank called out, "Hey, Claire!"

She turned to face Frank and smiled. "Yes?"

"You've got a heck of a brother. I really like that kid."

She smirked. "Yeah, I've heard he's pretty popular around here. I like him too."

Frank let out a laugh, and with that, the girls were off to the front desk to meet Vickie, and hopefully John.

The front of the lodge was very utilitarian. With a front desk, two chairs, and a few plants, this was not a place where guests were expected to spend much time. The most impressive part of the room was a large, four-by-six foot aerial picture of Wood Lake with the resort faintly circled. Claire narrowed her view on the picture until Abby said, "Let's meet my mom."

Behind the front desk, they found Vickie deep in her summer paperwork. She had just come home from teaching that day, but was already at the lodge to meet Claire. She often used summers and her other vacations to catch up on the batch of paperwork that John left neglected while he tended to other business. No one could really blame John since he and Frank basically ran the resort alone during the school year. All the maintenance and day-to-day chores were left up to them.

"Hi, Mom," Abby said.

Vickie looked up, adjusting her glasses and scanning the two girls, then her face lit up in a smile. "This must be Claire." She came out from behind the desk and gave Claire a hug. "It's so good to meet you."

After taking a step back, Claire responded, "It's nice to meet you too, Mrs. Whitworth." She snuck a look over at Abby, who was laughing quietly. The level of intimacy threw Claire a bit. Her family was certainly not affectionate with strangers.

"I'm so excited to have you here," Vickie said in a tone Claire found to be familiar, forced enthusiasm. Her own mother was the master of it.

"It's nice of you to have me. You have a lovely place."

Abby interrupted, "I'm going to find Dad."

"Fine, dear," Vickie said. "Claire and I have things to talk about." She took Claire off to talk while Abby went into the office to find her father.

After looking at the supplies in one of the storage closets,

Claire and Vickie discussed the different types of projects that had been done in the past and the responsibilities Claire would have running the arts program for the summer at the resort. It was a big undertaking, and Vickie had already purchased supplies that looked like they were used mostly for classroom art projects. Claire hoped to move beyond that a bit.

"Is there anything else you think you might need?" Vickie asked as she obviously looked Claire over for a second time.

Smiling knowingly, having been misjudged for her looks so many times before, Claire responded, "Not that I can see right now." She picked up some of the paints. "Is there an art supply store in town?"

"Yes. Abby's friend Meghan and her family own a store that sells art from local folks. You can order from them. We like to support local businesses, especially if they're friends."

"That's great," Claire said, turning to Vickie. "I'll have Abby make introductions. Mr. Whitworth gave me a budget, but with all of this, I'm sure I won't need to spend much."

"Well, it's settled then. We like to have the activity in the morning before lunch and then during afternoon recreation."

"That's what I was told. Around ten in the morning?" Claire wondered if John and Vickie actually talked or if this whole organization was done haphazardly.

"That's it. My, John was thorough."

"It seems so," Claire said. "That gives me a few days to get ready for next week. How's business if you don't mind me asking?" On the surface, this might be seen as an offensive question, but Claire had learned from her father that it's always best to get business out of the way at the beginning.

"Oh," Vickie said, putting a finger to her lips. "We're

booked from Memorial Day through Labor Day weekend. I think it will be a full house most weeks."

Nodding, Claire said, "Well, it will be an interesting summer. Thank you for the opportunity."

"It's our pleasure."

Meanwhile, in the office, Abby and John were discussing the week before Memorial Day weekend. About a third of the rooms were filled up for the week, but they were booked after that. The final cleaning and prep had to be done because after the coming week, it was buckle your boot straps until September.

Abby had been through the drill. What had to be done was clear. She simply had to agree with her father as he talked through his anxiety. He ran the place, but she was certainly second-in-command. There was a growing awareness that he was handing over more responsibility to her, but she was ready. She knew she could handle it.

"So, when is that boyfriend of yours coming up here?" John asked.

"Craig?" Abby responded, smiling.

"Well, unless you have another one we don't know about, yes, Craig. When is he coming?"

Abby could tell her father was stressed. He was curt with everyone and didn't like jokes or extended conversations.

"He will be here next Friday night."

John straightened up and looked directly at Abby. "Why so late?"

"His parents wanted him home for a week."

Nodding in acceptance, John continued, "Well, I hope he doesn't think he's coming up here on vacation. We have a lot of work to do this summer. I have some big projects planned."

"I've made him aware. He'll be ready to help."

"Good," John said, almost cheerfully.

Vickie walked in with Claire. "John, this is Claire, Craig's sister."

John stood to shake her hand. "It's nice to finally meet you in person."

A tall, strong, bearded man stood before Claire. He was lean, almost gaunt, but muscular, very different from her father. "Glad to meet you as well," she responded. John's formalism struck Claire as an extension of who he was. She picked up from the phone calls that he was a very serious man. Her initial impression matched what she was now observing. This man seemed to have very little time or patience for small talk.

"Vickie showed you the storeroom then?"

"Yes, sir."

"Need anything else?"

"Not for now, sir. But I'll have Abby introduce me to Meghan's mother. I'm sure we will come in well under budget."

"That would be nice," John said, shooting a quick glance at Vickie. She just smiled.

"Well, Abby, you need to show Claire the rest of the place and get her settled."

"Yes, Dad. Will do."

"It was nice to meet you again," Claire said as she and Abby walked out. John had already gone back to his desk.

"Sorry about my dad," Abby said as they reached the front desk area. "He's really stressed this time of year."

"Oh, no problem. This is a big undertaking. I doubt my father has ever worked a day in his life the way your dad works every day."

Abby felt the warmth and sincerity of Claire's comment. "Thanks. He does work hard."

They walked out the front door of the lodge and around the back to the cabin road.

Claire loved how all of the cabins were the same, but also had their own personalities. There were trees all around, and it was easy to see that only the trees that needed to be cut down to make room for the cabins had been removed. In the area she had grown up, the trees were largely clear-cut, and new ones had been strategically planted. Here, nature's randomness was barely interrupted, and the resort seemed as though it grew out of its surroundings. Looking closer, she noticed that each cabin was numbered with simple white paint on the side. This gave her an idea.

"You think your dad would mind if I made a sign for each of the cabins?" She was already pondering how she could attack the project.

"I don't think so. Sounds like fun."

They got down to a far cabin, off the water. It looked like it needed attention. One step was cracked, and overgrown shrubs surrounded the exterior.

"This is where you and Craig will be staying. It is a one-bedroom, but we put an extra bed in the living room," Abby said.

Claire looked it all over, walking the perimeter. 'Birch' was the name that came into her mind.

"No offense," Abby continued. "This is the farthest away

from the lodge, and it's usually the last to be filled."

"Oh, no problem," Claire said as she approached the steps. "I totally understand. It looks good." She knew this cabin needed care, and she intended to fix it up by the time she left.

They climbed the stairs of the little front porch. There was a swing hanging from the ceiling on one side of the door and two chairs with a small table on the other side. Claire could see the lake peeking through the other cabins and watch the setting sun.

"Let's go inside," Abby said as she unlocked the door. It was a bit musty inside, and she made a move to open windows. Claire caught on and began to help her, but then, she paused to look at the pictures on the wall.

She zoomed in on one of a fish under the water. "These are your pictures, right?"

"Yes. My dad has them hanging all over," Abby said, feeling a little embarrassed.

Claire noticed that there were issues with some of the lighting, but the framing was good. 'She really has an eye for landscapes,' she thought as her eye scanned the rest of the pictures.

"Come in here," Abby said from the bedroom. Claire followed her voice into a room with a bed covered in a green bedspread. There was a small closet, one dresser, and a separate entrance to the bathroom. More of Abby's pictures hung on the walls, but aside from that, there was little decoration.

"There are towels in the bathroom. If you need more, they are behind the office in the lodge. There's no laundry in the cabin, but you can always leave it in the laundry room in the lodge and get a new set."

Still looking around, Claire asked absentmindedly, "I can just do the laundry on my own, right?"

"Sure," Abby responded. "I can show you where the machines are later. There's also a small fridge in the kitchen area here and a stovetop and toaster oven."

Claire nodded. "Can I eat in the lodge?"

"Sure thing. Frank is cool with employees going and making their own food. Craig does that all the time when he's here."

"Good to know," Claire said.

"Do you want to see a few more things and then get your stuff? Parking in the lot would probably be closer."

"Let's do it," Claire said. "I'm going to check out the bathroom first."

"Ok. I'll meet you outside."

While washing her hands and running some water over her face, Claire thought again about how different Abby was at the resort. She was more confident, more alive. She seemed sure of every step. Claire smiled at the thought. Her brother had chosen someone outside of the norm, and in doing so, opened up a whole new world for himself, and her as well. Claire was determined to make this a good summer.

When she got outside, Abby took her to the end of the cabin road and showed her Frank's place. Claire immediately knew another sign would need to be made.

"The resort owns the next few hundred feet of shoreline, but it's mostly woods back there." Abby went on about the resort as they walked back to Claire's car, but Claire hardly said a thing. She was lost in the sights and pictures she couldn't wait to take.

Later that evening, Abby went back to her journal. She was working on a poem about Frank, and she only had a few lines so far:

When I returned for summer
There was a stool.
It followed him
Through the kitchen
Like a dog looking for scraps,
Always at his heels.
I wonder sometimes
How much more
He can take?

Abby was worried about Frank. He was different somehow, more tired, off a step. There were a few times he had forgotten to place items on a grocery list, and they had to switch the menu. He was even late for breakfast service a few times, Vickie had said, and John had stopped to ask if he was sick. But, he was the soul of the resort. No memory Abby held was free of his presence. She hoped Claire could bring him back to life and that her energy would do him some good. At least, on one level, Abby believed it could.

CHAPTER 2

Craig pulled into the driveway to find his usual parking spot next to the garage filled with a pile of bark chips. In lieu of this development, he parked at the end of the driveway behind his mother's spot because, he assumed, she would be home. It was strange to have a pile of chips sitting in the driveway because his father usually just hired people to do the landscaping. In fact, he usually hired a client so he could get a discount. It was a topic he could talk about with his father later. He wanted to get inside and get the week over with so he could get up north.

Craig had stayed a few extra days at school to see Abby off and meet with his education advisor to arrange possible field experience hours for the summer. He had also gone to Chicago another day to help Claire put even more of her things in storage. Her lease was up in May and she wasn't moving into her new apartment until the fall. Graduate school weighed heavily on her mind during the move and dominated the conversation. There were also a lot of questions about the resort. She had gone north that morning. In fact, she should already be there. He decided to get settled and then text Abby to see how Claire's first day had gone.

Craig went in through the garage and threw some of his stuff in the mudroom. He was surprised to find that his mother was not home. His sister Sarah and her new husband, Brad, lived in the same neighborhood, less than a mile away, so Linda must be there. 'How soon until that gets old?' he thought to himself. His father must have been forced to go along. Craig could only imagine how that conversation went. The Brewers were on tonight, and Craig expected his father would be entrenched in his chair with a few beers in him by now. Craig went to his room and dropped the rest of his stuff on the floor. He was only going to be home for a week. 'Seven days. I can make it.'

How was your day? Craig texted Abby, hoping to catch her at dinner. She was always so busy at the resort. Often their exchanges were after ten, when things began to wind down.

Good! You caught me just in time. I've got ten minutes before I need to help Frank clean up the kitchen.

Excited by the prospect of talking with Abby, Craig wrote, *K! Call me?*

His phone buzzed.

"Hey!"

"Hey. How are you?" Abby asked, almost breathless.

"Good. I just got home. Helped Claire again yesterday and spent the morning walking by the lake after she left, then had a late lunch before coming home. Traffic was horrible. Don't know why anyone would live there."

"I know. Claire made it up just fine."

"Good. How was her first day?"

"Good, I think. She met my parents and Frank."

Remembering his first meeting with Abby's parents, he asked, "How'd that go?"

"Well, she had talked to my dad already."

"I know. I heard."

Abby decided to blow off the last comment. "My mom did most of the talking when they met. And I think Frank's in love."

"I figured they would hit it off. Is she around?"

A tinge of jealousy was already developing in Abby with regards to Claire's ability to make fast friends with everyone. "No. She went to help Frank make some desserts."

"Making herself useful already."

"I think she'll fit in just fine."

"I'm sure."

"What are you going to do with yourself for a week?" Abby asked cheerfully, although it annoyed her to have Craig away from her for over a week.

"You know," he paused, "I really don't know. I think I'll go work out with some of the guys and play the role of the dutiful son."

"Oh, really?" Abby's sarcasm was fully engaged.

"I might go see Sarah too. She lives within walking distance, you know. I think my parents are there now."

Given the amount each McLean child complained about their parents, Abby found the whole Sarah living in the neighborhood situation very odd. "That will get old quick."

"You're telling me," Craig replied, smiling to himself.

"Well, I gotta go. There's a lot to do, as you know."

"Ok. Can't wait to come up there. It's going to be a great summer!"

"It's always a great summer. I can't wait to see you. Love you."

"Love you, too."

Craig was happy they had made their way back to "I love you." More and more, he had trouble seeing a life without Abby. He was determined to learn the resort this summer to show both her and her father that he could be in that future.

When Linda and Mike got home, Craig could hear Linda awash in her gossipy glory. She was going on about Sarah and Brad's neighbors and the rest of the subdivision. Craig knew his sister didn't want to rock the boat, but living under Linda's lens would be stifling.

After pausing on the steps to wait for his father to go into the basement, Craig walked into the kitchen to greet his mom. Without looking up she said, "You should go hang out with your father." Her tone left no room for compromise. "You're only home for a week. Both you and Claire…" She pursed her lips and shook her head. "What is it about that place? Don't want to come home anymore." She kept ranting to herself as Craig left the kitchen.

When he got into the basement, his father was surprisingly not in his chair with a beer. Instead, he was out in the backyard looking over the bushes that lined the back fence. Craig went out into the yard and walked over to him saying, "What's up, Dad? How was Sarah's?"

"It was good. She made some design decisions I would not have made, but it's her place. Lind…your mother loves it."

"That's good. I'll have to get over there in the next few days."

"Sarah would like that. You can walk. It's not that far."

Mike's demeanor was very subdued, and Craig didn't know what to make of it. Most of the time, his father was always either jacked up or asleep. This was not the Mike McLean Craig was used to.

"So, what's with the chips in the driveway? Going to have someone spread them?" Craig asked, trying to keep the conversation going.

"Yes. As a matter of fact, I was thinking you could do it before you went up north."

"That wouldn't be a problem," Craig said almost as a reflex.

Mike's head turned and cocked to the side. "Really?" he said sarcastically.

"Not a problem. I'll get started tomorrow." Craig was no longer bothered by physical tasks.

"There's a lot of them to spread."

"That's why I need to get started."

Mike walked over to Craig and patted him on the back. "Ok, son, let's go inside."

They stood at the bar. Mike fixed himself a lemonade and offered a drink to Craig. He declined. "So, are you and Claire getting paid for this summer?"

"Well, we get a cabin and food, and I think Claire is getting a stipend. I said I wouldn't take any pay. I think John will insist though." Craig leaned his arms on the bar.

"Well, that's noble of you, Craig, but if you're not getting paid, that might be weird. You know what I'm saying?"

"Yes. Maybe," Craig said plainly.

"Remember, you two are employees. I expect you to do a good job and be respectful. Finish what you start."

"I know, Dad," Craig said sternly. It annoyed him when his father struck an instructive tone.

"Do you have any other plans while you're up there?"

"I did get a lead on a strength and conditioning job at the high school for the summer."

"Really? What's that all about?"

"Well, I work out sometimes in the morning at the same time as the football team. I met this guy there named Will. He was also in my Intro to Ed class and mentioned that he was doing summer school up in Eagle River and getting field experience hours. He's doing hours in the summer so he can focus on football in the fall."

"So, is he getting paid?"

"Yes. He gets hours and gets paid."

"Sounds like a good deal to me." Mike took a big gulp of his lemonade. "Mom wants me to drink less. She said she'd get really pissed if I don't try. Not all bad, I guess." He finished the last of his glass in one swig and poured more in. Mike was a man of big appetites. "So, strength and conditioning…what would you be doing?"

"I think I would be working with the football team. Teaching them how to lift. I would just be an assistant."

"Like coaching them?" Mike seemed intrigued.

"I guess. I haven't told Abby or John. I hope he won't be angry. I don't officially have the job. It's just a lead."

Mike didn't seem to hear the last part of Craig's comment. "How long is it?"

"Just three hours in the morning. Four weeks."

"That's not too bad. I'm sure you could make up the time." Mike went under the bar and pulled out a bottle of wine, opening it and pouring a glass.

"You drink wine?" Craig asked.

"No. I poured it for you. I wanted to congratulate you on

your first year of college. With Sarah's wedding and all this shit with Claire, I didn't want you to think that we didn't notice what you had done."

Craig was confused. This was not his dad. Some other man had invaded his body. "Thanks?"

Mike poured a small glass for himself. "And Abby," Mike said, looking up to catch Craig's eye. "She's not the kind of girl we thought you'd be with, but you seem to be committed." He paused to breathe deep, and Craig stood stunned. Mike continued, "Treat her right, Craig. She's a nice girl. She's got a lot more figured out about her life than you do. She's a beautiful, confident young lady. Treat her right, you got me?" He reached his hand out and grabbed Craig by the shoulder.

"I will, Dad," Craig muttered and took a sip of his wine.

"I know you will." He patted Craig on the shoulder, downed his wine, and walked out from behind the bar and went upstairs.

Craig just stood at the bar and stared. His parents had seen more than they let on. He wondered why they had given him such a hard time before. Later, when he talked to his mother, he found out that his father had suffered a "heart episode," as she called it, shortly after they got back from spring break. She said he was fine, but changes needed to be made. Craig wasn't supposed to bring it up unless Mike brought it up first. She didn't want anyone to get all upset about anything. Everything was going to be alright. Craig noticed that his mother was repeating herself a lot and wondered if she was trying to convince herself more than him.

The next morning, Craig got up at six and went to check if his dad was smart enough to have borrowed a wheelbarrow and shovel. Mike had done one better. He had purchased new equipment. In addition to a shovel and wheelbarrow, there was a pitchfork and a pair of gloves.

Craig grabbed the gloves and pitchfork and walked around the property. There were several trees and two big berms in the front that needed chips. He decided to save the back bush line by the golf course until the end. 'Take care of what people can see first' was his thought. He pulled the wheelbarrow out and filled it up. After dumping too much by the first tree, he decided to spread each pile as he dumped it to conserve his chips. He got into a rhythm and the work came easy. Like chopping wood at the resort, the physical labor mixed with purpose provided satisfaction. By the time his father came outside, Craig was done with the entire front of the house and the chip pile had been reduced by half.

"Well, you've been busy. I thought you would be at this for a few days. If I let you keep going, you'll be done by noon."

"It's just work, Dad. Best to just get on with it."

"Is that what you learned up at that resort?"

"That and a lot more," Craig said with a smug look.

"Good," Mike replied. "Nothing like learning a work ethic."

"You taught me that."

"Ok," Mike laughed out. "Now, clean yourself up so we can go to the gym."

Usually, Craig would protest having to work out, but his dad needed support, and he was going to give it to him.

At the gym, the roles were reversed. Craig spent most of the time "encouraging" his father to keep moving from exercise to exercise while he also talked to some of the boys on the Whitewater football team who worked out at the same gym. Mike did well working through his personalized exercises and then went for a forty-five minute walk on the treadmill.

Craig took that time to get his lift in with Dan, a wide receiver from the Whitewater team.

"You ever think of playing again?" Dan asked as he stepped out from underneath the squat bar.

"Not really," Craig replied, smirking, not sure if he could lift the same weight as Dan.

"Why not, man? You were good! I could use you on the outside. I get doubled up all the time."

"It's been a year, man. I'm totally out."

"No. Come out and catch with us. I bet you could still run a heck of a route."

"I don't know."

"Just come hang out with the guys. We go out to the Pewaukee football field around seven some nights. It'll be fun."

"I'm only home for a week. Going to my girlfriend's resort to work this summer."

"Abby, right?" Dan said.

Surprised that he would notice enough to know her name, Craig replied, "Yeah, Abby. Her parents own a resort in Eagle River."

"That's cool. You should still come out this week."

"I'll think about it."

"Alright."

The rest of the lift went well. Craig was not at his usual numbers, but it felt good to work it through and get into a routine.

Later, Craig went to Sarah and Brad's for dinner without his parents. They lived around a mile away, so he walked. The opulence of the neighborhood was on full display. Unlike the summer before when Craig bounced from friend's house to friend's house without a thought, now, the extremity of the homes sickened him. He was no longer impressed by what type of car people drove or how big their pools and game rooms were. He was used to living with less. He just wanted to get north for the summer. The prospect of smaller dwellings and simple living was alluring.

A few loops down the road and he was at Sarah's house. When he walked in, Brad greeted him and turned with an arm out to show him around. He looked at Craig and shook his head. The blush on Brad's face showed Craig all he needed to know. The ceilings were high and the walls white and mostly unadorned. Despite the potential for light, Brad had the blinds drawn, and everything seemed dark.

"This is a really nice place," Craig said, his eyes searching for where it all ended.

Brad took a large breath in, then exhaled. "It's really too much, truth be told, but it will be a nice investment. Sarah loves it."

"That's good," Craig said, not sure how to respond. "Can you show me around a bit?"

"Sure. Not every room is furnished, but we've got a good start."

Brad wasn't lying. The living room, though brightened by floor-to-ceiling windows, was filled with patterned furniture, which seemed like a dated look to Craig, the kitchen contained stainless steel appliances with all the updates, and the upstairs family room, Brad explained, was his to decorate, but Craig could see his sister's influence in the choice of color and precise lines of the arrangement. Their bedroom was also done, and there was a bed in one of the other bedrooms for guests, but that was it. However, all the rooms had 42" flat screen TVs in them with surround-sound speakers. The only room in the basement that was finished was another family room, but it had a large leather sectional and a TV so large Craig felt he could climb into it if he were watching a football game. The rest of the bottom floor was all unfinished. Moving from a small apartment to a house was huge. Brad had been working at an investment firm since he finished his MBA, and Sarah worked as a trainer for the local gym Craig had been to with his father. In fact, she was the major player in trying to get their father back in shape. Mike had discussed it as they drove home. Craig listened to his father, and as his mother requested, he didn't pry. Much like Linda, Sarah was not to be denied.

"Sarah should be home in a minute. She just went to get a pizza and some beer. Do you want anything to drink?" Brad asked.

They had made their way back to the kitchen, and Craig sat down at the table. "I'll have a soda if you have one."

Brad looked in the fridge, which Craig saw was almost empty except for milk, eggs, and some strawberries. "Diet Coke ok?" Brad asked.

"Sure."

Brad tossed Craig the soda and got one for himself before coming to sit down.

"So, you're going up north for the summer? To your girlfriend's house? Sorry, what was her name again?"

"Abby," Craig said. He took a sip of his soda. "Yes, I'm going up there on Friday night to help with Memorial Day weekend and then staying the summer."

"Hmmm," Brad responded and took a big swig of soda. He had been around the family so long that Craig was used to him. They were never close, but he was a good guy. Brad was not an athlete. He played tennis and golf, but not seriously. Even for a casual dinner at home on a Saturday evening, he wore a polo shirt and ironed khaki shorts. However, he treated Sarah well, and that was all that mattered to Craig.

"What do they have you doing up there? Claire's there too, right?"

"I'm not sure. I think I'm doing maintenance work, but I don't know what that means, exactly. I'm also going to learn the kitchen with Frank."

"Who's that?"

"He's the guy who does all of the cooking. He's a great guy."

"And Claire?"

"I think she's running the arts program. They get a lot of kids up there in the summer, and parents like to be able to do things independent of their kids, so the resort organizes activities."

"That sounds fun," Brad said as he got up and walked to the counter. Craig knew he was never one for casual conversation. The garage door opened and Brad almost jumped towards the door to the mudroom to open it for Sarah.

Sarah came in with the pizza, and Brad grabbed the beer. "Hi, Craig!" Sarah said. She put the pizza down and came to give him a hug. The McLean children had always been close. That was the true accomplishment of their parents.

Brad pulled out three Lite beers, and they all sat down. No plates, just pizza from the box.

"So, when do you leave?" Sarah asked.

"Friday evening if I can stand it."

Laughing, Sarah said, "Right?" She took a bite of pizza.

"We should go up there for a weekend this summer. It might be fun," Brad said.

Sarah slowly turned and looked at him with scrunched eyes. "Really?"

"Yes. I think it would be cool," Brad said again while chewing his pizza.

Craig nodded his head. "I'll look into it. I can ask John."

Sarah smiled tight-lipped. "So, what do you think Mom and Dad think about the two of you being up there? Makes them empty nesters right away."

"I don't really know. Dad said something about being a good employee. I think they're resigned to it."

"What about Claire and all this art shit?" Sarah asked between bites.

"I don't know. She knows what she's doing." Craig paused to think about how to phrase his next statement. "I know you were on your honeymoon, but you should've seen her art show. It was incredible! I can't believe Mom and Dad skipped it."

"I know. And to come on vacation with us." Sarah sighed.

"That was bullshit," Brad coughed out.

"I'm sure," Craig said. "No, I think she'll be ok. Claire sees things differently. It'll be cool to spend the summer with her. She's so private. It will be like getting to know her for the first time."

Sarah seemed to consider Craig's statement. "I guess so."

"I still say we should visit up there," Brad reiterated. Sarah patted his knee. "We'll see." They went about finishing their pizza and discussing Mike's new reality and Linda's new choices of clothes. Sarah seemed to think that if their dad was going to get into shape, their mom thought she needed a change as well.

That evening, Craig wrote Abby an email. He didn't know why he didn't want to tell her about his dad on the phone, but he just needed to work out his feelings. He wasn't even sure she would check it.

Hey Abby,

I decided to write you an email. Not sure why, but I just thought "Hey, I'll write Abby an email instead of calling." I know you're busy, and I just talked to you last night, but there's more I wanted to tell you. I just didn't know how to say it. I'm feeling pulled by something I can't explain. I am being pulled to you. When I get out on the highway, I think sometimes I should just drive north and get on with it. However, I now know why my mom wanted me to stay here. My dad almost had a heart attack or something a few weeks ago after they came home from vacation. They didn't say anything cause Claire and I were finishing up school and stuff. I guess it was pretty bad because my dad is eating better and I haven't seen him have a beer since I got home. He's being nice too. It's weird. There's part of me that thinks I should stay home (my mom does too). But my dad insists he's fine and I should go. I went for a workout with him. He's doing pretty well. Guess you can't beat the athlete out of the old man. I met a few guys I used to play against. They still play,

and I worked out with them while my dad did his cardio. I miss you. I really have no idea what to expect from the summer, but if you are there, then it will all be good. Write me back. Love you,
  Craig

When Craig got to the Pewaukee football field on Monday at seven, he felt nauseous. There were a few middle-aged runners trotting around the track, so he decided to take a lap to warm up. He dropped his cleat bag and started to run. The track was still relatively new, and the surface felt fast. After half a lap, Craig came to the back stretch and let out his stride. For seventy-five meters, he built up and then slowed to a walk and shook out his legs. He decided he should probably do a good warm-up because he hadn't run fast in over nine months and he didn't want to pull anything.

As Dan and some of the other guys arrived, Craig went through his full warm-up routine. The moves came back to him easily, and he could feel his muscle memory begin to kick in. Many of the guys who came were players Craig recognized. Most were going to be sophomores, but one or two were older or younger. These were kids, like him, who just wanted to play in college, so they went to schools like Eau Claire, Oshkosh, and Whitewater.

Dan approached him first. "Hey, Craig," he said, jogging over. "Glad you came."

Craig nodded as he stretched his inner thigh. "Lots of guys," he responded.

Dan slapped his back, saying, "Yeah. We try to meet twice a week to stay sharp. Our own little minicamp."

"Cool," Craig said with little sense of enthusiasm. "We going to run routes and stuff?"

"Yeah," Dan responded. "We'll get to that. Let me introduce you to Josh. He's the quarterback at UW-Oshkosh. Good guy."

They made their introductions, and many of the guys started to warm up. Dan, Josh, and Craig played catch for a bit and then ran a few simple routes just to help Josh get loose. There were no linemen here. All of the guys were speed players save for two linebackers. They split into two groups of five. On offense, one of the running backs snapped for Josh while the other one lined up with him in the backfield. Dan and Craig were the receivers. On defense, the linebackers lined up in the middle to defend the run while two corners flanked the receivers, and a safety was ready to help over the top. With only ten players, it was far from perfect, but they did the best they could.

For the first play, Josh called a crossing route with Craig lined up in the slot. With all of the different jargon, it was easier for Craig to just hear the pattern. He lined up, and Kevin, a corner formally from Mukwonago, was across from him. The ball was snapped, and Craig took four hard strides right at Kevin then broke inside. The ball came quickly, and out of nowhere, Kevin rubbed up on him and snatched it right out from under his nose. Craig felt embarrassed. If he had run a crisp route, there would be no way Kevin could've jumped the ball. Craig looked back at Josh and tapped his chest. "My bad."

"No problem," Josh called.

As Craig was running back to the huddle, Kevin came up to him. "Lost a step, McClean?" He flicked the ball back to Josh.

They got in formation, and Josh called, "Same play," and went to line up.

Craig looked at Josh and flicked his head up. Josh nodded in acknowledgment. They were on the same page.

The ball was snapped, and Craig ran right at Kevin. Everything slowed down. Craig looked at Kevin's eyes as he planted his right leg hard to cut in. Kevin broke inside again, and Craig stuttered and went straight, right past Kevin. Josh hit him in stride as he reached the sideline. He broke upfield and almost made it to the end zone when the safety came flying over. Craig saw him and slammed on the brakes, letting him run right by. Then, Craig trotted into the endzone as Kevin came full speed, eight yards behind. Turning to Kevin, Craig drew a single finger on his mouth. "Shhh," he said and jogged back to Josh. He felt tingles from head to toe. The rush was great. He had not felt it in over a year, and it was invigorating.

They ran patterns for the better part of an hour and left around nine. When Craig got his phone out, there were three messages from Abby. The last one said, *Where are you?* He didn't want to tell her he was playing football, so he wrote back, *Out. Be home soon. Call you later.*

Ok, she wrote back a few minutes later.

Craig didn't know what he was going to say. But he knew he was going back to play on Wednesday.

Tuesday afternoon, Linda finally felt like starting in with her usual line of bullshit. "You know we're very concerned about you and Abby," she said before they got out of the car to go shopping. Linda had told Craig that she would take him out before he went north for the summer.

"Why, Mom? Cause she's not like you?"

Linda's mute, expressionless face spoke volumes.

"I'm just going to call you on it," Craig said. "I'm sick of it. Abby's great, and I'm happy. So that's all that matters."

"She just seems to have so much influence over you. And now Claire."

"She doesn't have 'influence' over us. What are you talking about? There is opportunity to be had up at Wood Lake, and we are taking advantage of it. Think of what I'm learning…"

"I guess. It just seems like she's the gravity and you're caught up in her orbit."

"So what if she is? I love her, and that's it."

"Really?"

It felt liberating to have said it out loud. "Yes. She's great, and I've never felt more secure in anything."

Linda stared straight forward into the distance, then turned with a prim, fake smile. "Well then, I guess there's not much more to be said."

"That's right. Let's just go home. The stuff I need for summer I can get at Farm & Fleet."

"Farm & Fleet?"

"Yes."

The rest of the week consisted of an almost silent understanding of differences that were not going to be discussed again. Craig played with the guys again on Wednesday and felt even more excited.

Surprisingly, Abby had checked her email, something she rarely did when she was home, and wrote Craig back. He received the response on Wednesday. He packed his bags that night and decided to leave Friday morning before his parents got up.

Hey Craig,

Thanks for the postcard and the email. I loved being with you in Chicago a few weeks ago for the art show. I think about it all the time. I don't think I have ever felt as close to anyone as I felt to you that night. I miss you too, even though it's only been a few days. I can't wait for you to come up. Summer at Wood Lake is the most special time, and I can't wait to share it with you. We are going to have so much fun. Claire is fitting in just fine. She seems to have a knack for figuring out what needs to be done next, and Frank and my dad really appreciate that. I am worried about my dad. He seems to be carrying a weight that is heavier than other summers. He is curt with everyone all the time. I don't know. Maybe I'm just reading too much into it. And Frank too. He just seems so tired. He's usually excited for the summer, but there's something off about him.

So sorry to hear about your dad. No problem about not telling me on the phone. It seems you needed to work out your thoughts, but know you can tell me anything. Sometimes, there's so much I want to say to you and I forget or get caught up in my thoughts. I'm glad you had time to connect with some old friends. Speaking of time, don't expect to have much of that here. There is always so much to do. Anyway, I am not sure I'm good at writing letters, but I wrote this quickly to be sure you got it before you left. Love you. Can't wait to see you.

Abby

CHAPTER 3

"They have a lot of stuff here," Claire said as she looked around the shop with Abby shadowing behind. "What do you usually do with the kids?"

"I've done painting, leaf printing, coloring. I don't know. I kinda do whatever, and if it works, I do it again." Abby shrugged her shoulders. "My mom does the art stuff. I mostly take the adults out after dinner for sunset pics. Sometimes, they want to paint too. It's pretty loose."

"That's what I figured. We'll just get some paints and canvas paper. Can we stop to get wax paper at Walmart or something?"

"Sure," Abby responded.

As they were gathering their materials, a guy came into the store. He was tall and thin, and his hair was pulled back in a ponytail that fell down over his neck. Sharp angles mapped his face, and his blue eyes burned. Claire found herself transfixed and compelled at the same time. She just knew she had to talk to him. 'Don't let an opportunity slip by' she thought to herself. While Abby picked up the rest of the stuff they needed and went off to check out with Meghan's mom, Claire went to the boy and said, "Hi."

The boy turned to Claire and looked down at her. "Hello," he responded in a very deep voice.

"I'm Claire. Are you looking for anything in particular?"

The boy smiled, and his eyes focused only on Claire, then he said, "Not really. I'm just seeing what takes hold of me today."

Confused, Claire asked, "What takes hold of you? What does that even mean?"

"Well, it means that I don't have a plan for today. I'm going to let the supplies I see here tell me what they want me to do. What about you? I know you don't work here, so what are you looking for?"

Claire scrunched up her face and thought, 'I'm going to let the supplies tell me what they want? What a load of crap.' "Well good luck." Claire chuckled at the nonsense. "I'm here getting supplies. I'm working at Wood Lake resort as 'Artist-in-Residence' for the summer." She made air quotes but quickly pulled her hands down, embarrassed.

Now the boy laughed. "Oh, 'Artist-in-Residence.' Sounds official."

His mocking tone made Claire laugh at herself. This guy was almost too handsome. She felt short of breath and tried not to look at him directly. Studying a sculpture carved out of wood, she asked, "What's your name anyway?"

"Shane Olson. I guess I'll be seeing you around. There's a pretty cool art scene here, so don't be afraid to jump in and see what you can see."

"Ok. I'll try. But you're not getting off that easy. I've got time to talk, and I'm going to talk with you." She turned to face him, noticing his hands as he reached for some paint. They were thick and large, and they didn't seem calloused. However, there was a scar that went from the base of his left hand down his wrist. It looked like a surgical scar.

"Well…ok then. Shoot. What do you want to know?" He

turned away from the bins, tilting his head slightly, and looked at Claire.

Abby looked on while Claire flirted with the boy. She thought his name was Shaun or Shane or something with an S. Abby wished she could walk up to strangers. The McLean children didn't seem to have a problem with it. That was how she and Craig had met. She just couldn't do it. But Claire seemed totally in her element. She was both animated and coy, tilting her head and smiling when the boy talked.

"How are you today, Abby?" Meghan's mother asked, drawing her attention away from Claire and the guy.

"Oh, I'm fine, Mrs. Fallow. Say, who is that guy who just walked in?" Abby asked, turning back to the couple.

"Oh, that's Shane Olson. He's a local artist. He's from here originally, but usually he leaves for a time and then comes back. It's been that way since high school. I think you girls were in middle school when he left town the first time."

"Ok, that's right," Abby said, still distracted. She knew she recognized him from school and around town.

"Meghan is working with you again this summer?" Mrs. Fallow asked. "That is so nice of your folks."

"Yes. She's going to lifeguard and run the boat for waterskiing. We're glad to have her."

Abby paid for the supplies on her parents' account and walked past Claire, winking as she went by.

Claire got the hint. "I gotta go." She smiled.

"Sure thing. Where are you staying again?"

"Wood Lake Resort."

"Oh yeah. I know where that is."

"Cool. See you around."

He smirked at her as she followed Abby out the door. Before they got to the truck, Abby started in, "So, who was that?" Even though she already knew, she wanted to get the details.

"His name is Shane. Really interesting guy. He's an artist. Works in all mediums. Sounds like he's travelled a lot."

"He was cute," Abby said.

Claire giggled quietly. Her pale skin reddened right away. "I suppose he was," she said calmly.

They stood by the tailgate of John's truck. "I don't know how you and Craig do it," Abby said.

"Do what?"

"Talk to people."

"Oh, it's not so hard. I made a promise to myself a long time ago to never let an interesting person pass if I had the time to talk. It's helped me meet a lot of people."

"Really?" Abby thought of how many people she had just walked by over the years.

"Yes. Craig does the same thing. But I think he stopped when he met you."

"You think?" Abby scrunched up her face. "Why's that?"

"I guess he figured he didn't need to meet anyone else." Abby blushed.

"Hey," Claire continued. "Let's do something."

"What?" Abby said.

"When do we have to be home?"

"Four thirty or five."

Claire checked her phone. "It's like one thirty. Let's go get your haircut and pick out a new outfit for when Craig comes."

"I've got a crazier idea."

"Really?" Claire was intrigued.

"If they have an opening, I want to get my hair colored. I want to really surprise him."

Claire was smiling. "Ok."

They dropped the supplies in the truck and walked down the main street to the hair salon that Abby's mother used. Luckily, they had an opening. Abby looked at the colors and chose a deep auburn with blond highlights. Claire was all for it.

"It's going to look really good, Abby. Craig's going to be shocked."

Abby's eyes sparkled.

Claire continued, "I'll leave you to it for a while. I'm going to walk around town and sketch."

Claire was filled with inspiration walking through the streets of Eagle River. The setting was so different from Chicago. The water was more contained and diverse. The small-town Main Street had lights and bridges that begged to be drawn. Even the people had a different look. They were determined and walked with purpose, not so distracted or preoccupied. Claire sat on a bench by the river, unbothered, something she could never do in Chicago. She began to zoom in and sketched for what seemed like an hour. Trees, shoreline, a man sitting in a chair with a fishing rod in his hand and a cigarette hanging from his mouth. He didn't care that he wasn't catching anything. His head followed a bird from time to time, and he seemed content to watch the water run by. Claire was completely mesmerized by the man. His every move and twitch simply enthralled her. She spent page after page sketching him and trying to listen to his story as it revealed itself before her. After being lost in the moment for quite a while, Claire realized it was time to get back to the salon.

When Claire got there, Abby had her hair rinsed from the dye and was getting it trimmed and styled. Claire went to the front to surprise Abby by settling the bill. From time to time, Abby smiled in Claire's direction. Claire winked at her and continued to sketch the ladies doing the cuts and coloring. She loved faces. She loved trying to capture the emotion of the moment. On this afternoon, there wasn't much business. The feel of the place was relaxed and easy. Much of the pace of the week at the resort had been the same. Although they were busy every day readying the resort, to Claire, it didn't seem like there was that much to do. She was sure things would pick up on Friday. Craig was coming Friday, so Claire wanted to help Abby welcome him. The hair was a good start.

Abby's face was poised to burst when the stylist finished the last few cuts. Claire could see exactly what Craig saw in her. She had a smile that could brighten your day. Her eyes possessed not only strength, but also a desire to experience the world. They darted everywhere, taking in every expression, searching for thoughts in others.

"The color looks nice," Claire called out.

"Really?" Abby almost laughed out. "I told them not to show me until it was done."

"You'll be happy," Claire assured her. She was happy to see Abby so filled with joy. After her own home life of anger and unfulfilled expectations, Claire longed for a summer of joy. She wanted to embrace every aspect of the resort and the life it provided. Frank had become a fast friend and mentor. The more she learned about him, the more she realized that she had found a fellow artist. He was the shadow in the forest painting. There was such care in his every action. Claire felt comfortable surrounded by the laughter of his kitchen. He was always so open and giving in ways her parents never were.

"All done," Claire heard the stylist say. She looked over at Abby, who was lightly tapping her feet against the floor. As the chair turned, Abby's hands came to her face and she looked at herself through her fingers. Claire got up and walked to her. All of the stylists gathered around. When Abby took her hands from her face, her eyes were welled up.

"I love it!" she said. She looked at Claire. "Do you think Craig will like it?"

Shaking her head and smiling, Claire responded, "He'll love it, Abby. You're beautiful."

"Thanks, Claire." Abby got up and turned to her stylist. "Thank you so much. How much do I owe you?"

"The bill has already been paid," the stylist said and winked at Claire.

Abby's eyes grew wide. "What?"

"I took care of it," Claire said.

"No, I can't," Abby stated as Claire put a finger up and fished out a card.

"It's on Linda." She smiled. "It's the least she could do after the way she's treated you."

Abby laughed out loud as she ran her hands through her hair. No one else seemed to get the joke. They said their goodbyes and left the salon.

At dinner, the response to Abby's hair was mixed. Vickie hated it and told Abby that there was no need to dye her hair. She ran her hands through her salt-and-pepper gray, almost to prove her point. Frank thought it was lovely, and he looked right at Vickie when he said it. Vickie dropped her protest.

Meghan loved it! She kept looking at Abby from across the table. She seemed a little miffed that Abby was spending a lot of time with Craig's sister this past week. There had been a few times during the week when Meghan had popped in to talk with Abby and ended up just following her around instead of being helpful. There just didn't seem to be enough time in Abby's day to check in with everyone. Besides, Meghan just wanted to talk about the boy who broke up with her right at the end of the semester. Abby had heard the story nine different times and had run out of things to say.

This was the dinner before Memorial Day weekend. John, who hardly noticed Abby's hair, had all the summer help minus Craig in the lodge. There were not many meetings before the season, so this larger dinner was important. Abby could see her father was nervous. His face was red and perspiring. He was taking deep breaths at the head of the table and had not eaten more than a bite or two. She was concerned about him. These dinners had been a regular part of her entire life, but this summer seemed different.

"So, people," John announced, signaling that it was time to go from dinner to meeting, "we've got a big summer. We have a few changes to the place. Meghan is lifeguarding this year instead of working the cleaning crew. Thank you, Meg, for being flexible." Meghan nodded in acknowledgement. John continued, "We have Claire, Craig's sister. Some of you still need to meet Craig, Abby's boyfriend. Claire is our Artist-in-Residence this year. She is going to be running our arts program, giving tours, and, from what I've been told, helping Frank in the kitchen for food service. Abby is going to be working with Vickie in the office, learning the business. Craig, when he gets here, will be working with me. We have some big projects to finish this summer. Daniel, Jackson, it's good to have you back. Taylor will be helping you with cabins. Welcome all. We are going to have a good summer. Starting this weekend, we are ninety percent booked for the summer weekends, one hundred percent for this weekend, the Fourth of July, and Labor Day. There is a block on some of the cabins for work to get done, but we will use them for overflow if needed. Ted already got two of the roofs on the smaller cabins done this spring and is working on the two-stories." He clapped his hands together once to signal the end of his speech. "Let's eat, drink, and be merry tonight so we can get to work tomorrow." He paused. "Abby, can you go for a walk with me after dinner?"

She nodded.

After dinner, everyone got up to clean the table. The cleaners, Daniel and Jackson, went to the bar while Claire, Meghan, and Frank went to the kitchen. They had something planned and told Abby to go with her father. Vickie shooed her out. Abby stared back at the kitchen, trying to see what might be going on, but couldn't tell what they were doing.

Out on the deck, Abby found her father waiting. "Let's go down and sit on the dock," John said, looking out at the lake.

"Ok, what's up?" Abby asked as she followed her dad down the steps and across the green. He said nothing. They walked out on the main dock and reached the bench at the end. John took a seat and reached his arm out, inviting Abby to sit. When she did, he put his arm around her and looked out over the lake.

Abby didn't talk. She took in the sounds of the waves coming ashore and the twinkle of the sun off the water. The two of them had sat on this bench for years, often in silence.

One of the times Abby remembered most vividly was after her grandma died. She found her dad out there, staring at the water. He said nothing when she sat down, but when she leaned her head against his shoulder, he began to weep. It was one of the only times Abby had ever seen him cry. Now, even with the few words spoken, so much was said in silence. It was the unspoken that had convinced Abby that this was the only home she would ever need. She often saw her father sitting out on this bench in the morning when she went out to fish. He was a part of the lake. Abby imagined that he was drawing his strength for the upcoming day from it. She knew this feeling. The mist of the morning that rose from the lake gave her the strength to do what needed to be done. She had tried to explain this to Claire when they went fishing and toured the lake over the past week. Claire's wry smile and the speed of her hand as she sketched everything told Abby that she got it.

"So, another summer," John said, breaking the silence. "What is this? Fifteen?"

"Fifteen or sixteen?" Abby questioned cautiously.

"I lose count too," John said. He looked right at Abby. "Craig coming tomorrow?"

Abby smiled at the thought. "Yes. He should be here around noon, I think."

"That's right. Good." John looked back at the lake for a moment and then turned his body to fully face Abby. She looked at him, not really knowing what was going on.

"I'm glad Craig is coming for the summer. He's a good young man." John paused and took in a deep breath. "He's staying with his sister in Cabin 13?"

"Yes."

"That will be good. You put the extra bed in there?"

"Yes. I got an extra dresser in there too. He and Claire will be fine."

John nodded. "No funny business then," he said with a chuckle.

Abby winked and responded, "Well, not too much of it, I guess."

John laughed out loud. "Good for you."

"No offense, Dad, but is that why you called me out here?"

"Not exactly." John took another deep breath. "So, Abby, you probably noticed that you're not going to be working with Daniel and Jackson this year. They can handle the cleaning on their own. And with Taylor helping, I guess. God knows how that will go."

"Ok…" Abby said. She still wasn't sure where her dad was going with all of this, but she tried to stay engaged. He often rambled his way to a point, and if you didn't follow, you missed the entire message.

"You're going to work with your mother at the desk and in the office. I really want you to learn the business."

Abby's eyes narrowed, and she tilted her head slightly. "I can still take out my tours, right? And fish in the morning?"

"Of course. I just want you to get familiar with how the systems work and what the books really look like." John paused but never took his eyes off Abby. "I need you to know the truth about the business."

Abby narrowed her eyes. "Ok. What truth?"

John looked to the lake again. "It's not always good." He took his arm from around Abby's shoulder and rubbed his hands together before grabbing one of hers. "Don't get me wrong, we make a living." He breathed in heavily through his nose. "That seems like all we've been doing lately."

"Dad?" Abby asked, but couldn't remember the rest of the question.

"Don't get me wrong. We aren't in debt. We have yours and Taylor's college set aside, and we don't carry a mortgage on either the resort or the land north of town. Your future is secure. It's just that, some years, we live off your mother's salary. The resort breaks even."

"Really?" This was the first Abby had ever heard of any of this. She always assumed the resort at least pulled in a little profit.

"Yes. Really. I just need you to know."

Abby's head was spinning. She crossed her legs, letting go of her father's hand, and looked out at the lake herself. The water was calm, and there were only a few boats out. She breathed deep. "Are we going to be ok this summer?"

"I think so. We are pretty well booked, but we can't have anything major happen."

Abby just nodded. Then, after what seemed like quite a while, she said, "I'll get to work on things tomorrow."

Nodding, John replied, "I'm sure you will, dear. I'm sure you will. By the way, nice hair."

Abby laughed.

When they went inside, there was a small birthday cake to celebrate Abby's nineteenth birthday and the first year of college for her and Meghan. Everyone was in on the plan, including Meghan. There wasn't always time to spend together as a family, but it was these small moments Abby loved most about being home.

Later, out on the dock, Abby wrote in her journal. She decided to write Craig a letter to put by his bed when he went to sleep that first night. After finishing the letter, she sat, waiting for the last sliver of the sun to finally descend.

Craig was coming today. He would be getting to the resort after noon, and Abby wanted everything to be perfect. She had other responsibilities but got up early to get them finished. Now, she was in full prep mode. The cabin needed to be cleaned, although Claire said she would handle it, and Abby wanted to prepare a special meal. She wasn't sure why she was so nervous. It wasn't like she and Craig hadn't talked lately, but she had not seen him in almost two weeks. It was the longest they had ever been apart.

Claire cleared out of the cabin. She had started working with Frank in the kitchen, a job she looked to continue throughout the summer. Claire watched Abby running around all morning, and it seemed as though she had not stopped. From fishing in the morning, which Claire went along with to "learn the lake," to lunch prep, and now in the early afternoon, it made her happy to see how in love Abby was. She smiled at Abby's affectionate behavior, although she had to admit, she was jealous of their relationship.

With all in place, Abby only had to wait. She paced around the green in front of the lodge and even took a lap or two around the cabins. She texted Craig a few times, but it seemed as though he was making her wait. It wasn't like him not to return a message, so she looked at her phone every other minute. It was twelve fifteen.

As Craig came into the lot and parked, he closed his eyes for a moment and took a deep breath. Ever since he had received Abby's email, his excitement had grown. This was home. Instead of going left towards Abby's house, he had parked on the right side of the lot, right near the entrance to the cabin road. He turned off the car and checked his messages. There were six from Abby. Craig laughed. The thought of seeing her made him feel energized. He could barely feel his legs. They had the whole summer to explore and be in the moment.

There was another message. It was from Will, the local football player who was on the UW-Whitewater team. It read, *Sure, we can work out. Love it. You playing next year? Definitely have something for you this summer. Call me.* There was the question again, "You playing next year?" Craig wasn't sure. He was also not ready to discuss it with anyone, especially Abby.

The air was already hot at midday, and trees were swaying in a breeze Craig recognized as stronger than usual. He walked over to Cabin 13, his new home. No one was there. He checked his phone again after dropping his bags on the porch. *Meet me in front of the lodge.* Looking between the three-bedroom cabins, he saw the lake. It was that body of water that brought life to this place. Wood Lake held the resort together.

Abby saw Craig walking down the cabin road. A rush went through her so hard, it almost hurt. She ran to him, and he lifted her off the ground. Nothing else existed beyond the strength of his arms and the feelings of their love. A moment later, he let her down and ran his fingers through her hair. Abby looked up, still holding onto his arm.

Craig's face grew serious. "What did you do here?"

Smiling, Abby responded, "Do you like it?"

Bursting into a smile, Craig nodded. "It's great. Red?"

"I thought I'd try something new for the summer."

Abby grabbed Craig by the hand and led him away from the lodge and back to his cabin.

"Where are we going?" Craig asked.

"I have a little surprise for you."

They got to the cabin, and Abby went to open the door while Craig picked up his bags. She let Craig go in first. He looked around and saw the bed against the back wall. There was a dresser and a rod that had been placed on the wall to hang clothes. Craig went to put his bags by the bed, and when he turned around, Abby embraced him and kissed him gently. When he reached around to pull her in, she turned quickly and walked away. Craig stayed standing at the bed, confused.

"Come over here," Abby said. "Are you hungry?"

Craig strolled over to the small table and for the first time smelled the food. Abby had a meal prepared, and they sat down to eat. Saying almost nothing for a few minutes, Craig finished his plate. Abby ate sparingly, content to just look at him.

"That was great, babe. I missed this at home. My mom didn't really cook much, and I had to fend."

"Well, we will eat well this summer." Abby looked at all the food she had left. "Do you want the rest of mine?"

"Why? Don't you want to eat?"

"I don't know," she said, pushing her plate over to Craig. "I guess I'm just so excited to see you." She smiled.

Craig winked at her and ate up the rest of her food.

What Abby really wanted to talk about was the resort. She wanted to share with him all that her father had told her, but she was afraid. Instead, she asked, "So what have you been up to?"

Craig finished chewing. "Not much. Been working out again. My dad is going to the gym."

"Yeah. You mentioned that." Abby thought about Craig playing football with his buddies. They had spent so much time getting past it in the last year.

"Yeah. He stopped drinking, and he's trying to get in shape. His doctor said he had to do it."

"Good for him." Craig had told her all of this in his email, but Abby played along.

"So, yeah. Some of the guys from the team work out there. It was cool."

"That sounds like fun. Did you see Sarah?"

Craig chuckled. "Yeah, I went to their house for dinner." He shook his head.

"What?" Abby asked, one side of her face cracking a smile.

"It's huge! The thing is so big, they can't even furnish all the rooms. It's going to take them a year to get the place done."

"But, how are they?"

"Sarah's great! She got a job. Brad's nervous as ever. They don't have a mortgage, but somehow he's still worried about money."

Abby breathed deeply through her nose. A feeling of complete contentment washed over her.

Craig continued, "We going to go see everyone else? What's Claire up to?"

"We can go to the lodge. Everyone should be there, somewhere. Claire has found a new calling in the kitchen. I thought we could go for a boat ride," Abby said, eyes wide.

Craig was trying to take all of her in. He wanted to be alone with her and knew she wanted the same, but there was nowhere to go. Claire could be back at any minute. Instead of indulging his fantasy, he got up with the dishes and went to the sink. As he washed them, Abby came over and scratched his back. He turned off the water and pulled her in. They kissed, and he felt her back, finding his favorite spot just above her waist. He just wanted to take her to the bed and run his fingers over that spot for hours, but there were people to see, things to do. They would have to make time for the intimate moments and take advantage when they could.

They took their time walking to the lodge. Abby was in no hurry to share Craig with her family. She longed for a time they could be alone, but there was a lifetime for that. Now, Craig had to be given over to the resort, and that included being shown off. Just before they went up the lodge deck stairs, Abby saw Meghan. "Hey, Meg," she said.

Meghan smirked and turned her back to Abby, then headed down towards the lake. Abby watched her walk away. 'Maybe she's just busy,' she thought to herself. But not saying "hi" struck her as rude.

In the kitchen, one could almost mistake Craig's arrival as the return of a conquering king.

"Craig!" Frank yelled, getting up from his stool and hugging him so strongly that he almost lifted him from the ground.

Claire looked on with amazement. Abby had talked to her about Frank's strength, but also her perception of his weakness since she had come home. Claire was asked to keep an eye on Frank, not only by Abby, but also by Vickie. There seemed to be a collective worry, but this display gave Claire reason to believe that the whole affair was overblown. Frank came alive for Craig.

"Wow! Frank! You look good."

"Shut up. I'm an old man. You're the one who looks good." He stepped back as Abby came up behind Craig and put her arm around his waist.

In a formal voice, Craig said, "I'm fit, trim, and ready for work."

"That's good," Frank replied. "I think John's going to try to kill you this summer. It's been a while since we've had a young mule to work around here. You might be singing a different tune come July."

"I'm sure it won't be all bad," Abby chimed in, knowing that Craig's eyes would be opened to a new world in the coming months.

Craig walked over by his sister. "Hey, Claire, how are you getting along?"

"Don't worry about her," Frank called out as he walked back to his make table and sat down. "She's fitting in just fine. It's nice to have some help in the kitchen again."

Abby felt stung by the comment since she had been Frank's constant companion over the last several years, but she was sure he meant nothing by it.

"I'm doing good, little brother. Frank's teaching me a lot, and I'm looking forward to experiencing a real weekend." Claire winked at Abby.

Abby turned to Craig. "We should go check in with my parents so we can get to work and have time to go out on the boat later."

"You bet," Craig replied. There was a twinge of nervousness in going to talk to John. He could always make Vickie laugh, but John was a tough nut. Craig had yet to figure him out.

Craig's nerves proved to be unfounded. Both John and Vickie were inviting and gracious hosts. Walking back to the cabin to put on work clothes, Craig exhaled. "Well, that went ok."

"What do you mean?" Abby questioned.

"I don't know. I always get anxious around your dad. I guess I haven't quite gotten used to the idea that this place is his job."

"It's more than a job, Craig. It's a lifestyle."

Nodding, but not fully understanding what Abby meant, Craig replied, "True."

The rest of the afternoon and evening got away from them. Craig helped in the kitchen during dinner service and cleanup because Frank went back to his cabin after the last plate went out. Claire mentioned to Craig that he had been doing that, and Abby said it was his "new normal." Rather than going out to fish in the evening, Abby told Craig that she would meet him in the morning. She left him on his front steps to breathe it all in. There was a calmness to the exhaustion of a day full of tasks to be done. The promised structure of the summer was exactly what Craig needed to calm his mind.

Right before he went to sleep, Craig found the letter Abby had put right next to his lamp, as though she knew he would turn it on to read.

Dear Craig,

I just wanted to write you a quick note to tell you how excited I am for this summer. Even though there is a lot to do, I have some fun things planned. I am hoping you will begin to feel connected to this place as I think you are to me. You have been so good about not talking about the future since it scared me back in February, but I am starting to see it now. This could be our place someday. I feel like something has been missing this past week without you here. Now I feel whole again.

    Love you,
    Abby

Craig wrote in his journal at the end of day one:

God, I love this place. The lake, the forest, the people. There is nothing not to love. Abby's right about her dad and Frank. I've never been here for a summer, but both of them do seem off their game a bit. Claire told me she is going to help Frank as much as she can, and I guess I will do the same. It was so great to see Abby today. Her hair is sexy. Damn, I'm a lucky guy. Remember that, Craig. I can't wait to get down to business. I think the work will do me good. Excited to see what comes next. Great first day.

CHAPTER 4

Memorial Day weekend came and went like a blur. After fishing on Saturday morning, Craig and Abby set to the work of the day. Abby hoped that fishing could become a daily event for them because their work schedules and living situations would allow them little time to spend alone. Until afternoon check-ins started, they had worked together to get cabins ready and make sure the grounds were as clean as they could be for the official start of the summer season.

Knowing in advance from the reservations the number of children who were supposed to come, Claire was ready to offer art experiences starting that Saturday. She was looking forward to working with the kids. There was a space she designed up in the loft of the lodge devoted to all the things she would need, that is, if she wasn't outside. In the meantime, she was spending her days with Frank. They fell into a nice rhythm, and John was happy not to hire more help for the kitchen. Claire had no problem cleaning fish or anything else they might serve. Her presentation was far above what Frank put out, and she was a sponge for information, able to reproduce almost any recipe from memory after one time. They laughed and smiled their way through most lunch and dinner services, but Frank warned her that she still had not seen a holiday weekend. Claire was at ease with the "impending doom," as Frank called it. She had learned a long time ago to take each task as it came. No need to do more than what was in front of you.

When people started to check in around noon on Saturday, Abby went off to help her mother, and Craig made himself useful by offering to help people get their things to their rooms and cabins. He knew the place as well as anyone by now and made up the rest as he went along. There were a few faces Craig recognized from Thanksgiving and Christmas, but most were new. By dinner, their capacity had reached sixty percent, with many more promised by later that evening. Kids already wanted to swim, and there was even a boat tour and a campfire ready for the evening.

"Wow! This is going to be quite a ride," Craig said, sitting at the bar with Abby.

"Yeah. It's always like this. Pretty soon it'll be Labor Day and we'll be back at school." Abby smiled.

They ate their walleye and drank their Mellow Yellow. Claire brought them some dessert, a marble cake she had made for the occasion.

"Y'all just sit and eat now," she said in her bad Southern accent. "Me and Frank'll take care of the folks." Abby made to get up almost by rote, and Claire patted her back, saying, "It's fine, I was just kidding."

Abby sat down and took a deep breath. As relaxed as she usually was when at home, Craig could tell by her silence and hunched posture that she was tense.

"I've got to get ready for the sunset tour. You coming?" Abby asked, trying to sound cheery.

"Me?" Craig answered.

Abby snorted. "Yeah."

John moved down the bar towards them. He must have heard Abby because he said, "Craig and I have a little walk to take after dinner service. Take Claire on the tour. She knows the route by now. See how she does with the people. I want her to take that over in a few weeks."

"Ok," Abby said without emotion. She was upset by Claire taking over the sunset tour, but she understood. Despite her usual shyness, Abby loved giving that tour each night. She could be on the water, and she knew all the best places to go, and the pictures always turned out great. Claire was picking it up though. She was a bit short on the history of the place, but her eye was impeccable. Abby couldn't deny that the way Claire framed a shot was far superior to hers. Abby, mostly, hoped to get a good one. Claire rarely got a bad one. Abby had talked to Claire about using her pictures for the improved website John had requested, and Claire, who knew a lot about digital media, said she would be willing to work on the whole setup. Once the summer really got underway, Abby planned to do a complete overhaul. The only issue was finding the time.

When they finished dinner, Abby went to get the cooler stocked and gather the regular guests who always took the tours. The pontoon could take anywhere from twelve to fifteen people, including the driver. With Claire going along, they had about ten guests, mostly women, ready to go. Fishing tours, which John led, went in the morning and after lunch, but the evening tour was a popular one during peak times, often filling up early and sometimes requiring a fishing boat to trail after with overflow.

They toured around the lake, taking in rock formations

and trees of interest. Abby stopped at the river and creek entrances to check on wildlife. There was an old beaver dam that was occupied intermittently, and then it was on to the middle of the lake for sunset. They could get the beauty of the trees in the background and the reflection of the sun in the foreground. Abby knew the tour by heart, but she never tired of it. She loved listening to people coo about her home. Tonight though, with the sun setting so beautifully over the pines, she wondered why people would ever stop coming to the resort. It was a conversation she had with her father after she told him of her intention to stay and run the place. The beauty of it kept drawing her home. Why would people not love the wonder of the outdoors and return time and again? Why would generations of people not keep their traditions?

Claire helped a few customers with the high-priced cameras they brought. Most people just snapped a few pics on their phones and had another beer or wine cooler while chatting about things Abby didn't care for in the least.

Meanwhile, John had caught up with Craig while one of the "regulars" took the bar for a while. "Hey, Craig," John said as he put his hand on Craig's shoulder.

"Hello, Mr. Whitworth," Craig said as they walked out on the deck. "Going to be a good summer?" He realized the awkwardness of the question as soon as he said it.

Laughing softly, John responded, "It sure will. I hope you and Claire are going to be comfortable. She's already a big help."

Smiling, Craig said, "We are very comfortable in the cabin. Yeah, Claire's great."

John held a straight face. "We have a lot of work to do here. Let's take a walk to look it over."

They walked off the deck and started down the cabin road. Craig could see the pontoon out on the lake along with several other boats of different types. He had not seen this much activity on the lake during his previous visits. There was a lot of life to be enjoyed. As they moved down the road, the trees and three-bedroom cabins started to obscure his view. They stopped at the first cabin.

"So, Craig, ever do any roofing?" John asked, looking up at the roof.

"No, sir," Craig replied.

John chuckled. "Not afraid of heights or anything, are you?"

"Not that I know of." Craig looked up to determine the height. The roofs of the cabins did seem higher now that the prospect of being on top of them had been introduced. As he gazed around and counted the cabins, he failed to notice that John had begun to walk down the path again. He scrambled to catch up. There was life all around. People were walking about, and children were running. Craig supposed they were going to the game room or to play on the beach before it got too dark. John nodded at a few of the adult guests, but he said nothing until he got to the end of the cabin road. There, he paused and looked back. Craig turned around. Opening up on both sides of the road were cabins and the lodge, which stood looming in the half-light. Craig could take in the entirety of the resort from the end of the road. Up until that very moment, it was not a thing he had paused to do.

"So, we're going to try to get new roofs on all the smaller cabins. I had a second layer put on when we moved here years ago, but it's past due. You can see chipping, and we've lost a lot of shingles over the years."

Craig looked up at the roof of his cabin and saw that there were only a few shingles that still had square edges. Most were rounded and chipped.

"So, when do we get started?" Craig tried to sound eager, but he was nervous.

"Well, Ted, the guy who did the roofs last time, he's retired now, but he said he could come by next week and help show us what to do. He already did two of the smaller ones this spring. There are eight more to go. I have a schedule where one of the cabins is unoccupied each week so we can get it done before August. We have a tight timeline."

"Yes, sir," Craig said, but in the back of his mind, he was thinking about the opportunity Will had for him and the possibility of training camp if he returned to playing football.

"I'm going to try to get everything in good shape over the next few years." He started to walk back. "Don't want to give Abby a crap place, right?"

"No, sir."

"Well, it's going to cost money to make money. We better get back to build the campfire."

The rest of the weekend went by in a blink. Morning fishing was really the only time Craig and Abby had to be alone. Craig was not always happy to get up that early, but when he saw Abby down by her boat at her home dock, he smiled and broke into a jog. She was always ready at six. They had an hour to talk and be with each other. The rest of the day was filled with a list of tasks as long as it was diverse. Craig basically took orders from John. Wood, pickups and drop-offs, and helping in the kitchen were most often called for. Saturday night, Craig quickly learned, was party night. While not as big as Thanksgiving, Saturday evenings brought the resort together. Frank did it right with grilled food, steaks and burgers, while Claire's desserts were a hit. Craig and Abby sat together at meals and campfires both Friday and Saturday nights. Over the first few days, Abby had not come back with Craig to his cabin. He didn't mind though. With Claire being in the bedroom and him sleeping in the main room, there was little time for privacy.

Morning fishing was in its third day when Memorial Day came. Craig wasn't used to the early mornings, but he valued the time they got to spend together. Today promised to be a full day. Many guests would be leaving in the early afternoon, and rooms would need to be turned for any early summer guests who would be taking advantage of a less populated resort before most of the schools let out and they would be filled to capacity.

"Today will be tough," Abby said between casts. "Then it should be a little calmer until Thursday or Friday." She threw the lure back out.

Craig had not picked up fishing yet. Abby taught him a few things, but he could only get his casts to the right place one in every five tries. Aside from the two fish that basically swam onto his hook, Abby was pretty sure he was hopeless. He couldn't even be persuaded to wrap his hand around the fish when he pulled it out of the water. Abby found his squeamishness hilarious.

"Yeah," Craig finally responded. He was not fully awake. "Going to be a late night." He tried to cast to the reeds again but came up several feet short and reeled in what he knew would be an empty line.

"What does my dad have you doing with the roofs?" Abby asked without breaking her concentration, which after years of fishing, no longer needed much focus.

"We're going to do a full tear-off and replacement on the one- and two-bedrooms. I have a week to do each once I get started." Craig cast to the reeds this time.

"Big job," Abby said as she snagged another fish and dragged it in.

Craig marveled at her ability. It was as though she willed the fish to her hook. She casually took the fish in hand, pulled out the hook, and put it in the cooler. Then, she cast again, perfectly. Craig nodded his head and said, "Yep."

Mornings went on like this. Their conversations were punctuated by long pauses and chopped sentences. Neither of them minded though. They were content to be together.

Later, in between cleaning cabins and turning over rooms, Will stopped by. He had arranged a meeting with the Eagle River football coach so Craig could work with the strength and conditioning program over the summer. The meeting was set up for Thursday afternoon. Craig walked the resort with him, and Will talked about what the coach was like. He was sure Craig would not have a problem getting the gig. Craig knew he would have to tell John and Abby soon, but he wanted to get the first cabin knocked out this week so he could tell what he was in for the rest of the way.

That evening, Abby figured out a way for her and Craig to be alone. They ended the day as they began it, in the boat, out on the water. This time, there was no purpose. Abby drove the boat to the middle of the lake after dark, cut the engine, and let it drift. There were mats in the front of the boat and a blanket. Craig could tell Abby had been planning this. At first, they just lay there. Craig, on his back, looked up at the stars, more numerous than he had ever seen in his entire life. Abby lay on his chest. She had counted those stars all her life. Now, she only cared about sharing all of it with Craig. "God, it's beautiful," he said.

Abby lifted her head to watch Craig as he took in the sky. His eyes were gleaming, and he moved his head slowly, scanning the whole sky. "I'm so happy right now," Abby said.

Craig kissed her on the lips, and she laid her head back on his chest. "I am too. This is perfect." He meant it too. As Craig slowly ran his fingers through Abby's hair, he thought about the moment he was in and wished it could last forever. A sense of stillness invaded him with each breath. Nothing could come in to break the moment. He could think of nothing that ever would.

After some time, Abby sat up and stretched her arms up high. She glanced at her watch and said, "It's almost midnight. Damn. We better get going." She stood up and started the engine.

Craig stood up and looked around. In the dark, he couldn't tell where they were. He tried to find any marker on shore that could help, but no reference could be found. "Yeah," he responded. "We better get back. I have to be up early to work with Ted and your dad."

"They will be ready to go at seven," Abby said tentatively, biting her lower lip.

They sat down, and Abby slowly pointed the boat towards home.

CHAPTER 5

With the art supplies they ordered the week before and a few other items John asked her to pick up in the trunk, Claire decided to take in more of the town before lunch service. She had not left the resort since the day she and Abby went to the store and salon, almost seven full days, and she hoped to observe more characters like the man she sketched the first day. The memory of him had not faded. The story her pencil outlined was still speaking to her as loudly as ever. But now, Wall Street invited exploration, and she meant to accept. The small-town feel of this main street was what many suburbs tried to emulate with one or two blocks of carefully scripted "small" shops and bars. Quaint as they were, this was real. With brick buildings and neon lights, the street had a bygone feel, but it also had energy. It was an energy of lives lived, and, as Claire walked, she could feel this energy fill up her heart. The stories the walls of these buildings held went back nearly a century and were as varied as the people who created them. Claire longed to discover the secrets of only a few. There was simply too much to bring into her field of view. She narrowed her frame and focused in on capturing the perspective. After a few snaps from her camera, there was a tap on her shoulder.

"Hello," a deep voice said.

Claire turned to see the guy she met at the art store a week ago. "Hi, Shane," she said as a smile washed over her face and a shot of adrenaline ran through her. She was surprised by the feeling. His piercing gaze stared back at her.

"What are you doing?" Shane asked, smiling.

"I'm exploring. Seeing what I can see."

"Do you want me to show you around?" he asked with his arm extended.

"That would kind of defeat the purpose of exploring," Claire responded, tilting her head. "But sure. I don't want to get lost. Lead away."

They walked down Wall Street a bit. Shane pointed out a few bars and a toy store named Grandma's Toy Box. It was a combo toy store and bookstore, and it reminded Claire of a little store in downtown Waukesha named Martha Merrell's. She would stop there from time to time and talk with the owner, who was an interesting lady full of fun stories and memories.

Shane paused for a moment, looking in the window. "I used to love this place. It was the store to go to before there was Amazon. They can find anything. I was a bit too old to enjoy it as a toy store, but the family that owns it has been around here for almost a hundred years. I like stories like that. Local people making a life by sticking around."

Claire was confused. "Didn't you say you traveled a lot?"

Confidently walking ahead, Shane said, "I do travel, but I always end up coming back here. There's too much history in this place to walk away for good."

"I guess. I kinda feel that way about Chicago." The statement came out flat, as though Claire didn't really believe the words.

"I see a lot of people from Chicago. They come here to

get away." He looked down the street. "Hey," he said suddenly. "Have you heard of the Warehouse?"

She cast a sarcastic smirk in his direction. "I've only been here a week. I haven't heard of much."

Shane laughed. "You're cute." He recovered himself. "The Warehouse is an art center. They have classes and plays, and they sponsor events. You'll love it."

As they walked further, Shane outlined all the things they did at the Warehouse and the various festivals and markets held in town. Claire knew that she wouldn't have time to indulge in all the town had to offer, but the art scene seemed robust and intriguing.

"You want to get a cup of coffee or something?" Shane asked.

Claire wrinkled her nose slightly and said, disappointed, "Not now. I have to get back to help with lunch service and get ready for the weekend."

"Where are you working again?"

"Wood Lake Resort."

"That's right. I know the place." He looked away, down the street again, as though indifferent to what she had said. She was a little annoyed.

"Yeah. My brother is dating the owner's daughter. They gave me a job so I could get away for the summer before starting grad school."

"Grad school?" Shane said sarcastically. His smile was almost unnerving.

"What?" Claire shot back a little more sharply than she intended.

"Grad school for art? What can you learn in school that you can't learn with a library card and a museum pass?"

"Is that what you think?" Claire asked, looking past him at a corner she would like to get a quick snap of before she left town for the day.

"Yeah. The art is out here." He spun around playfully. In Claire's head, time slowed down and she could see every muscle on Shane's forearm flex. His skin was bronze already, even this early in the summer. "It's all around us. Why go to some stuffy school?"

"Because I want to," Claire said with a hint of sassiness meant to end the discussion.

"I suppose to each…" Shane didn't finish the phrase, but instead held up his hands in apparent surrender.

Claire took a deep breath. "Maybe another time for coffee?"

"Sure. Can I get your number?"

They exchanged numbers and said their goodbyes. Claire watched as Shane bounced away. 'He doesn't have a care in the world,' she thought to herself. She gently bit her lip and wondered what that would feel like. Quickly, she took a few more pictures of interesting corners and buildings before heading back to the resort.

Craig met Ted up on top of his cabin. Coolness filled the morning air, and mist rose from the lake. The roof was still damp and slippery. Craig was a bit unsure of his footing as he stepped off the ladder.

"Welcome to the top, son," Ted said in a higher-pitched voice than Craig expected. "We are going to tear off today. Got the two cabins done down near the lodge for you to look at, but thought we'd start with yours so we had time to get it done."

Craig nodded enthusiastically, almost losing his balance. Catching himself, he observed that Ted was a short man with a belly on him, but his forearms looked like he had swung a hammer most of his life.

Ted continued, "The tear-off…it's messy work. Nothing to it, really." He reached down with a crowbar and popped up a sheet of shingles and threw them off to the side. "See?"

Craig put on his gloves and grabbed another crowbar from Ted. When he got his first set of shingles off, he was stoked. The work went quickly after that. Ted took one side of the roof, and Craig took the other. Where Ted used precision and technique, Craig was filled with boundless energy. By the time Craig cleared his side, Ted was about finished.

"Done already?" Ted asked.

"Yes, sir."

Ted got up and went to Craig's side. "Nice work."

Craig had already begun to finish up Ted's side. Ted pulled up a bit of the tar paper, and it cracked in his hand. "I suspected we would need to replace this."

"Will that take a lot longer?" Craig asked, already concerned by how long each roof might take.

"A bit. I budgeted it in. Not too big a deal. We need to get it off and get the nails up."

"Cool. We can do it this afternoon?"

Ted took a deep breath. "You can. I'm getting a bit tired. Working in the afternoon is not my cup of tea anymore."

"Not a problem. I'll get it done."

"I'm sure you will." He patted Craig on his shoulder.

Craig could tell he was going to like Ted. He was no-nonsense and had a wry sense of humor. He cleared the rest of the shingles while Ted began on the remaining tar paper. By lunch, they had cleared most of the roof. There were still a number of nails, but Ted told Craig to finish it after lunch. When Craig got down from the ladder, he looked over the roof. They stripped the whole thing in a little more than three hours. There were shingles scattered about, but mostly on the side facing the lodge. Craig began to pick up the scraps.

"Don't worry about that right now," a voice called from behind Craig. It was John. "You'll have to clean it up by the end of the day. But for now, go to lunch. It looks good so far."

Craig walked down to the dock in front of the lodge. He looked out over the lake and took a deep breath in and held it. The work of the morning washed over him, and, exhaling, he walked out on the dock to sit on the bench at the end of it.

"Hey, Craig," Meghan called from the right side of the dock. Startled, he turned. Meghan was standing up to her waist in the water, wearing a bikini top and washing down a boat. There was a paddle boat, two canoes, and a handful of kayaks for guests to use. She was washing down the inside of one of the canoes by dunking the side in and letting the water swish around. Then she picked the boat up and let the water flow out. The move revealed her considerable strength, which Craig had no occasion to see before. Wet and with a boat raised over her head, Craig found Meghan to be fairly attractive.

"How are you, Meghan?" Craig asked as courteously as he could.

She set the boat back in the water. "I'm great," she said, smiling. "It's nice and warm today." She dipped her head in the water and threw her wet hair back behind her head.

"Yes...it is."

"You got a lot done this morning."

"Yep. Mostly done for the day. Just have to clean up."

"Good for you." Meghan lay back in the water and began floating. "I just love the summers up here."

Craig recognized Meghan's flirting. He laughed to himself and said, "It should be fun." Then, he walked to the end of the dock. Sitting on the bench, the entire lake came into view. The water rippled with a gentle breeze and glittered in the sunlight. A forest of pine and birch rimmed the lake with homes, big and small, visible through the trees. A few boats were anchored in the fishing spots he had been to with Abby. 'Too late in the day to catch much of anything,' Craig thought. 'Maybe it's really about the experience.' He gazed around again and found himself losing focus, lost in the moment. Awareness was all there was, and nothing existed beyond the lake, the breeze, and the sound of water lapping against the shore. He was aware of his thoughts, but somehow beyond them at the same time. As he breathed in and out, nothing else mattered. He didn't even notice Abby walking down the dock.

Abby stood for a moment, watching Craig. She knew exactly where his mind was. There was no past or future. He was lost in the present. Lost in the lake. She had been in that place so many times. It was the reason for living at the resort. Why live anywhere where the past haunted you? Do the task that's before you, then move on to the next. That was how she had been living for as long as she could remember. The problem was that she now knew the finances of the place, and the tasks before her seemed so numerous that she wasn't sure where to begin. At that very moment, she decided to leave the office behind and enter Craig's world and see if she could be restored. "Hey," Abby said as she got to the bench.

"Hey." Craig grabbed hold of her hand as she sat down. He smiled and looked back at the lake. Abby laid her head on his shoulder. Their perceptions merged. She saw what he saw.

Craig finished pulling the nails and cleaning the debris from around the cabin. A dumpster had been delivered next to the basketball court in the parking lot. The four-wheeler and trailer made quick work of the job, and Craig finished by three. With no rain in the forecast, Ted said they could wait until the next day to finish the tar paper and to begin the new shingles. He hoped they could be done on Thursday morning, which was good because Craig had to meet with Coach Granger that Thursday afternoon. Ted told Craig to go up on the two finished cabins so he could see what they were shooting for in the end.

With two cabin cleaners and the additional help of Meghan and Claire, most everything around the resort was well in order. The weekend promised to be busy, and the weeks that followed promised the same. Craig went to the lodge to see Abby and found her sitting at her father's desk in the office. The office was small, but amazingly well-kept from Craig's point of view. John, being a former engineer, had adopted computers early, so the clutter of paperwork was really nonexistent save for receipts that had yet to be scanned in and the things he couldn't get to on a daily basis. "Hey, babe," Craig said since Abby hadn't seemed to notice him walk in. "Nice digs."

"Not really." Abby looked up at him with a straight face. "I don't even have a window."

"Yeah. Bummer."

"What's up?" she asked.

"Nothing much. I'm done for the day."

Abby looked at her phone. "At three?"

"Yeah. I guess I could always go chop or something, but I'm done with the roofing. You?"

"I guess I could be done."

"Want to take a walk?" Craig asked energetically.

"Sure. Let's check with Frank first to see if he needs help in the kitchen."

"Ok. I'll go change out of my work clothes."

"No need. We're just going for a walk, right?"

"Sure thing."

They walked to the kitchen and saw Claire at the make table preparing some fish while Frank seemed to be missing.

"Hey, Claire," Abby said. "Where's Frank?"

"So," a voice from the freezer said. "We have some chicken, but not too much. We will need to add that to the list."

"There he is," Claire responded and went back to her work.

"Oh hi, you two," Frank said as he walked out of the freezer towards the make table and put the food down. "Claire's helping me with dinner prep."

"That answers my question," Abby chimed in.

"How's that?"

She clarified, "You don't need any help with dinner prep?"

"Oh, no. We're good."

Claire held up a knife, flashing it in the light, then picked up a filet and put it in the spice rub. She winked.

77

Craig and Abby left for their walk. They made their way past Frank's house into the forest where the trees, mostly birch, looked old and untouched. The next house was several hundred yards down the shoreline. With enough room to walk along the lake, they enjoyed the warm air and nice breeze filtering through the trees. Craig grabbed Abby's hand, interweaving their fingers while they walked in silence for a while, peering at each other from time to time. Nothing really needed to be said. Both of them were reaching the point where they knew when to speak and when to stay quiet. This was a moment to reflect and refocus on a shared purpose, each other.

Finally, Craig asked, "Who owns the property next to Frank's house?"

"Either Frank or the resort," Abby replied. "You know, I'm not really sure. Why?"

"No reason...just wondering. You're quiet. Is everything ok?" Craig stopped and took a seat on a fallen log about ten feet from the shore with an unobstructed view of the lake.

"I don't know. I guess so."

"Come on now, Abby." Craig smiled.

"I guess it was just a surprise to see Claire so integrated into the kitchen. That used to be my spot."

"It still is," Craig said in a reassuring voice.

"I know. It's just, seeing the resort from the office point of view, I can see the work that goes into it."

"Well, that's part of it, right?"

"I know, Craig." Abby put her hand on his knee and squeezed it.

Craig began to lightly scratch her back. "Come on. Is

everything ok in there?" He knocked lightly on her forehead.

Distracted, Abby answered, "In where?"

"In your head? In the office? Wherever you are?"

Abby snickered and shook her head. She wanted to tell Craig everything, but she knew not to. 'Not yet. Let him learn to love the resort before seeing it for all that it truly is.' she thought. Speaking quickly, she said, "Not really. There's just so much to learn. Website could use some work as well, but Claire said she could help me with that. I don't know, it's just a lot."

Craig nodded. He didn't really know anything about how the place was run or what added responsibilities Abby had, but he knew enough to just let Abby speak. She would tell him what she needed to tell him in her own time.

Abby continued, "Sometimes, I wish I could just carry some towels around and take a tour."

"Aren't you going to do the photo tours?"

"I think so. This weekend and after. We'll have afternoon tours as well as evenings. If I stayed in that office all the time, I think I would go batty."

Craig laughed.

"How was the roof?" Abby asked, trying to change the subject.

"Not bad. I think putting on the new roof will be more tricky than tear-off. Ted seems nice. I think it will be fine."

"Good. Yeah, Ted is nice. He's been out here before, teaching my dad stuff about repairs and things."

"We get along well. It will be a challenging summer. I like the work though."

Abby patted his leg and leaned in. They sat quietly again for a time. The summer was coming, and with it, work that would fill their days. It was good to spend time together and feel a sense of calm. Craig had never been in a world where he had time to feel peaceful. Mostly, before coming here, he would have described his summers as a whirlwind of activity with camps and practice and the occasional job. Here, the stress of the day faded and never overwhelmed.

Abby held onto her secret. She longed to return to a moment where the reality of the resort didn't threaten to consume her. Finally, she broke her silence. "Where are you going again on Thursday?"

"Over to the high school to meet the football coach."

"Why's that?"

"Will set up the meeting. I think I can get some field experience hours through coaching."

"Do you need that to be an English teacher?"

"It's like getting Gen Ed credits. I don't have to do the specific hours for a while."

"Will you be able to get your work done around here?"

"Oh yeah. I'm sure it's only like two or three times a week. I just need twenty-five hours total."

"Why don't you do it in the fall?"

Craig felt a pang of guilt, but he held his form. "Why not knock it out in the summer?"

"Good point."

"You want to keep walking or stay here?"

Abby stood up. "Let's walk a bit further."

"Ok."

They headed past the neighbor's house and down the lakeshore. Abby went into tour guide mode. Craig listened intently.

CHAPTER 6

The tar paper went pretty easily. Cut to size, nail down, seal the seams, no problem. Ted and Craig were done quickly. The shingles were a different deal. What seemed light in tear-off were now heavy and awkward when putting on. They needed to be straight and layered in the right pattern. Craig mismeasured the first row, and a gap developed that caused him to remove all but the first two sheets and start over. Ted didn't trust Craig with the power hammer, so every strike was done by hand. His feet were sore from standing on the ladder, and he dropped his hammer or a handful of nails at least a half dozen times. Meanwhile, Ted had finished his half by lunch and cut all the corners.

"Not so easy, huh, kid?" Ted said as he walked over to Craig's side of the roof. He snorted and knelt down to line up the first set on the third row.

"No, sir, it's not," Craig replied, defeated.

"Well, it's sealed up, so we can be done for the day if you like."

"I think I'll come back after lunch and see what I can get done."

"Suit yourself. It's getting hot out here, and I'm retired. You do what you like."

After lunch with Abby, Craig got back to his work. He thought about using the power hammer but decided to continue by hand. He took off his shirt and tied his long, shaggy hair up with a bandana. He had lamented to Abby all through lunch about the heat and the number of times he messed up or dropped something. She laughed at him and said, "Welcome home." That was funny to Craig. "Home."

The work was tedious but rewarding as more and more of the roof was covered. Keeping a straight line was less of an issue, and Craig thought he might be getting the hang of it. He had his music on, so he didn't notice Meghan come up on the roof. He felt her vibration before he heard her.

"Just thought I'd bring you some water," she said, holding out a bottle.

Craig took out his earbuds. "Thanks," he replied, taking the water. He sat back, digging his heels in so he didn't slip down. The water was cold, and he drank deeply, then pressed the bottle to his face.

"How's it going?" Meghan asked as she sat down and stretched her arms above her head. She was wearing nothing more than a bikini top, shorts, and Teva Sandals. Craig could see that she was already acquiring tan lines where her suit was riding up. She smiled at him.

"It's fine. I'm a bit tired."

"Well, you've been working hard." She lay back on the roof. "It's so warm up here."

Craig's eyes narrowed. "It's getting that way."

"So, what are you listening to?"

Craig couldn't believe Meghan was actually flirting with him. He seized on the opportunity. "I am listening to Sarah Jarosz. She's an artist I discovered on Pandora. She's pretty cool."

"Really? What's she like?"

"Bluegrass, country, folk. Kinda hard to pin down." Craig looked her up on his phone. "She looks like Abby I think."

Meghan looked at the picture. "Wow. She really does."

"Yeah. It's like I have Abby singing to me while I work."

"That's a little cheesy," Meghan said with a forced laugh.

"Yeah. But if you listened to her, you'd get it."

"Maybe. I'll give her a listen."

There was an awkward silence before Craig picked up his hammer and said, "I have to get back to work. Thanks for the water."

"You're welcome. See you around."

Craig put his earbuds in and went back to work. When he heard Meghan leave the roof, he relaxed.

The warmth lasted into the evening. With it being midweek, there was no bonfire, so Craig and Abby decided to go fishing so they could sleep in, although Abby was sure she'd be up early anyway. The rhythms of the resort had taken hold of her, and the days seemed to dictate her schedule, not the other way around. In the evening's embrace, Craig and Abby found themselves reviewing their day between casts. Craig actually managed to catch a fish and remove it from the hook by himself, and Abby, as darkness set in, could still land her lure in a circle the size of a volleyball. Craig continued to be amazed at her skill. She was revealed to him day by day, and nothing sent him running. He had been waiting for this time of the day for most of the afternoon. The visit from Meghan had only intensified his desire for Abby. If Meghan was flirting, he didn't mind, but it made him think of Abby more than anything else.

"What is the office looking like? Are you going to be able to get out over the weekend?" he asked.

"I think so. I told my dad that I wanted to work four days in the office and get out Friday through Sunday. He seemed ok with that."

"That's good. I think we'll get this first roof wrapped up by Friday unless there are surprises I don't know about."

"There are always surprises, Craig," Abby said with a twinkle in her eyes. "Something always comes up."

"You're probably right." Craig took one more cast and got it stuck in the weeds. "I just want to work with you sometimes so we can see each other more."

Abby reeled her line in and helped Craig get his unstuck. "We have our nights for now," she said in a low voice.

Craig looked at her. The corners of her mouth went up, but not quite in a smile. The motor sounded quietly, and they moved away from the fishing hole. Darkness surrounded them, but the evening chill wasn't there and the air continued to embrace them in warmth and humidity. There were no other boats out on the lake, and the wind had died down on this Wednesday, leaving the water a smooth plain.

Abby maneuvered the boat to a place where there were no homes along the weedy shore. They were about fifty feet out, and no one was around. Aside from a few crickets, there was no sound. She dropped the anchor and let the boat come to a complete stop. Craig watched as she took out the blankets and pads from the side compartments and made a place for them to lie down. When she waved him over, he came to her and laid down on the floor of the boat. Abby stroked his rough face, and Craig reached for her back. She nuzzled closer and began to kiss him softly. Craig's hand rode up her back and found that she was not wearing a bra. He rubbed the entirety of her back and felt its smoothness as they continued to kiss and she pulled him in closer.

For a moment, Abby hesitated. She moved her hand to Craig's back and squeezed his butt, then pulled away, saying, "Let's go swimming."

Confused, Craig responded, "Here? Won't someone see us?"

"No one will see us, Craig. I know just where we are. We can be quiet."

"Ok." Craig stood up and took off his shirt. He left his shorts on and slid into the water.

On the other side, Abby slid in a moment later, not making a sound. The water was cool but not too cold as she swam around the boat to meet Craig. He beckoned her to follow him, but instead, Abby grabbed hold of the boat, pulling herself up to reveal a bare shoulder. "Why don't you come here?" She slid back down into the water.

Craig made no protest. His heart was racing as he came closer. Still holding onto the boat, Abby grabbed hold of Craig with the other hand and wrapped her legs around him. She kissed him as he reached for the boat to support himself. With the other hand, he began to touch her. She guided his hand at times until he gave in and allowed her to take the lead. After a few minutes, she put her head on his shoulder until he felt her tense briefly, then release, almost melting into him. He felt her hand move over his body and pulled himself away.

Abby felt immediately unsettled and sick to her stomach as she stared at him through the darkness.

"It's fine," Craig said. "Really." There was a shakiness in his voice. Confused, Abby swam away. Craig slowly swam after her.

The First Touch - Abby

I let Craig closer tonight
Out in the water
Where no one else could see
Hidden from the world
He was shaking, unsure
Where he was going
What he was doing
But I am safe and sure
Because he makes me feel
I want him, only him
He is the only one
I will ever
Share my secrets with
No one will ever know
What we know
It is only for us

Craig's Journal

I don't know what she wants from me. Who am I kidding? I know exactly what she wants, but why? Why do we need to go there? I mean, I kinda want to, but what's the deal? Is she afraid she's going to lose me if we don't go further? She should know better. I'm not going anywhere. Sex or no sex, I'm in this. I don't know what to say to her. I don't want her to think I'm rejecting her. I don't know. She's just so, I don't know, incredible. She's incredible and I don't deserve to be loved the way she loves me. I mean, who am I? I'm just some guy she met. Why does she want to share her life with me?

Letter to Abby (maybe never given)

Abby,
  I love you. Know that first and always. Just because I'm not as ready as you doesn't mean that I don't love you. It doesn't mean I don't want you. I think about it all the time. I just, in the moment, can't go that next step. I'm scared. I'm scared I'm going to screw it all up. I will go too far. I will hurt you, and I would never want to ever do that. I'm just so confused. My brain gets in the way of my body. Did I blow it tonight? These are the days I miss having someone to talk to besides you. Sorry if that sounds bad.
  Craig

The next day, on the roof, Craig was having trouble shaking the night before. Even the work, while still commanding his attention and structuring his day, was not enough to distract him from replaying the moment over and over in his head. Abby had led him there. It was beyond doubt that she had taken the initiative, but why? He loved having the ability to take her where she wanted to go, but it scared him too. He decided to focus on the task at hand. Zone in on each sheet of shingles and each swing of the hammer. It worked for a while, and eventually, he met Ted at the top. Craig left the top seam to Ted and went to have lunch before his meeting.

Meanwhile, Abby spent most of the morning staring at a blinking cursor. From time to time, she laughed to herself. She wasn't sure what came over her the night before, but she couldn't say she didn't enjoy it. Craig seemed to know what to do, but at the same time, he pulled away. She couldn't figure out why. It made the whole thing end kinda weird.

There were accounts to be settled and estimates to be fleshed out for the summer. How much was the roof project going to set them back, and what other maintenance could they afford this year? These were all new questions for Abby to grapple with. Her dad wanted the numbers from Memorial Day weekend finalized and printed to review. They had a good weekend, one of the better ones in a few years. However, the loss of revenue from the cabin Claire and Craig were staying in coupled with the loss of one additional cabin a week for the roofing would have an impact. Neither Craig nor Claire were accepting their pay, so Abby was instructed to just put it aside for the time being. She tried to get lost in the numbers, but every time she thought of Craig and the boat, it gave her a shiver.

Craig had grabbed a bite to eat and went to his cabin so he could shower before his meeting. When Abby arrived in the kitchen at their normal lunchtime, he was already gone. She found Claire in the kitchen and grabbed an apron to join in. "What are you working on?" she asked. "Can I help?"

"We're getting some meat prepared for the weekend."

Claire noticed that Abby was just walking around looking at the spices and other ingredients. She wasn't touching anything. "We're trying some longer marinades. Seeing what works."

"Really?" Abby looked at Frank.

"Yes, deary. We're going to try a few new things this summer. Spice it up a little." Frank laughed at his own joke. He looked tired to Abby. Despite the energy Claire seemed to be providing, the bags under his eyes were larger and his movements seemed labored and more deliberate.

Abby repeated, "Can I help?"

"Sure." Frank walked towards her. "You want to break down these birds? Just hand them off to her." He looked at Claire, and Abby understood instantly.

Abby smiled. She wanted to get her hands into something, literally. "Totally broken down?"

"Sure thing," Frank replied.

"Ok." Abby got to it. They were about a half hour into their work, mostly silent except for an occasional comment regarding techniques or tasting this or that, when Abby asked, "Hey, Frank, where are you in the mornings? I haven't seen you out on the lake in a few days."

Frank walked up behind her and put his hand on her shoulder to watch her work. "You and Craig have been doing such a good job this week, I decided to take a walk this morning. Even with what you brought in last night, I still think we will be good for a while. Not sure what you were doing out there, but I don't want you to fish the lake out before the summer really gets going." He laughed as he walked away.

Abby was left unsure of what to say. She focused on getting her last bird done.

When she handed the bird over to Claire, Claire asked in a whisper, "What the hell happened last night?"

Abby shot her a look.

Claire continued, "Craig came in all flustered, and he stayed up half the night writing in his journal."

"His journal?" Abby asked.

"Yes. He writes in it every night."

"I didn't know that."

"Well…whatever. What happened?"

"I really don't want to say here."

"Ok." Claire stopped what she was doing and called out over her shoulder, "We're going to take a walk."

"No problem," Frank replied, not even looking up from his table.

"Come on," Claire said, taking off her apron. Abby held up her hands. "Oh right." Claire looked at her own hands, and they both went off to clean them.

The breeze on the dock had picked up. A few kids were splashing around on shore or lying on the diving raft, taking in the sun. Abby sat quietly. She was amazed at how confident and forward Claire always was, but now she seemed to have gone mute.

"Soooo, last night," Abby said as she looked out over the lake and rubbed her hands.

"Yeah. Craig was acting really weird. This morning too. I found him asleep with his pencil still in his hand. Did you guys have sex or something?"

Abby's head snapped around. She blinked several times, instantly feeling hot.

"I knew it."

"No. No. Well, sort of. No. This is too weird."

"I'm not looking for details, but it seemed like a logical conclusion."

"Well, no. We didn't. Sort of." Abby felt herself getting overwhelmed. "Claire?"

"What?"

"Is Craig ok?"

"What do you mean?"

"Last night was kind of intense. Craig backed away. He always backs away. Is it me?"

Claire looked directly at her. "No. I don't think so."

"Then what?"

"Abby. Craig never does anything halfway."

"I know that. I love that about him. But what does that have to do with us?"

"When you guys go all the way, that's it. Craig is only going to do this thing once. He's all in. I think he's scared of that moment. He's always been that way. Apprehension until the moment is there before him, and then that's it. Decision made. That whole confidence thing, it's all bullshit."

"You think?"

"I know. Enjoy this time. You don't get another try at it. Believe me." Claire turned towards the lake herself and put her arm on the bench behind Abby. She was already starting to feel closer to Abby than to her own sister. However, it was a different feeling being the one giving the advice. The decision to come up to Wood Lake for the summer held a meaning for her that she hadn't quite figured out yet. As with everything, Claire assumed the meaning would reveal itself in due time.

Craig made his way to the football field to meet with Coach Granger. Even with Will there to make the introductions, Craig realized he was nervous. His palms were sweaty on the walk to the field, so he rubbed them on his shorts. The facilities were nothing like Arrowhead, where he had gone to school, but they were nice. The building looked like it had been renovated with a new gym addition, and the field was in mint condition. Craig was impressed with the place and being back on a grass field reminded him of his childhood. Will met him just inside the entrance to the fence and shook his hand. As a linebacker, Will was a solid guy. Craig always tried to avoid the quick inside routes so he wouldn't get hit by guys like Will.

"Hey, man," Will said with a warm smile. He had on a Northland Pines football shirt.

"Hey."

"Coach is finishing up with a few kids. He'll be with us soon."

Craig saw kids running patterns out on the field. He remembered all the days after school when he would run play after play. At this time of the year, the state track meet was almost underway, but he would still go out after track practice and catch a few balls. The only adult on the field, Granger, was a taller man with a healthy beard. Craig touched his own face. He hadn't shaved since he arrived at the resort, and he didn't intend to.

Coach Granger called to Will and Craig, so they jogged over to him. Craig's high school coach never let them walk on the field. It was a tough habit to break.

"Craig McLean," Coach Granger said, reaching out his hand. "It's good to meet you."

Craig shook his hand firmly. "Nice to meet you as well, sir."

"I saw you last year at the state track meet. Man, you're fast. I'm leaving tonight for La Crosse actually. Got a thrower competing."

"Cool, and thanks," Craig said.

"Will says you want to work with us this summer?"

"Yes. If I can, that would be great."

"I think I can arrange something." They began to walk towards the building. "We do it pretty simple around here. Speed, agility, and weight room. I'd like you and Will to run the weight room. We do that first. That way I can get out and work drills with the boys. How's that sound?" They stopped.

"That will work great." Craig looked at Will.

"Yes, Coach. We can do that," Will agreed.

"Good. We'll send you some paperwork to sign and drop off next week. You have an email?"

"I have it, Coach," Will said. "I have the paperwork too."

"Well, great. We don't get started until the week after next."

"Sounds good, sir," Craig said. "I'll get that paperwork to you next week."

"Great," Granger said. He started walking again. "Where you staying anyway?"

"Wood Lake Resort."

"Oh, John's place. You must be Abby's boyfriend."

"Yes, sir," Craig answered proudly.

"Great. She's a sweet girl. Love that place. You know, they should turn that lodge of theirs into a restaurant. Frank's a great cook. They'd make a killing."

Craig smiled. "I'll be sure to mention that."

"Will?"

"Yes, Coach."

"Show Craig around the weight room and get him acquainted." He started to walk away. "Nice to meet you, Craig." Will nodded. "You got it, Coach. Come on, Craig."

Claire and Abby sat in the office with Claire at the computer and Abby looking over her shoulder. "You see here," Claire said, pointing to the menu on the side of the main page. "This type of side navigation is not very intuitive. People tend to go to the top of the screen for menus now. Also, we have to get more pictures on every page." She clicked to the 'reservations' page, which had no pictures, to prove her point.

"You mean more pictures of the resort?" Abby asked.

"Yes and no." Claire opened another window to log on to her cloud drive. "You need pictures of the resort, but also pictures of activities people can do at the resort. See here." She showed Abby some of the pictures she had already taken this summer. There were pictures of people on the tours, kids swimming, and even pictures of wildlife from around the lake. "You need to put people in the experience so potential guests can see themselves being here."

This approach was new to Abby. She had never thought of what it was like to be the person viewing the website. So much of their business was word of mouth. They provided a positive experience when people were already here. Claire was showing her how they might invite new guests.

"Should we make a Facebook page?" Abby asked.

"That would probably be a good idea. Then, if guests post pictures of their vacation, the resort gets tagged and it spreads to their friends and family. Let's set up the Facebook page and a dummy website for now and see how that goes. We can work out the kinks on the dummy site and then take it live later this summer. We can use some of my pictures for now."

"Great. Thanks, Claire."

"Not a problem. My pleasure."

Later, after dinner, which really doubled as a strategy session, Abby and Craig went to watch a movie in the basement. Claire mentioned she was going out, which was noted, but not discussed, while Taylor complained about her increased workload with Abby in the office, and, more immediately, the fact that Abby and Craig were using the TV down in the family room and she had no place to watch her show. Her father suggested she finish some of the work she had left undone in the game room at the lodge. This suggestion was met by Taylor retreating to her room.

After finding a movie, Craig laid his head on Abby's lap as she ran her fingers through his hair. They stayed silent for most of the movie. Craig thought about his meeting with Coach that afternoon. How would he tell Abby and John about the schedule change? How would he get all his work done on the cabins? He wanted to tell Abby and discuss the other thing, but he was scared to bring up either subject.

Abby just wanted to ask Craig if he was ok. She felt the tension as she rubbed his head. She wanted to go out in the boat again to feel him close to her, but she didn't want to scare him. Not wanting to push him away, she, instead, sat in silence.

Finally, Craig said, "You want to walk me home? Lots to do tomorrow."

"Yeah. Final prep on all the open cabins and rooms and whatever else pops up."

Craig nodded and sat up. "Seems like a lot. I'll help you if I can. I need to check on the roof and see how Ted finished it."

"How was that this week?" Abby asked, standing up.

"Good. I like to see things get done."

"I know you do." Abby reached out her hands to pull Craig up. He hugged her tightly.

"Let's go," he whispered and kissed her gently on the forehead.

They made their way upstairs, and Abby called out, "Going to walk Craig back to his cabin!"

"Ok, honey," Vickie called back. "Don't be too late. Lots to do tomorrow."

"Ok."

The evening was almost eerie. One family, who came a few days early to claim the best cabin on the lake, was expecting the rest of their extended family tomorrow. They were a younger couple with kids and were still hanging out on the deck. Other than them, the rest of the resort had grown quiet. Rather than stopping in at the lodge, Craig and Abby went straight to Cabin 13. Abby went to the bathroom while Craig tried to make his bed and straighten his clothes. When Abby came out, he was sitting on his bed rather than the couch or chair. Abby lay down next to him and coaxed him to lay down and face her. Craig stroked her arm while she played with his beard. After a while, she asked, "Are we ok?"

Craig smiled. "I think so."

"Things got intense last night."

"Yeah." Craig paused. "They did." He found his favorite

spot on her back and rested his hand on it.

"Are you ok with it?" Abby asked.

"I think so. Are you?"

Abby blushed and pulled herself a little closer. "Yeah."

"Really?"

She closed her eyes for a moment, then opened them, focusing directly on him. "Yeah. But I don't want to do anything that makes you uncomfortable."

"Thanks."

She kissed him softly and rolled over so he could spoon her. He did exactly what she wanted, and they soon fell asleep.

"So, what do you want to do?" Claire said as she sat down on the bench near the river where she and Shane had decided to meet. Truth be told, it was the only place in town she really knew how to get to besides the art store. She examined Shane, who seemed to be studying the river intently, watching the water rush by. He didn't answer right away. Frustrated, Claire remarked, "What are you looking at?"

"There's a fish, right there," he answered, pointing at a small pool of water gathering behind a rock. "If I had a rod and a fly, I'd drop it right in there and have a nice meal."

"You fish?"

"Do you draw pictures?" He looked at Claire and smiled widely.

Claire was struck by his big brown eyes. He was more alive than anyone she had met in quite some time. "I'm going to ask one more time. What do you want to do? I love sitting here, but I didn't come to town to watch the water go by or dream of fish you cannot catch. Let's do something fun. I've been working all day."

"Ok, ok. Something fun." Shane put his hand to his chin in a mocking gesture. "I know. We can go throw pots."

"Throw pots?"

"Yeah. Remember that place I told you about, the Warehouse?"

"I think so?" Claire said, still a bit confused.

"There's a beginners pottery workshop tonight. Do you want to crash it? Might be fun."

Claire chuckled and nodded her head. "That might be fun."

"Yeah. Let's go throw some really bad beer steins or something."

"Ok. Can't remember the last time I got clay under my fingernails."

Shane chuckled. "I don't think you'll have any problems. Let's go get dirty."

They walked into a studio-like space and sat down at wheels in the back. Claire saw Shane nod at a few people before the instructor started in. He obviously knew most of the people there. Claire tried to listen, but found herself looking at Shane most of the time. He leaned forward like an eager child who was attending his first class. There was a bounce to his presence. He rubbed his hands together, and his focus never varied. Claire felt the urge to draw him. She wanted to capture the shape of his thin face, every angle. She wanted to study his eyes long enough to give them the life and energy they contained. All the lines and shades were coming into her head as she watched him. Then, the clay came. "Are you with Shane?" the instructor asked, breaking her attention.

"Yes," Claire said as pleasantly as she could, smiling up at the older man.

"Welcome then, I'm sure you know what you're doing."

Laying her hands on the cold clay, Claire replied, "I'll do my best, sir."

Shane was already spinning his wheel. His hands moved seamlessly from the water to the clay and up and down. He looked at Claire. "Need help?"

"No. I think I got it," she said unconvincingly. Claire moistened her clay and began to spin her wheel. She had taken a ceramics class or two in high school and undergrad. The feelings came back pretty easily. Clay rose from the wheel, and soon, she had a six-inch cylinder and was ready to create an indent. Shane was almost done with his mug. He came over to Claire's station. She had formed a nice stein-like pot, and Shane moved his fingers lightly up and down the inside.

"Nice job. Very consistent. Should be a good piece."

"Do they fire them?"

"Yeah. We can pick them up next week."

Claire winked at him. "I guess that means I'll have to see you again."

Shane smiled. "That's my plan."

Claire stood up. "Where are you going?" Shane asked.

Putting her hand on his arm, Claire replied, "To get some clay for a handle." She ran her hand along the length of his forearm to the middle of his hand.

Shane looked down at Claire's fingers on his hand. "Oh. Ok."

They went back to work adding handles. Claire made a

simple handle, while Shane was obviously trying to show off a bit. After finishing their mugs and putting them aside, they thanked the instructor and washed up.

"What's next?' Claire asked as they walked out into the light evening sky.

"There's a place we can go hear some live music and get a bite to eat."

"That sounds great."

A few blocks away, they found a bar with a small stage where a guy was playing an electric guitar. Claire watched him for a moment. He was lost in his music, as though no one else existed in the room. Claire loved that kind of focus, both feeling it for herself and seeing it in others. It was the feeling she was most comfortable with.

"I found a place to sit," Shane called out from a table further back.

Claire made her way to the table. The bar was about three-quarters full, and, surprisingly, most of the patrons were listening to the artist. The whole vibe was pretty chill. Claire took her seat and looked at the menu. It was bar food mostly, but she saw "Fish Tacos" and settled on that quickly. Setting the menu back in the stand on the side of the table, Claire started in, "So, who is this Shane character I'm sitting across from tonight? An artist? A drifter? The local boy who knows everyone? What's his deal?"

Shane slowly set his menu down. "Wow. Ok. We're doing the life story thing then?"

"I guess we are. Is that a problem?"

"No, but you already pinned me down with a few labels, so let me have a turn." Shane straightened his chair and locked into Claire as though he were trying to read her mind. "You are an artist of a sort, a suburban girl, a rebel without a cause and…someone who wants more out of life and thinks you have to go bigger, but really needs to let go of a great many things before you realize that what you need is all right here." Shane pointed to his heart.

"Well, that stung a bit," Claire said meekly. The problem was that he'd nailed it. Without even knowing her, he'd pegged her perfectly.

"It only stings when I hit a nerve." His eyes were unwavering.

"Pleasantries aside now, who are you?"

"Ok. Fair enough. Who am I? I guess I'm trying to figure that out."

"Cop out. According to you, I'm the one trying to figure that out. You're just being a dick."

Tipping back in his chair as though he'd been blown over by a stiff wind, Shane said, "Wow. So…I guess I'll start at the beginning. I'm from around here. Not lately, but recently enough. I live with my mom when I'm home. If there's something I want to do or see, I go do it or see it. I can always seem to find a place to stay or work. I stay in hostels if I can't find a place, or I sleep on people's couches. I don't know. That's about it, I guess. I don't really know my dad that well. He lives in the Twin Cities. I've only seen him a few times over the years. My parents broke up when I was pretty young."

"Did you go to high school here?"

"Yeah. I didn't graduate. There was really nothing I could learn that I couldn't read about in a book. If I want to learn about a place, I go there."

"So, you travel?"

"I don't really call it travel. I just live I guess. I mean, I go to places and just try to live for a while and see what I can see and learn whatever I want to learn."

"That must be stressful."

"Why would it be stressful?" Shane asked, looking confused.

"Not knowing where you're going to live or what you're going to do?"

"That's the beauty of it. I get to go wherever I want. And, as for work, there is always work in a restaurant or kitchen. I've cooked all over the country. I just got back from a few months in Washington, D.C. It was great. So much to see and learn. I just spent all day in the museums, walking around. Have you ever been?"

Claire nodded.

"So, you know. The weather is solid, and there is so much to see. History around every corner. I got lost a lot, but if I could find a Metro, I could always get back to where I came from. Found a room at the end of the line to the south and lived there. The guy who owned the house ran a restaurant in the Georgetown area. Gave me a job as a cook. That's how I do it..."

After they ordered, Claire was swept up in Shane's descriptions. She had been to Washington, D.C. on a school trip in high school, but it was scripted and boring. Shane talked about little food trucks and corner places, but mostly, he told stories about the people he met. After working in a Vietnamese restaurant for several months, Shane was obsessed with Southeast Asian spices. It seemed to Claire that he was obsessed with a great many things, but they were all short-lived. He could throw himself wholeheartedly into a place and its people, but then he became obsessed with something else. "Dang, sorry. I've been talking for a while. So, how are things over at Wood Lake?"

Between bites, Claire said, "Good." She finished chewing. "I'm getting acquainted with the place. Lots of work, but fun, you know? I enjoy the kids and their little projects. And Frank, he's the best. He's invited me into his kitchen, which is big."

"It is. They're good people from what I hear. I remember Abby from when I was around here. She was little, but I remember her. Good people. I think Mrs. Whitworth works at the school?"

"They really are. I'm glad I came up here. And yes, Vickie teaches at the elementary school."

"That's right. I thought I knew her. I'm glad you came up here too," Shane said with a return to the intensity he showed at the workshop.

Claire smiled and finished her meal.

They stepped out into the late evening coolness to streets still bustling with people. "Is it always like this?" Claire asked.

"During the summer, yes. The population of this town is triple its size or more in the summer and winter, and then for a few months in the fall and spring, everyone forgets we exist. At least, that's how it feels."

"What made you come back this time?" They were walking down the street, and Shane had taken hold of her hand, which almost disappeared in his. It felt nice. She had not held hands with a boy in quite a while.

Shane looked off in the distance, and after a long pause, he replied, "I missed my mom."

"Aw," Claire responded sarcastically.

Shane squeezed her hand and gave her a sideways glance. "Hey, I did. Washington was tapped out. I needed to come home. I guess I thought I might meet someone this summer."

Claire looked over at Shane. He winked. "I guess this is me," Claire said as they reached her car.

"Really? So soon? Let's sit down for a while."

They were at the same bench where they had met earlier in the evening. Claire couldn't think of a reason not to sit down, so she said, "Sure." They sat down, and Shane let go of her hand and looked out over the river.

"I told you all about myself at dinner. I talked through the whole meal. You never got to tell me about who you are and where you come from."

"Not much to tell, I guess." Claire turned to Shane and smirked. "I am the suburban girl. I'm the rich kid trying to act like she's from the gritty city."

"No. I was just joking earlier. I bet there's a lot more to you."

"I want there to be. Sometimes, I wonder though. I know all about these artists because I've seen pictures of their work and memorized facts about their lives or their use of color or whatever. But who does that make me? A girl who can draw pictures and take photos?"

Shane shifted his position to face Claire. "I don't know. Is that how you see yourself?"

"Sometimes." Claire was afraid to really let him in. She guarded herself from most people, but for some reason, she felt as though she could talk to this guy.

Shane spread out his hands as though framing her in a picture. "I see a girl who can see people. It's not like you're just drawing people or taking photos. You're capturing moments. You're trying to feel those moments with the subjects. I sense you want something more, but you're looking for meaning in the wrong places."

"What do you mean?"

"Don't take this the wrong way, but I'm guessing you come from a neighborhood with big houses on loopy streets and manicured lawns where all the moms drive big, expensive SUVs."

Nodding, Claire replied, "That's accurate."

"And you thought if you went to art school in the big city, you'd find some meaning in the middle of a great big world that was unlike your own?"

"Ok. Maybe."

"You're looking in the wrong places. You've got to get small. See the little things. Look in a person's eyes. That is where the meaning of life is. Go see the paintings and sculptures of the world."

"How do you do that?"

"You are already doing it. The picture you drew of Manny, the old guy on the bench down that way. I saw you drawing it when I walked out to my car after I met you at the art store. I didn't stop and talk because I didn't want to mess up your flow. You wanted to know his story. Or at least you were trying to capture his story in the picture. You weren't concerned with technique or where a line went, art school shit. You were interested in the moment you were seeing. That's the meaning."

Claire stared at him and shook her head ever so slightly. "You're something, you know that?"

"Something, huh? I guess that's a start."

"Listen, I gotta go. Breakfast service is going to come soon enough. Besides, I gotta check in with my little brother and see what I missed this evening."

"Ok. I'll pick up the mugs and hold them until I see you next."

"Why don't you just bring them over to the resort?"

Shane's expression went blank. He stuttered, "Oh. Ok. Maybe I'll do that."

Claire got up and patted him mockingly on the head. "See you around, Shane."

"Yeah. It's a small town."

"So it is." Claire walked to her car and hoped she could figure out how to get back to the resort in the dark.

When Claire finally got home from her date with Shane, she found Abby enveloped in Craig's arms. Both of them were still in their work clothes, peacefully asleep.

CHAPTER 7

The first weekend of June was a whirlwind, as Craig suspected all the weekends would be. His only connection to home was checking the state track returns as they came in on the web. He tried to help at the resort where he could, but "the boys," as they came to be called, Daniel and Jackson, had the cleaning down to a science, and Frank had Claire in the kitchen. Claire had Vickie, unable to fully give up her duties as art leader, to help with the kids' projects. Abby didn't need him to come on the fishing tours or late afternoon photo tours. He would just take up room on the boat. So, he ended up playing with the kids. Craig joined Taylor for soccer games or played water polo while Meghan watched on. No one bothered him as long as he looked busy. While he was leading a game of football with the late elementary and middle school kids, Abby caught his eye and winked on her way out to fish with a few guests for the second time of the day.

The weekend tours were Abby's thing. She always had a mixture of regulars who wanted to go to the old holes and newbies who had never put a line in the water before. The only problem was that they had to take the touring pontoon, and it took so long to get anywhere. She loved the speed of her boat because she could spend more time fishing and less time getting there, and all the unpleasant side talk could be avoided. The afternoon tours were more newcomers, or those who wanted to get away from the hustle for a while. They needed more instruction, often providing Abby with a lot to do. Gone was the temptation to throw in her own line.

Claire, although distracted by thoughts of Shane, occupied herself with food prep and her twice daily art projects. There were lots of fun activities at the resort, and she loved what the place afforded. Kids would come and go, and she would try to tailor her projects to their desires. Some kids wanted to draw or paint while others just wanted to play with the materials. She let kids do as they pleased for the most part but always made it mandatory that they clean up. This scared some away, while others, it seemed, would stay the whole day with her if they could.

Claire also started taking the lead on some Friday and Saturday meals. Frank stepped back and marveled in the new creations Claire offered. There were Greek- and Italian-inspired spice mixes that garnered mostly positive reviews from customers. Even John, who was as resistant to change as a piece of granite, enjoyed the flavors and encouraged her to continue with the experiments.

The weekend flew by, and cabins needed to be turned on Sunday and the whole lodge cleared only to be filled halfway again on Monday. A few were staying the week and had fallen into their own rhythms of rising early to fish or sleeping until the noon sun warmed the air for swimming or boating. Some guests brought their own boats, and Abby overheard discussions John had with them about permanent cabins and "places up north." Those talks were always uncomfortable because the resort depended on regular visitors who didn't buy their own places. For the past few years, John had often complained about the ownership trend over family dinners.

Many years ago, John had a conversation that threw him completely for a loop. Abby remembered it clearly. He came into the house in a huff, midday, which was unusual. A regular, whose family had been coming to the resort for years, even before the Whitworths had owned the place, had just bought a "family compound" on the other side of the lake. He described the encounter to Vickie, who told him that a lot of the Chicago folks were thinking the same thing. It seemed like people loved coming to the area, but they wanted the freedom to come whenever they wanted, no reservations and no planning. John, despite being an intelligent man, could not wrap his head around the idea. He was upset for weeks and never fully recovered from the blow. It didn't help that he saw the former guest at least a half dozen times every year. Instead of thinking of him as a friend, John simply thought of the entire family as lost revenue.

On Sunday afternoon, after the last art project, Claire and Shane snuck out in a canoe before dinner. There was a spot on the lake that Claire knew no one ever went, and they got there easily. Shane was a very skilled paddler.

"This is a nice place," Shane said.

"Yeah, I like it. You know, I've only been here a few weeks and I already feel so at ease."

"Really? I get bored around here sometimes." He gently turned the boat, and Claire flipped around in the front seat to face him.

She put her paddle down, still dry from lack of use. Not that she would know what to do with it even if she tried. "I'm far from that. There's so much to do! You never think about how places like this are run."

"I do. This type of place is all I know, here, Colorado, California. I've never really worked anywhere else."

"I guess. I like it. John's nice, and Frank is really cool. He's letting me cook. You should try some of the stuff I've come up with." Claire dipped her hand in the water, making a small wake behind it.

Shane leaned his head over, following Claire's hand. Then he straightened up, catching her eyes. "Where did you learn to cook?"

"College. If you can read, you can cook, right?"

"No." Shane almost laughed out loud.

"Well, that's where I started, and then kinda expanded from there," she said, shrugging her shoulders.

Relenting, Shane said, "That's cool. What do you cook?"

"Greek and Italian. Not big on pasta. I just like the spice palate."

"It's a good one. Have you ever thought about using Middle Eastern spices? I worked at a Middle Eastern joint in Austin for a few months, and that stuff will kick your butt."

"Maybe you could cook something for me," Claire said quietly.

"Sure. Might have to use your kitchen. I could throw something together."

"Nice." Claire moved so she could sit back against Shane's legs. "Hey, do you do any of that wood-burned sign work I saw downtown?"

"Yeah," Shane said. "Why?"

"I was thinking of putting new signs on all the cabins.

I thought wood burn would look nice."

Shane nodded as though he was already thinking of what they might look like. "What should they say?"

"I don't know. Maybe tree names or fish or something. All they have now are numbers."

"I'll get right on it."

Claire looked up at him. "I can pay for materials."

"It's wood. There's no need for money." He pointed to the woods all around them. "I think I have plenty of material."

When they got back to the resort and docked the boat, it was nearly time for dinner service. Claire didn't need to be there, but she decided to report out of habit. Shane was quiet as they approached the lodge. He tried to say he needed to go, but Claire insisted that she could quickly throw something together for him to taste. He sat at a table on the other side of the dining room, near the deck, as Claire went into the kitchen.

"Who's the guy?" Daniel asked as he stopped in the kitchen for a snack.

Frank growled from behind a large pot on the stove, "Shane Olson."

"How do you know Shane?" Claire asked.

"I'll tell you later. Short answer is, I don't like to see him around here. You be careful with that one."

She narrowed her eyes. "Shane? He's harmless."

"Like I said, be careful, Claire. We'll talk later." He left to go into the fridge.

Claire rolled her eyes and shook her head.

Daniel just shrugged his shoulders.

Claire brought out some food, and Shane ate it quickly. He

complimented the flavor and the look of the lodge but said little else. He stayed quiet as Claire walked him to the parking lot.

"Craig," a voice said as he sat on the steps of his cabin writing in his journal. Craig looked up, then stood quickly when he realized it was John. "Yes, sir."

"At ease, kid," John replied. "We have a few more guests than normal for a summer Sunday, so we're going to have a fire tonight. I need you to get some wood cut and set up right after dinner is served. Don't want to have too late a night. Got it?"

"You bet." Craig went inside to store his journal and put on a ratty shirt.

While he was chopping, Craig could tell that someone was watching. He heard a rustling in the trees coming from the lodge's direction. Hoping it was Abby, he turned with the sledge up on his shoulder, trying to strike a manly pose. It was Meghan. "Oh, hi," Craig said haltingly.

Smiling wide, Meghan responded in a lower voice than normal, "Hello." She walked over and began to pick up the logs and sticks, putting them in the trailer.

"Thanks," Craig said pensively. He set the wedge, chopped the last two logs, and then started loading them up as well. Meghan watched him.

"Do you need any more help? The kids aren't swimming anymore, and tomorrow's my day off, so I'm just trying to pass the time."

"Not really."

She looked down and kicked at the dirt. "Ok. What's with the wood?"

"We're having a fire tonight."

"On a Sunday?"

"Yeah. I guess there are more guests than expected, and John wants a fire. Lots of kids or something."

"Oh. Maybe I'll stick around. Eat with Abby's family." She picked up another piece of split wood. "Hey, did you see the guy your sister was with today?"

Craig remembered seeing Claire and a guy go out in a canoe in the middle of the afternoon. He never worried about Claire. She could handle herself. "Yeah, I saw them. Do you know him?"

"I think his name is Shane O-something. Good for her though. He's a cutie."

Craig really didn't know what else to say to Meghan. He kinda just wanted her to go away, but he was too nice to say anything mean. "Cool. Well, I gotta get this over by the pit, and Cabin 6 wanted some wood for their fireplace. Not sure why, it's been so warm."

"It sure has," Meghan replied. "Well, see you later." She walked away and disappeared into the woods.

Craig got on the four-wheeler. 'That was weird,' he thought to himself, shaking his head.

Claire found Abby walking some towels to one of the far cabins close to Frank's place. She asked to lighten the load, and Abby complied, handing her three of the towels. After they dropped them off, Claire asked, "Can we go for a quick walk before dinner?"

Abby checked her watch. "Sure. We have about twenty-five minutes."

"Good. It won't take that long." Claire knew that it was in Abby's nature to be structured, and the resort had a way of drumming that into you. There really was no other choice.

"Wanna walk past Frank's house?" Abby asked.

"Sure. I've never been down that way."

They walked into the forest with the lake still visible to their left. There was a path of sorts, more overgrown, not like the shortcuts worn in throughout the resort. Claire was still getting to know these paths almost three weeks in. She saw moss growing and small bugs scurrying about. A few trees leaned against others, and some had fallen completely. Nature, in all its glory, was constantly around her. Although the Chicago skyline no longer closed in on her, the trees had a similar effect.

They reached a tall tree that had fallen. The scene was perfectly peaceful. A gentle breeze moved the water slowly, and only an occasional bird call punctuated the silence. This was where Abby had sat with Craig, and it was quickly becoming a favorite place for her. "Let's sit here," she said.

Claire sat on the fallen log. "This is great." The trees framed the lake perfectly.

Abby looked over at her. "What's up?"

Claire didn't answer right away. She caught sight of a heron gliding down to the shoreline. "Nothing much. How are you?"

"Busy. It was good to get out of the office this weekend."

Claire shifted to face Abby. "I bet. Pretty stuffy in there when you have all of this just outside."

"Yeah. Hopefully I'll get a handle on things soon so I can get out more. The newly released Facebook page is already showing some activity. People posted pictures from Memorial Day."

"Really? Good." Claire paused to take in her surroundings. "So you and Craig are good?"

Abby blushed and looked out towards the lake. "We are. We talked it out. You were right."

"Yeah. So…"

Abby could tell Claire was avoiding something. "What's up, Claire?"

Claire knew that Abby was waiting for her to start. She looked down at the ground and drew a circle in the dirt with the toe of her shoe. Then she turned and just said it. "You know Shane Olson, right? The guy we met at Meghan's mom's store?"

"Yeah, I know him. Or at least I know of him."

"Is there anything I need to know about him?"

"What do you mean?"

"I don't know. Frank mentioned he knew him. Not sure how. I know he's from around here, but Frank seemed angry."

Abby took a peek at the lake, seeing some familiar boats out for an early evening ride. "Hmmm. I don't know specifically why Frank would be angry. Shane's always been a little, I don't know, shifty? He's like a guy without a home. He drifts in and out on a whim. I guess that's all I really know."

"Ok, thanks." Claire looked out at the lake, getting lost in it.

"Sorry I couldn't give you more."

"That's ok," she said, turning back to Abby.

They stayed quiet for a while. Then Claire said, "I really like it here."

"Really?" Abby replied. "You don't miss the city?"

"Not yet. There's such a rhythm to this place, you know?" She chuckled. "Well, of course you know."

Abby laughed as well.

Claire continued breathing deliberately, focusing her mind. "I like the hustle of the city. It's alive in a way, but not like how this place is alive. Even on the weekends, life seems to take its time. It allows you to come to it rather than being in your face." Claire looked right at Abby, whose tight smile and watering eyes showed her that she had hit right on it.

"That's it. You know, school sometimes overwhelms me. All the artificial deadlines and waiting around. I can't do that with my life. I need more control," Abby said.

"That's funny. Cause I think I need less, and that's what I feel I have up here."

"Interesting. I guess we feel exactly the opposite about the same thing."

"That is interesting. Different perspectives from the same picture, I guess." Claire got up and reached out a hand. "We should probably get back."

"Yeah. Frank will be wondering where we are. You should just ask him about Shane. I'm sure he'll tell you." Abby grabbed Claire's hand.

Pulling her up, Claire said, "Maybe I will."

Craig got a bucket of water from the lake and poured it on the fire to make sure it was out, then kicked the ashes and stomped on the coals just to be sure. Later that night, he was supposed to meet Abby at the dock to go out fishing. With the fire sufficiently out, he walked over to his cabin to get his suit on just in case Abby had something else in mind, but someone was sitting on the steps. It was Meghan.

"Hey, Craig."

"Hi," Craig said, unsure of why she was there.

"That was a good day, huh?"

"Sure." He stood at the base of the stairs.

"Can I ask you something?"

"I guess. I'm supposed to meet Abby soon."

"Oh." She looked down and kicked her heel against the step. "Maybe some other time then?"

"No, what is it?" Craig tried not to sound annoyed, but this was the second time she'd snuck up on him today.

"My boyfriend, well, ex or whatever…he called me and invited me to come down next weekend to Milwaukee."

"Ok?"

"Should I go?"

Craig was not sure why she wanted to know what he thought. "Do you want to go?"

Meghan got up and slowly walked in a small circle, dragging her toes in the dirt. "I don't know."

"Well…do you like the guy?" Craig took his bandana off and ran his fingers through his hair.

Meghan stopped and looked squarely at Craig. "Yeah. He was great. But he broke it off to get back with his high school girlfriend. I guess it didn't work out."

Wiping his face with the bandana, Craig replied. "Well… go then."

"You think?"

Craig took a step up the stairs. "Yes, go. If nothing else, you get to go to the city for a weekend."

Meghan nodded. "You're right. Thanks, Craig. I should jet then." Just before she left, Meghan said, "Hey, Craig?"

He turned. "Yes?"

"I listened to that singer you told me about, Sarah Jarosz."

"What did you think?" Craig asked cheerfully.

"I think my best friend is a lucky girl." She walked away around the side of the cabin before Craig could respond.

Abby watched the exchange from the grass in front of the lodge. She was going to get Craig because he was late, but stopped. Neither of them had seen her, she was sure. 'What were they doing?' She waited, motionless, until Craig emerged, then she walked towards him.

Craig saw Abby and broke into a jog. Reaching her, he said, "Hey."

"Hey."

"Sorry I'm late. Had to get the fire out and then Meghan stopped by." He scrunched up his face. "Weird."

"Oh really? What did she want?" Abby's voice was as normal as she could make it, but if Craig looked at her, her eyes would have burned through him. She didn't like secrets.

"She's having boy problems. I don't know why she would talk with me about them."

"That's weird."

"Yeah." Craig grasped Abby's hand tightly. "Let's go." The two of them jogged off to the boat and ventured out on the lake.

The One - Abby

Craig says I sing songs
To him all day
While he works.
I think he's cheesy
And sometimes full of crap.
But then, I tried
Listening to his songs.
I tried to hear
What he hears
When he is listening.
What does he think
I'm trying to say to him?
One song says something
Like "I think you
Just might be the one."
I hope that is what
He thinks of me.
Because, when I'm alone
With him, I know
He's the one. The only
One that will ever be.

CHAPTER 8

The second cabin went much smoother than the first. Craig had tear-off done with all the nails pulled by the end of the first day. He even got a few rows of tar paper measured and cut so he could get on it early the next day and start laying rows of shingles later. Ted checked in on him both Monday and Tuesday morning, but felt that Craig had everything pretty well in hand. The days went fast. Craig found a rhythm, and he and Abby spent the beginning of the week seeing each other when they could. By Wednesday afternoon, Craig had reached the point where he had only finish work left, which Ted would need to show him.

Sitting at dinner that evening with Abby, Vickie, Taylor, and the boys, Craig got a call. "I have to take this," he said, excusing himself from the table. "Hey."

"Hey, Craig," Will responded.

"What's up, Will?"

"Me and a couple of the guys are going to start lifting tomorrow. School's out, and I got a key."

"Really?" Craig said. The thought of getting back to the gym excited him.

"Yeah. I just thought you might want to come join us. We're going to start tomorrow at seven."

"Ok. I might be there." Craig had reached the deck outside.

"Cool." Will hung up.

Craig sat out on the deck. The lake danced in little ripples with the low sunlight, the pines were in full bloom, and the world was awash in blue and green. Abby came up behind him and put her hands on his shoulders. He raised his hands to touch hers.

"Who was that?" she asked.

"Will."

"Oh. What did he want?"

"He invited me to lift with some of the football players from the high school."

"Really. When?"

"Tomorrow."

Abby was confused. "Are you going to go?"

"I'm not sure."

"Don't you have work to do?"

"I'm pretty far ahead. Only the finish work is left, which Ted has to show me."

"Oh. Ok."

She moved one hand to his face and ran her fingers along his beard. The roughness had started to give over to smooth curls. She liked the look. "I just want to make sure you finish your obligations."

Obligations. The word sank deep into his consciousness. "No problem." Craig turned and pulled her down onto his lap. "I'll get it done."

Abby laid her head on his shoulder. Although she didn't like when Craig got cocky or overly confident, he had rarely failed. She had to trust that he could balance the work. "So you're going to go then?"

"I think it's a good opportunity to meet the kids."

"Ok. Fishing tonight?"

"Sure."

"Let's go," Abby said and kissed his ear.

He turned and pulled her in to kiss her lips. She shivered. "What?" he asked.

"Fuzzy kisses." She smiled.

Craig drew his hand to his face. "Should I shave it?"

"No. I like it." Abby kissed him again and got up to go to the boat.

When Craig got back that night, Claire had fallen asleep on the couch while watching a cooking show, but Craig turned off the TV before he could tell which one. Just as he was about to cover her with a spare blanket, she sat up, stretching. "Hey, little sister," Craig joked.

Yawning, she asked, "What time is it?"

Craig put the blanket down on the arm of the couch and took a seat next to Claire. "I think it's almost eleven. I'm not sure entirely."

Claire blinked a few times, trying to wake up. "So, were you out fishing?" She smiled.

Craig chuckled. "Yeah. Something like that."

"So, you guys are good then?"

"We're good." Craig smiled.

"That's excellent. I'm happy for you. How's the work going?"

Craig thought about all the cabins he had left. "It's ok. It's necessary for the resort, but it's a lot of work."

"Yeah. This place is like that, I guess. Lots of work that needs to be done." Claire turned awkwardly, cracking her neck.

"It's so different from anything I've encountered."

"It is," Craig said, nodding. "Don't get me wrong, I love this place."

"Oh no, no. I love it too. I'm just saying, it's nothing like how we were brought up."

"You got that right. I sometimes find it hard to believe that Abby grew up here."

"It's certainly unique. But it's cool."

"It's just that there's so much to learn about the place." Craig yawned too. He knew he needed to get some sleep if he was going to get up early.

"Hey, what do you think Mom and Dad would think of this place?"

"I don't know." Craig tried to imagine what Mike might be like wandering around the grounds. He shook the thought from his head. "I don't want to think about it."

Claire smiled at the thought. "I hope Dad's doing ok."

"Me too. He seemed good before I came here. He just needs to stay consistent."

"I guess. I think I'll stop over there before going back to school. I'm sure Mom would like that."

"I'm sure."

Claire moved to get up. "I'm going to bed. Frank will be expecting me in the morning."

Craig watched Claire walk to her room, but before she made it through the door, said, "Hey, before you go. How's it going with that Shane guy?"

Not willing to get into it, Claire said, "Goodnight, Craig."

"Ok," Craig said, knowing the non-answer was her answer. "Goodnight."

In the morning, Craig wasn't there to fish. Abby went to another hole and had a pretty good day. She took her time to see if the fish would flash and dropped her cast in just the right spot, allowing the fish to come to her. The sense of control Abby had over herself and the activity was comforting. She barely thought of Craig the whole time. The moment found its way into her soul, and she tried to recognize it the way she and Kate had talked about throughout the past year. 'I wonder how she's doing?' Abby thought. Aside from a few text messages, she had not heard much from Kate, but they had decided to room together again during the upcoming year.

When she came back to the dock, she found John wrestling with the pontoon. The engine was partially taken apart, and parts were sitting on the dock. Abby asked, "Everything ok?"

"Not really," he replied, kicking the boat. It drifted a few feet before he pulled it back to the dock. "This piece of shit is just shit. That's it. Going to have to replace the engine probably. Where's that money coming from?"

"It will be ok, Dad. We're fine."

"I know. But if it's not one thing, it's another. You know? Where the hell is Craig this morning? I could have used his help."

"He's at the high school, lifting."

"What? Why?"

"He's doing some student teaching, or field hours…I don't know what it's called. Something for school in the fall. He'll be there a few mornings a week."

"Is that so? When did this come up?"

"Last week. He said he talked to Coach Granger. I thought he told you."

"First I'm hearing of it."

"Interesting," Abby said, stepping out of her boat to tie it to the dock.

"I hope he has time to get his work done."

Abby reached into her cooler to get her fish out. "I know he's way ahead this week."

John reached down to look in Abby's cooler. "Wow."

"What?"

"Nice fish. Where'd those come from?"

"I tried a hole over on the north end."

"Nice." He closed the cooler. "But, like I said, Craig better get his work done around here. I'm not giving up a whole summer's revenue on a cabin for nothing."

"He knows. Claire's pulling her weight so far."

"Yes, she is. She's an impressive girl."

"She sure is. Well, I better get these fish over to Frank."

John winked at his daughter. "Love you, Abby."

"Love you too, Dad."

On Friday, Craig worked through lunch to finish the cabin to Ted's specs. The finish work was still difficult for him, but he snapped some pics and took a video of Ted working and was sure he could master the technique. Ted chuckled at the action. While he worked, Craig thought about the kids he was going to work with. 'Kids,' Craig thought. It was a funny word given that he was only a year or two older than most of them. They had gone over two lifts the first day, squat and clean.

Craig was happy with how many details he remembered. The pointers he gave on body position and angles of attack were gobbled up by the players. Helping these kids gave him a new sense of accomplishment.

While he was touching base with Abby, John mentioned that there was a group leaving the resort at noon on Sunday and challenged Craig to get started on the roofing as soon as they left. "That way we can possibly tackle two cabins this week to get ahead."

"I'll try, sir. The tear-off isn't the problem. It's the shingling."

"Well, Ted's going to visit his son in California for the first two weeks of July, so we need to get ahead."

Despite his apprehension about flying solo, Craig tried to sound confident. "I'll get right on it."

"Hope you can fit it into your schedule," John said in a sharp tone.

Craig wrinkled his eyes, then looked at Abby for some guidance. She shrugged and looked away.

"Well," John said, "break time is over, and we have another weekend ahead of us. Time to go to the bar. Abby?"

"Yes, Dad?"

"Frank probably needs help in the kitchen. Craig?"

"Yes, sir?"

"Time to get a fire set up. Might as well get ahead. Check the wood levels at the cabins as well."

"Yes, sir."

"Taylor?"

"What?"

"You should go to the game room and see if you can get some fun going."

"Fine," Taylor responded without protest. She was getting better as the summer got underway.

"Vickie, I'll see you later?"

"Yes, I'll be over later. Jane and the kids are in from Chicago, so I'm going to catch up with them."

"Is Richard with her?"

"No, he had to be in Atlanta for the weekend."

"Righty-o."

Everyone got up and went to work.

"Another weekend," Abby said, looking at Craig with a smile.

"You bet," Craig responded, trying to match her enthusiasm. He was tired but wore a smile for her.

Abby could see that Craig needed rest. His movements were slow, and he had been fighting to keep his eyes open all through the meeting. No nights out on the boat this weekend. 'Maybe I should let him sleep tomorrow,' she thought. As they walked to the kitchen together, she squeezed Craig's hand. He turned and smiled, swinging their hands in rhythm with their steps.

Claire urged Shane to stop by Saturday afternoon to help some kids whittle during afternoon art since several of the upper elementary boys had knives and wanted to make something. He agreed, but the nervous tone in his voice concerned Claire. When he got there, she was set up with some easels and a couple blocks of wood on the grass. Shane set down the first few cabin signs he wood-burned, then sat with the boys, immediately engaging them with his abilities. They did more watching than carving, but when they did get going, Shane moved from boy to boy, getting down close and walking them through their cuts.

As she painted, Claire caught his eye from time to time and laughed at his funny expressions. He was just so handsome and intense. It seemed to her that he could do anything. She knew it couldn't be more than a summer fling, but she meant to enjoy it. When art time was over, the kids all left with creations they loved while guests (mostly women) started gathering by the dock for the photo tour. Abby met Claire and Shane with her clipboard, already registering guests.

With Shane along, there would be one too many people on the boat, but Claire still didn't feel comfortable driving.

"I can drive, Abby," Shane said in a low voice that only she could hear. "If you have something else to do."

"I always have something else to do, Shane." She laughed. "Claire, you know where to go, right?"

"Sure thing," she replied, squeezing Shane's arm. "I'll take this little charmer and the ladies to all of the pretty spots."

"Ok, y'all have fun then," Abby said, handing over the registration clipboard.

Abby found Craig chopping wood and asked if he wanted to help Frank with dinner prep. He agreed but needed to change first. She told him to meet her in the lodge in fifteen minutes.

Frank was surprised to see Abby when she entered the kitchen. "Aren't you supposed to be out on the tour?"

"Claire's out there. I thought I'd help you today."

"Lovely," Frank replied, giving her a hug. "It's good to have you." He went back to his work station. "Who's driving the boat?"

"Her friend, Shane."

Frank dropped his knife, and his face went red. He reached for a towel to wipe his hands and started to walk quickly towards the door. "Like hell he is. You keep prepping… breaded lake perch and pheasant over rice. There are baked potatoes in the oven."

"Frank?" Abby called as he stomped through the door.

"Not now." He marched right up to the bar and motioned for John to follow him to the deck. Abby could see them through the window. Frank was throwing his arms in the air, shaking them violently. Her father was trying to calm Frank by laying his hands on his shoulders, which he abandoned the second time Frank slapped them away.

Craig walked by, but John waved him off, so he went in the kitchen by Abby. "Wow. I've never seen Frank that pissed."

"I know. I don't know what's going on," Abby stated with concern.

"They were arguing about that guy, Shane, that Claire's been seeing from town. Other than that, I don't know."

"Well, we better get to work or he'll be pissed at us too."

"Right. What can I do?" Craig went to the wall to get an apron.

"Begin prepping the veggies?"

"No problem."

They both got to work. When Frank came in, not a word was spoken. Dinner prep continued, and dinner went well, as it always did. Claire came back in to finish dessert, and Abby continued to prep for the next day. Craig went out to charm the guests and serve drinks to the tables. It was as though nothing had happened. When dinner was over, Frank excused himself, saying he was not feeling well, and left the kids to close down the kitchen.

Around nine, when everything was shut down except the bar, Craig and Abby went to sit out on the deck. John asked Claire to watch the bar while he went to talk with the couple.

John walked out on the deck over to where Craig and Abby were sitting. "That sister of yours can do it all, can't she, Craig?"

"Seems so, sir."

"So," John started in as he pulled up a chair. "About Frank earlier."

"Yeah, what was up with that?" Abby asked.

"Frank was pretty mad. That Shane guy, the one who Claire's been hanging with? Well, Frank doesn't like him one bit." John's tone was more serious than usual.

"Why? Is he a bad guy?" Craig asked, leaning forward.

"Well...it's hard to say. Let's see, where should I begin?" He looked to the lake as though waiting for an answer to come to him. "Shane's kind of a drifter."

"Everyone knows that," Abby chimed in.

"Let me finish, dear," John continued looking at Abby, then back to Craig. "Like I said, he's a drifter. Restless, I would say. See, Shane was a good student when he was younger. His dad was a realtor around here, right during the housing boom. People were buying land and snatching up old places to fix up. He was doing really well. Everything was fine, Shane was a great kid, talented artist, and a good singer at church according to your mother. His mom could stay at home. But then the crash of '08 came, and they lost almost everything. Things got bad when his dad lost his business. His parents split up, and his dad moved to the Twin Cities to start over. Shane must've been fourteen or fifteen at the time. He seemed fine, played football, heck of a player according to Frank. Running back or receiver or something. But his mom couldn't find steady work, and the money his dad sent wasn't enough, and that dried up too, I guess. Shane got hurt and couldn't play football anymore, so he went to work for a few places around town, but never quite fit in. Then, when he was sixteen or seventeen, he was working at Rick's Place. You know the one, right, Abby?"

"I know the place." Her eyes had not wavered from her father.

"Well, one day, must've been mid-fall, right around Halloween, a bunch of money went missing, and so did Shane. Everyone knew what happened, but it seemed he gave most of it to his mom and skipped town. No one ever gave her a bit of trouble about it, and now she works at Walmart I've heard, as a resort cleaner sometimes. Meanwhile, Shane comes in and out of town as he pleases. Supposedly, he works the winters in Colorado at resorts and then travels in the off-season. Frank doesn't trust the kid. Rick's a good friend of Frank's. They go way back."

"What do you think of him?" Craig asked.

"Well, I believe in giving people a second chance. I don't know. I guess I'll trust him until I don't. You know what I mean?"

"I think so, sir," Craig replied.

"Now, we aren't going to tell Claire about all this. Let her find it out. Who knows, maybe he's a changed man. Besides, I think she could handle him if she needed to."

"Probably," Abby said.

"Frankly," John said, looking in on the bar. "I'll bet she'd kick his ass." They all laughed and sat back quietly. John interjected, "Either way, I'd keep an eye on things. Let's get that bonfire going, Craig."

Getting up and stretching his arms above his head, Craig replied, with a sigh. "Yes, sir."

CHAPTER 9

"Where are we going?" Claire asked as Shane had her take a left off a very bumpy paved road onto a dirt one.

"I have to pick something up at home for a guy. I promised I would have it done after the festival over Memorial Day weekend, and I just got it done last night. Here." He pointed. "This is us."

The home was a double-wide trailer set up on a little rise in the woods. There was a small, white, rundown shed with a car parked in front and another car along the side, although the second one looked like it hadn't run in years. Smoke billowed from the top of a large kiln that sat between the house and the shed. Claire suspected there were a lot of "cabins in the woods," but so far, she had only seen homes in town or around the lake.

"Home sweet home," Shane sighed as the car came to a stop. "I'll only be a second. You can wait in the car if you'd like."

"Is your mom home?" Claire asked as she pulled the door handle.

"I think so," Shane said as he got out of the car and started walking towards the house.

Claire followed him. "Wouldn't it be rude to stay in the car and not say hello?"

Shane stopped walking and turned towards Claire. "I suppose. There aren't really any rules with my mother. She just goes with the flow. If you want to say hi, I'm sure she'd appreciate it." He waited for her to catch up.

"Ok." Claire moved close enough to hold Shane's hand. She liked how it felt. There was a childishness to the gesture that she appreciated.

As they walked to the door, Claire observed a pile of broken pots sitting next to the kiln. Other pots, that looked like they had been shot with a gun, were littered all around the property.

"Hey, Mom," Shane called from the door as they entered. A small TV sat in the living room, while a wheel and table covered in clay dominated the small space.

"Hi, Shane," a voice called weakly from a room past the kitchen.

Claire had been in small apartments in Chicago, but they had always been decorated with trendy colors and furniture. This place looked worn. Nothing here belonged in the current decade. The small couch against the far wall was beaten and half-covered with a yellowing sheet. Clay dust permeated every inch of the home. The side table in the kitchen was covered with papers, and the two chairs on either side of it didn't match.

Shane waited as his mother came down the hall and greeted him with a peck on the cheek, then he disappeared down the same narrow hallway once it was clear. There wasn't enough room for two people. Shane's mother turned to Claire. "And who are you?"

"I'm Claire," she said. "I came by with Shane."

"Oh. And how do you two know each other?"

"We met in town a few weeks ago."

"So, you're here for vacation?"

"No. I work at a resort on the other side of town. I'm here for the summer." Claire looked her straight in the eyes. "Pardon me for asking, but I didn't catch your name."

"Janie."

"It's nice to meet you, Janie. You have some lovely pieces around here. You're a potter?"

Janie looked in Claire's direction, but with a vacant stare, as though she was looking past her. "What resort do you work at?"

Claire was trying to be pleasant, but Janie had totally ignored her attempt. "I work at Wood Lake Resort. John Whitworth owns it."

Janie's eyes opened wide. "I know the place. How'd you come upon that job?" She went over to her wheel and began kneading a new piece of clay.

Claire noticed a bulletin board full of pictures of Shane in the same shirt, but in front of different landmarks. She refocused on Janie. "My younger brother is dating John's daughter, Abby. They met at school last year. She asked if I wanted to come teach art classes for the kids this summer. It's been fun so far. I also work in the kitchen."

Janie looked down at her clay, and Shane came back down the hall with a framed painting. "I got what I need. Can we get this to the guy today, or do you have to get back to work?"

Claire turned to Shane. "Where are we going? I have to be back by four."

"No problem. It's over by Wood Lake. I can get a ride back to town with a buddy if we run short on time."

"Ok," Claire said and made a move towards the door. "It was nice to meet you, Janie."

Not looking up, she replied, "Nice to meet you too. Say hi to Frank for me."

As they walked back to the car, Shane said, "So, you met my mother."

"Well, yes. I went inside to do that." Claire opened the door so Shane could slide the painting in the back seat.

"I guess you did," he replied, straightening up to close the door.

Claire threw him the keys. "You drive. It'll be faster that way. I have no idea where we are."

"You sure?" Shane replied, looking suspicious.

"Yes."

When they got out on the highway, Claire relaxed a bit. She always worried that her little VW would bottom out on a rough road or driveway around here. Even though her dad would pay for it to be fixed, he'd give her the third degree before he paid the bill. Her thoughts drifted back to her conversation with Janie. She obviously knew where Wood Lake Resort was, but how did she know Frank? Claire decided to ask Abby about it.

"Hey, what were those pictures on the board in the kitchen? The ones with you in a pink shirt?"

Shane's cheeks reddened. "My mom…she gave me a shirt, like *Where's Waldo?* You know the books, right?"

In a mocking voice, Claire answered, "Yes, Shane. I know the ones." She put her hand on his thigh.

"So, my mom bought me a shirt that says, 'Where's Shane?', and she said she'd be ok with me traveling around if I sent her a picture of where I was with the shirt on. She puts the pictures up on that board. It's a little embarrassing."

"It's cute." The response was genuine, and Claire was

beginning to think Shane was pretty cute too. She leaned her head on his shoulder, and he gave her a peck on the forehead.

Frank had not liked it when Shane came by the resort the last time, so when the time came for him to drop off the painting, Claire decided to drive him back to town. His mom was going to come into town for an evening shift, so he said that he could just borrow her car to go home, or maybe see what the town had in store for him. Claire laughed at the last part. She was pretty sure that, outside of his art jobs and the street festivals, Shane didn't have a plan for what he was going to do an hour from now. She could never live that way. But she longed to.

"Hey, Craig?" Abby said as they lay back on the bed in Craig's cabin.

"Yeah, babe?" Craig responded, aimlessly running his fingers through Abby's hair.

"You want to go on a little trip?"

"A trip?" He turned to meet her eyes. "Where?"

"To the Porkies. The Porcupine Mountains."

"Mountains?"

"It's just a place a little north of here, in Michigan. A state park for hiking and camping." She smiled and leaned her head in, waiting for an answer.

Craig was happy to see her so excited. He gave her a quick peck on the nose. "Sure. When?"

"I don't know. Next week sometime?"

"I would have to check with Ted and your dad. And maybe Coach."

"Yeah, that's fine. I was thinking we could leave early on a Wednesday and come back late on a Thursday. You'd have time to get a cabin started and then finish it up on Friday. I don't know."

"You mean we'd stay overnight?"

"Yeah. We could camp, or if the weather's nice we could sleep out."

"Ok. I'll talk to Coach."

"And my dad?"

"Yeah. And your dad."

Abby snuggled in close to Craig and kissed the side of his cheek. "How was coaching today?"

Craig shifted again. "Lots of fun. The kids are nice, and they listen. It was great!"

Abby bit her lip slightly. "Good. I'm glad."

"Yeah. They're eager to learn. I didn't realize how much I really knew. I led the warm-up and could actually explain why we were doing what we were doing. And in the weight room, I remembered all the lifts." He barely took a breath.

"Sounds fun. How did you do on the cabins?"

"Got two torn off. Started with shingles on one and got the tar paper on the other one."

"Wow," Abby said, sitting up and stretching. "You had a long day."

"It's not so bad. Tuesdays and Thursdays are long. The rest of the week I feel like I'm running out of time."

"Lifting every Monday/Wednesday/Friday?" Abby was concerned that Craig was never going to keep up with the workload, but he was managing it all so far, so she had no reason to doubt.

"Yep. Going in early has been good. I'm going to be really fit between the weight room, hammering all day, and chopping."

Abby felt Craig's unflexed arm and said sarcastically, "Ooooh. My strong man."

Craig grabbed her swiftly and tightly, pulling her down on top of him. He pulled her head to his, kissing her. It was the exact reaction she was hoping for. With Claire gone almost every evening, they were hoping to fall into a pattern like at school. The only difference was that Abby had to sneak home each night, leaving Craig to his cold bed and his journal.

"You ever thought about developing the land north of town, Mom?" Abby asked from her computer in the office.

"No. Your father's pretty adamant about holding onto that the way it is for now."

"What about the land by Frank's place?"

"Where?"

"Over past Frank's cabin. There's got to be room for five or six more lakefront places or timeshares or something."

"I don't know about that, Abby." Her mother turned to look at her. "What are you getting at with this?"

"Well, I'm just throwing out ideas. How to turn this place around."

"Does it need to be turned around?" Vickie asked.

"I don't know. We barely break even most years. Projections for this year look good, but most of that is going into repairs. I'm reworking the website, and the Facebook page is catching on. I guess I feel like we just need to generate more revenue."

Vickie sat down next to Abby and looked at the computer

screen. She scrunched up her eyes, studying the pictures on the website. "This place is not about making a profit. Never was." She turned to Abby and leaned in. "It took me a while to adjust to the idea. Your dad was so passionate about it. He wanted it so badly. Not just for himself, but for me and you, and eventually Taylor too. He just couldn't make it in the big city." She took a breath and continued, "It was never about getting rich, and I love him so much. The whole thing just swept us up. This place, his father's death, and then his mother. I was never really close with my parents. One of eight, so there wasn't much room. I'm grateful for those who came up all these years. But it's different now. People have lives, activities with the kids. Heck, a few have grandkids."

"I know, Mom. I see them all the time."

"Less than we used to. I get what you're saying about the business. I warned you about it. It's not really a business, it's a lifestyle. If this place is going to survive, I agree, you will need to think of something new. But good luck getting your father on board. God, he's optimistic. It's lovable, but sometimes realism is what we need."

Abby pointed to the screen. "I have another question."

"Yes?" Vickie scooted her chair closer and lowered her glasses down her nose.

"What's with all of this 401(k) investment? There seems to be more paid out here than there is in salary. I don't get it."

"You should ask your father about that, honey." Her voice became almost sharp.

Confused by the lack of a clear answer, Abby pressed. "Why?"

"Because he can explain it better. When I do the books,

that's all I do. I'm not the one making the decisions around here. I just try to make sure the number at the bottom of the page is in the black. Other than that, I stay out of it." She got up and walked towards the door.

"I have one more question." Abby turned her chair toward her mom.

Vickie looked back at Abby after a moment of silence. "What is it?"

Abby felt her eyes beginning to water, and she bit the top of her lip. "I don't know."

"What? Is something wrong?"

"No, nothing is wrong." Abby got up and reached for her mother's hand. "Can I make an appointment with Dr. Johnson?"

"Why would you need to do that? Can't it wait for your appointment at the end of next month?"

"I don't know."

"What is it, Abby?"

Abby took a moment to compose herself. "I think I want to start birth control."

Vickie squeezed Abby's hand and let out a breath. "Ok, that's serious." She walked back to her chair and sat down, Abby following close behind.

"Yes. But I think it would be best," Abby said, trying to sound mature.

With a tear slowly dropping down her cheek, Vickie said, "Is this your decision, or is there something else going on?"

"What do you mean?"

"Is Craig pressuring you?"

"No. It's not him." Abby's breathing was becoming labored.

"Then what is it? What's bringing this on?"

Abby sat up straight and pulled her hands back to her legs, saying plainly, "It's me, Mom, not Craig. If anyone is doing the pressuring, it's me."

Vickie stared at her blankly.

"I haven't even talked to Craig about this. It would freak him out completely. I'm the one pushing him."

"Ok?" Vickie said as if asking a question. "This is a lot for me right now, Abby."

"I know. But I love him, and I don't want to get in trouble if things keep moving along."

"You love him. I know you've said that before, but how do you know?"

Abby smiled and looked down at the floor, blushing. "I can't wait to see him every day. I don't want to leave him every night. I can say anything to him, and he just listens or knows what to say. He's everything I could have hoped for. He loves this place. He loves me."

"That sounds about right," Vickie sighed, pausing for a few moments. "Be careful."

"That's what I'm trying to do."

"And so you are, I guess." Vickie got up and hugged her daughter. "Go ahead and make the appointment. We'll tell your dad it's girl stuff, if he even notices."

"Thanks, Mom."

"I love you."

Claire worked hard to get all the prep done for the weekend so she could get downtown to see the opening of the Early Summer Art Festival sponsored by the Warehouse and various downtown businesses. Shane had a booth set up with a mix of work: log carvings, drawings, and a few paintings, as well as "The World's Best Venison Jerky" with his own blend of North African spices, a palate not often used on this type of meat. He had been telling Claire about the festival since they first started going out, but until this night, she had never seen any of his work outside of the pot he made on their first date and the cabin signs. Even the painting they picked up at his house had been wrapped up.

She walked through the main street and let the moment invade her. Little street markets like this one were all over Chicago at all times of the year, save for winter. The variety of goods, jewelry, paintings, drawings, and clothing was impressive to her. She barely noticed Shane's booth until she was on it.

"Hey," Claire said, almost surprised by how excited she was to see him.

Shane jumped up from his seat and smiled. "What's up?"

"Not much. Got a lot of prep done for Frank so I could come out here this weekend. Still have to run my classes tomorrow, but I'll come out after that. How are things here?"

"Kinda quiet. Sold two pieces."

Claire looked at his drawings. Shane had a lot of raw talent. Some of the techniques were rough, but for having no formal training, his renditions were very realistic. "Nice."

"Yeah. It's a start. Tomorrow will be better. This place will be thick. All the Chicago folk want to take a piece of the Northwoods with them."

"I guess. Where do you keep all this stuff?"

"At my mom's. The garage, remember? It's cool. She mostly lets me explore whatever medium I want."

"I wish my parents were like your mother."

"Maybe. I'm sure your parents are cool. They raised you."

"They raised Craig and my sister Sarah. I raised myself."

Shane chuckled. "Really?"

"It felt that way. It was always sports, sports, sports. I never played anything. Did you?"

"I played football." Shane ran his finger over the scar on his wrist. "I quit."

Claire nodded knowingly.

After coming into the booth and sitting down, Claire took out her sketchbook and began drawing a guy who was selling homemade cuckoo clocks at a booth across the way. He was older, well-built, with strong arms, and had a salt and pepper beard. He wore a trucker hat and flannel cut-off. Claire made a quick gesture drawing and started in on his face.

Shane watched Claire's pencil dart across the page. "Wow, you're fast."

"Well, he just seemed so calm. I wanted to get him before he changed."

"You always have that book with you, don't you?" He chuckled.

Claire punched his shoulder. "Yes. I just want to capture this whole experience."

"No, no, that's very cool. I could never remember…" Just then, a customer came by. Shane's whole demeanor changed. He was committed and engaged, just like he was on the boat a few days before. He could charm the pants off people. Claire loved it.

Craig was behind on the cabins. Missing three mornings because of lifting left him still on the roof as guests arrived on Friday afternoon. The first two-bedroom was done, but John was forced to apologize to the family as Craig finished. They didn't seem to mind though. The kids ran out to the lake, and soon after, the mom and dad emerged, and Craig assured them that he'd be done by six.

True to his word, at five forty-five, Craig came down off the roof and went to his cabin. He wanted to shower before the night's festivities, campfire, and late-night fishing with Abby.

When he got to his cabin, Abby was inside, sitting on his bed, waiting for him. Surprised, he said, "Hey there."

"Hi."

"Claire here?" Craig asked.

"No. She's in town for the night with Shane."

"Oh. Who's helping in the kitchen?"

"Claire got way ahead, so all there is to do is service. Frank said he could do it."

"Oh, ok."

"We'll probably have to help tomorrow since it's Saturday. 'All hands on deck,'" she said with air quotes.

"Yep," Craig stated, still standing in the living room area. "I gotta take a shower."

"Ok. I'll wait." Abby smiled.

Craig went into the bathroom, turned on the shower, then undressed while the water got hot. As soon as he got in and put his head under the water, he heard the shower door open. His head whipped around to see Abby briefly before she put her arms around him. Hugging her in the warm water felt so good. They kissed and melted together. Exploring this new world, Craig got lost in the moment, and apprehension faded away. In the light of the late afternoon, a secret was shared. They washed up, saying nothing, and got out to dry themselves. Craig approached Abby while she was wrapped in a towel and kissed her gently.

When he pulled away, she smiled at him and ran her fingers through his beard. "I love you."

"I love you too."

"Off to work now?" She winked.

Craig fake yawned and said sarcastically, "I think I'll take a nap."

Abby hit him on the stomach.

"Ok," Craig said, giving her a quick peck. "Let's get to work."

With the weekend winding down, Craig jumped on a cabin right after the family checked out. It was a two-bedroom, and he wanted to get the tear-off done Sunday afternoon and evening. Since he and Abby were planning to go to the Porkies on Tuesday or Wednesday, he had to get the tar paper on, if not the shingles started, before the trip. He worked until the only light left was the campfire that Abby started. The tear-off went well, but cleanup became challenging with the lost light. Abby ended up bringing a flashlight to help find any loose nails.

When they got back to the cabin, Claire was there. "We're supposed to call Sarah. She left me a message."

Craig went over by his phone and saw a message as well. "I guess we should call."

They put Claire's phone on speaker.

"Hey, Claire," Sarah answered.

"Hey. What's up?"

"So…I have some news."

All three leaned in.

"Yes?" Craig said.

"Oh, Craig. You're there too."

"And Abby."

"Oh great. I'll just say it. Mom and Dad are coming up to the resort over the Fourth."

Craig and Claire looked at each other with the same wide-eyed expression. "What?" they said together. Abby sat back against the wall.

"Yeah. So, I tried to talk them out of it, but they said they wanted to see their children."

"They said that?" Craig asked.

"Well, Mom said it. They're staying for the week."

A panicked look crossed Craig's face. "The whole week?"

"Great," Claire said. "Thanks."

"Yep," Sarah said, still cheery as ever.

"Bye," Claire said, hanging up. "Shit."

"Yep," Craig agreed.

"It won't be so bad," Abby stated cautiously.

Both Craig and Claire looked at her sideways.

CHAPTER 10

After informing a not-so-happy Coach Granger and getting the tar paper on the cabin, Craig and Abby set off for the Porcupine Mountains Wilderness State Park. Vickie told Abby to be careful since she just had her appointment and, as she remembered, it took a while to kick in. Abby assured her not to worry.

Craig knew he needed to be back Thursday to work the rest of the day before a family came that evening. Secretly, he was hoping Ted would help him out before leaving to visit his son. Craig didn't want to shirk his responsibilities, but Ted agreed that young people needed their time alone. Craig had never gone camping before. His parents were hotel people. Besides, they never vacationed anywhere that wasn't a resort. This would be new.

Abby watched Craig as they drove north. His eyes darted around, taking in the dense forest and broad vistas as they rose and fell on the curvy, hilly road. A few questions were asked about a town or interesting sign, but for the most part, they drove quietly and content in the fact that they had almost two full days to themselves. Craig felt as though they were moving even deeper into Abby's world and farther from anything he could recognize as familiar.

When they arrived and parked the car, Abby told Craig

they had a six-mile hike to the place she planned to camp. The route she mapped out was a big circle. There were a few places she wanted to show him, and she hoped the campsite she had in mind was still available.

"How do you know so much about this place?" Craig asked.

"I've been here with friends a few times," Abby said, taking the packs out of the trunk.

"I thought you were always working."

"Well, yes. But over the years, I did have a little fun." She winked at Craig.

They pulled on their backpacks, which had Abby packed. Craig hadn't done anything to prepare. The only thing expected was for him to show up and be present. He was kinda nervous but meant to enjoy the time with Abby as well as he could.

"Let's get started. There are a lot of cool waterfalls I want to show you, and then we can hike back to a campsite overlooking the lake." Abby started up the trail.

"Great." Craig secured the chest strap on his backpack and followed. At first, he struggled to keep pace with Abby. She was steady and sure-footed. Nothing she did was ever fast, but Craig had come to appreciate the precision of her movements. She rarely made mistakes. It was as though every move was thought out in advance, and there was no room for error. Craig was built for speed. Before he met Abby and came to the resort, he just wanted to get everything done now and check off tasks from his list. But that idea held a different meaning for him. Slowly, he was realizing that it was about getting things done right. He was working for the benefit of others. The resort had slowed him a bit, but his mind was still racing.

A series of waterfalls appeared as they hiked further

inland, each more beautiful than the last. Stopping at one for lunch, Craig sat against a tree while Abby leaned against him, and they both watched the water run by. Craig remembered the first time Abby sat against him under a tree down by the lake in Whitewater. At that time, he was so nervous and unsure of the new relationship and what his future held. He felt as though he never knew what to say next. Now, he knew that things did not always need to be said. Feelings of contentment, ease, and momentary drift set in as surely as any experience he had ever known. There was nothing but the moment. Craig ran his fingers through Abby's hair and down her back. This place was real in a way Craig had never experienced before. The feelings he was having, mixed with the setting, created an intensity he simply tried to ride. No judgment, no evaluation, just enjoy.

Abby, too, was lost in the now. She felt every stroke of Craig's fingers. The rush of water was the only sound. They were together with nothing pressing against their time. The ripples of water danced through the rocks going this way and that, all falling to the great lake below. The eddies seemed to jump at random, sometimes going left, sometimes right. Life was determined by chance in much the same way. What if she had walked into biology a minute later on the first day of college? Would Craig have seen another girl and gone to talk with her? What if the breakup had stuck and they didn't find their way back? Life was a random jumble of accidents that people responded to in the moment. The leaf floating down the river doesn't know how it will get to the lake. It just lets the water rush it along. Was life like that? Abby felt Craig's arms around her. She felt her head against his chest and heard his breathing. The rhythm was a constant reminder to stay present. But still, she wondered.

"Hey. Where are you?" Craig asked quietly.

"Here," Abby said confidently as she nuzzled closer. "I'm here."

Craig squeezed her. He loved the fact that he could be content in the slowness of life, but he was also ready to move. "Where are we camping tonight?"

"There's this place," Abby began, then turned her whole body to face him, "down by Superior, just off the beach. I hope no one is there." She paused to smile. "It's just so peaceful."

"Sounds cool. Should we get going?"

Stretching as though she had just woken up from a nap, she said, "Yeah. Let's go."

When they emerged from the forest, they found that the place where Abby wanted to camp was not only available, there was no one else on the shoreline. They would have the beach to themselves. A wide-open strip of sand bordered by trees on one side and an endless expanse of clear blue water was all that could be brought into the frame of vision. As she took out the tent and sleeping mats to place on a small patch of grass that was elevated from the sand, Craig walked down to the lake to dip his feet in. Abby watched as he danced in and out. She knew how cold the water was. Craig, she assumed, had no idea.

"Craig!" she called loudly to be heard over the waves.

"Yeah!"

"Get over here and help me with this tent."

Craig immediately bounded across the beach over to the green. Abby laughed at his overly exaggerated motions and the fact that he left his boots down by the water. They made quick work of the tent, Craig more of an observer than offering any real help. Abby sent him to find some wood as she arranged rocks for a firepit. When he came back with more wood than they could possibly need, they built the fire, then had a snack and played frisbee. Running into and out of the water and tackling each other, they chased their love up and down the shoreline well into the late afternoon. There was nothing and no one to interrupt them. Their thoughts centered only on the here and now as the half-light of early evening set in.

Having totally lost track of time, it was hunger that awoke them from their lover's dance, reminding them of the close of day that gripped them despite the sun that lingered just above the horizon. Abby took out some marinated meat and cut veggies, putting them onto the grilling apparatus she had packed. Craig just followed directions, and fifteen minutes later, they had food for dinner.

"Wow. I never thought I'd eat so well on a camping trip," Craig said, still chewing his food.

"We do it right up north," Abby said. She wore a tight-lipped smile and began to clean up the garbage to pack out in the morning.

Craig could see her eyes flicker in the fire as he finished his meal.

Abby noticed Craig staring at her. "What?" she asked, blushing.

"Nothing."

"What?" she repeated more forcefully.

"I love you, that's all. I think you're beautiful."

A smile washed over Abby's face, and she was glowing. "I

love you too, Craig," she replied. "Now, go scrub the dishes off in the lake."

"Yes, ma'am."

"Ma'am?"

Craig laughed.

Abby arranged the campsite and put all the food away in a scent-proof bag. When Craig returned, she had already put out the fire and had crawled into the tent. The backpacks were set up in such a way that they could sit up and read or talk before going to sleep. Craig came in and handed the dishes to Abby, which she put in her pack. She had a book out and adjusted a headlamp she rigged to provide light to the whole tent.

"What are you reading?" Craig asked.

"A book of poems by Frost."

"I like some of his stuff. Which poem do you like most so far?"

"I like 'Birches.' I love the imagery. It's about a boy who grew up in the country and liked to swing on trees."

"Sounds about right," Craig laughed.

"What do you mean?"

"Well, you like to be out in the woods and out on the lake."

"I do. It brings me peace. It takes me back to a simpler time."

"I can tell."

"Really?" Abby's eyes narrowed slightly.

"Yeah. When we got up here, I could see a weight lifted. It's just like when we pull into the resort from school. A wave comes over you and washes you clean."

Abby smiled. No one had ever explained it so perfectly. "I just like the randomness of it all, you know?"

"Randomness?" Craig inquired, confused.

"Yeah. Being out in nature, you don't really know which way it's going to go. There is no agenda. It does what it wants."

Craig tried to feel the moment she was describing but couldn't quite grasp it. He replied, "I don't see it that way."

"You don't?"

"No. I sense a rhythm, everywhere...listen." Craig turned his head and put his finger to his ear.

Abby turned her head to mimic Craig. "What am I listening to?"

"Listen." He moved his finger to his mouth. "Do you hear it?" He paused. "The waves."

Abby listened.

Craig continued, "There's your rhythm. Everything out here has a purpose. Just like you."

"Like me?" Abby questioned.

"Yeah. You say you like the randomness of it all, but you also like the order. It's comforting to return to what you know."

Abby couldn't quite make sense of what he was getting at. "I guess, but how is that like me?"

Craig reached over and pushed her hair off her shoulders. She nuzzled her face against the back of his hand. "The world is full of chaos, right?"

"Yes," Abby said cautiously.

"You're my rhythm in all that chaos. Home is where the people you love are, and you are my home. You're my purpose." Craig's eyes locked in completely.

Abby didn't know what to say. She simply stared back at him.

A moment later, Craig gave her a peck on the cheek and fished his journal out of his pack.

Abby broke her stare. "What do you write in that?"

"I just try to write what happened in the day. Sometimes, I try a poem, but that usually doesn't go well. Just thoughts and stuff."

"Why?"

"I don't want to forget. One of my profs turned me on to it last semester. It helped a lot when we weren't together."

Abby looked down. She fumbled with the pages of her book for a moment as though looking for a poem that could explain her thoughts. "Craig?"

"Yeah."

"Do you think, maybe, you settled for me?" After she said it, she looked Craig squarely in the eyes, trying to remain steady.

Craig put his pen down and closed his journal. "What do you mean?"

"Well, after you met me, you kinda put blinders on and didn't talk to anyone else. You literally stopped talking to everyone but me for a while."

"You mean other girls?"

"That and…well, everyone."

"It wasn't me putting blinders on at all."

"What was it then?"

"When I met you, I wasn't blinded, I was overwhelmed. It's not that I didn't look at anyone else, it was that I couldn't see anyone else."

Abby's eyes stayed fixed on him as she continued to listen.

"Abby. It was like being set on the right course, a course where I discovered myself by discovering you. Like I said earlier, you are the rhythm I was looking for without even knowing it."

"Are you still on the right course?"

"You haven't steered me wrong yet. Listen." Craig took her hand. "Life is about discovering, right?"

"I guess."

"Well, I'm still discovering you. I'm still discovering this place. I know it scares you when I talk about the future, but I hope this moment never changes."

"I hope it never changes either."

"Hey, you've been writing a bunch too, haven't you?" Craig asked. He had often seen Abby writing in a journal out on the dock. It was always present on her desk at school.

"I like to write poems," she replied.

"Really? Why poems?"

"I don't know. I guess I like the challenge of them. I have to fit my thoughts into a small package. I have to think it through."

"Can I read one?"

She was tempted to just take out her journal and let him study it page by page, but then looked at her pack, seeing the corner of the journal sticking out. "Maybe someday."

With a gracious tone, Craig responded, "Ok, Abby."

"You should try to write a poem again. I'd like to see one of yours."

Craig smiled.

They had exhausted all feeling and said what they could. Going back to their poems and writing, each tried to quell the growing desire that had built to a near breaking point. But Abby wasn't going to push things further, and Craig was not making any first moves. He was content in the slowness and felt a connection to Abby more intimate than the physical.

When they woke the next morning, they packed up their

belongings and hiked out, stopping to fish at a lake on the drive home. So much had been said the night before with both words and gestures that speech was unnecessary. They returned home content and refreshed, ready to face the weeks that lay ahead.

Craig's Journal

Abby said I should try to write a poem. So, here goes:

The day begins with a list
Too long to be completed.
Smiles and hardy handshakes
Are the currency of thanks,
My only compensation.
But she moves seamlessly
In and out of each task.
Check one box, on to the next.
With winks and gentle gazes,
She fills her soul with service.
If Wood Lake has a heart,
It beats in her.

Why do I Write? - Abby

Why do I write these silly poems?
Craig journals to remember,
I write to discover.
No reason to replay
Memories I will never see again.
No reason to find words
In woods older than me
That will outlive
All that I see. Gathering years
In rings, around and around.
Maybe that's all we do too.
Maybe we just go around
In circles, making new rings
To hold ourselves in.
Rings to remember,
Rings to forget.
If that is what we do,
This last year's rings
Will have a lot of room between.
The growth may be too much
For the bark to contain.

CHAPTER 11

The work of getting ready for the Fourth was more than Craig expected. Abby had fallen into cleanup duty, abandoning the office, and Craig was expected to follow suit. He tried to get another cabin started but was often thrown off by this errand or that task which demanded immediate attention. The place was getting a spit shine, like over spring break, but with guests moving around constantly and checking in and out, the mission seemed almost hopeless. He was beginning to suspect that the cabins may not get done if he left for camp early. Panic was slowly sinking in.

Having worked the whole day on an endless number of tasks, Craig told Abby he needed to go to town to meet Will and get ready for strength and conditioning the next day, but really, he was going to run routes with Will, a guy named Kayden who played for Northern Michigan, and some of the high school guys. The routes came back quickly. Craig was crisp in his cuts and fast downfield. He broke down the plays with the cornerbacks and safeties on the way back to the huddle. The high school kids presented no challenge for him, but he could help them get better. He was the field coach, and it filled him with pride to see all the players hang on his every word. At the end of practice, Craig was encouraged with the progress and looked forward to more sessions like this one throughout the rest of the summer.

In the parking lot, Coach Granger walked up and said, "Hey, Craig, can you come over here for a minute?"

Nervously, Craig responded, "Sure, Coach, what's up?"

"Take a little walk with me," Coach said, strolling onto a grassy area in front of the school. "You look pretty good out there."

"Thanks, Coach," Craig replied, still breathing hard.

"Have you ever given any thought to playing again?" He patted Craig's shoulder as they kept walking.

Craig stopped. "Honestly," he began, "I've thought about it quite a bit." He felt scared saying it out loud.

"Really?"

"Yes." Craig tried to sound confident.

"Well, you quit before the season last year, right?"

All confidence dissolved with a single question. Craig replied, "Yes."

Nodding, Coach continued, "No need to get into that. If you want to go back, I can give your coach a call. When he was recruiting Will, I had a couple of conversations with him. If you want to go back and are ready to stay committed, I'll put in a good word for you."

Craig stared at him. "I'll think about it, sir. Thank you."

"Don't wait too long. Camp starts in about a month."

"I know, sir. I gotta get going. Lots of work to get done at the resort."

"Oh, I know. The Fourth of July week is upon us. The whole town is buzzing. I might stop by and talk with John for a bit and eat some of Frank's cooking."

"That would be great, sir. So, no strength and conditioning for next week?"

Coach Granger shook his head. "No way."

"We might still come and run some plays."

"Not a problem, Craig. Have a nice weekend."

'Do you want to play again?' 'Committed.' These words rolled around in Craig's head over and over on the drive back to Wood Lake. How would he ever explain this to Abby?

Meghan and Abby caught a few minutes out on the deck of the lodge as Meghan wrapped up the open swim part of the day. She had just come back from a few days in Milwaukee with her boyfriend and was eager to talk with Abby. "Milwaukee was so great! Dan and I had so much fun, and we did so much stuff. I couldn't begin to tell you everything. And being in the city…" Meghan was almost cooing.

"That's great. What all did you do?" Abby pretended to be interested but was preoccupied with all she had to do.

"We went to the art museum and out downtown and to the mall, and he even took me to the zoo. It was so much cooler than what we have around here."

Ignoring the last part of the comment, Abby asked, "How was his family?"

"They were really nice. I think they like me. I helped his mom with dinner one night, and we talked about Madison and home."

"What did you say about home?" Abby asked, actually interested in her answer to this question.

"I don't know. I don't always know what to say about my mom. It's always been hard. She acts like she's some sort of artist, but she owns a craft store. It's like impossible to talk to her about anything serious…she's just weird."

"I love your mom," Abby said.

"I know. It's just like, you know, sometimes, I feel like I grew up here as much as I grew up at my house. John and Vickie are like my parents too."

"Yeah," Abby said. "I get it."

"Hey, do you mind if I sleep here tonight?"

"No problem. There's so much to do. I have to get the dishes done from supper," Abby lamented.

"I'll do that, and then I'll go see if Vickie needs help with anything."

"Thanks, Meg. I'll bet my mom is in the office."

"Good deal." With that, Meghan ran off towards the kitchen.

Abby was left wondering what to do next. It wasn't for lack of things to do. Quite the opposite actually. She walked down the cabin road and found Frank walking home from dinner service. It was odd for him to be going home so early, so Abby jogged to greet him. Catching his hand from behind, Abby leaned into his shoulder. "Hi, Frank."

"Hey there, girl. What are you up too?"

"I could say the same for you. Aren't you going to keep the kitchen open for a bit longer?"

"Not tonight. We had so much turnover today, and it'll be the same tomorrow too. I thought I'd take a night to rest up. Big weekend and week coming up."

"Yeah. It's going to be busy, isn't it?"

"I hate when the Fourth falls in the middle of the week."

"Right?" Abby laughed out.

Frank let go of Abby's hand and gave her a quick hug.

"You're a good kid. You know that, right?"

"That's what you tell me."

"Well, it's true. You're going to do a heck of a job running this place someday."

"I hope so. After working in the office, I wonder sometimes about how the place is really doing and what I can do to turn it around."

"I have a feeling you'll be ok."

"How do you know?"

Smiling, Frank let out a hearty chuckle. "This old guy still knows a few things. Anyway, where's that guy of yours?"

They stood at the end of the cabin road. "I'm not sure. He said he had to run to town for something."

"Well, I guess I'll see him tomorrow. What's the use of taking a night off if I can't turn in early?"

"I guess you're right."

"Then this is where I leave you. Goodnight, Abby."

"Goodnight, Frank."

CHAPTER 12

Fourth of July week was upon them. The lodge was decked out with red, white, and blue ribbons and bows. The linens were changed to a bright red that played well with the wooden decor. Everything was ready to go. The boats were in tip-top shape, including the pontoon, which, it turned out, only needed a new wire and a fan belt. Nothing was left undone. According to Abby, around fifteen percent of the resort's yearly revenue came from the ten days surrounding the Fourth. She had been running around nonstop since she and Craig had come back from their camping trip. Craig had only managed to finish one roof the week before, and with no work being done during the week of the Fourth, he had four cabins left to do and only three weeks to get them done if he was going to leave for camp. None of his developing plan had been shared with Abby. He wanted to get through this week before throwing anything else on her.

With many cabins turning over Friday and Saturday, Abby stayed by the front desk, leaving Craig to run from cabin to cabin with the cleaners, getting whatever they asked him to get. Claire was either in the kitchen or out doing art classes with Vickie and the kids. No rooms or cabins were left unoccupied. About half of the week's residents had checked in on Friday, while the rest were coming Saturday. Many were staying until the Wednesday after the Fourth, with a full turnover promised by the end of the following week.

The lodge was humming for lunch when Mike and Linda arrived. Abby greeted them at the front desk. "Hello, Mr. and Mrs. McLean. We're so happy to have you this week. Welcome to Wood Lake."

Putting down their bags, Mike replied, "Why, hello there, Abby. Nice to be here."

Linda looked around the front lobby, seeming to barely notice Abby.

"You will be able to drive down the cabin road to drop off your bags. Looks like we have you in Cabin 8. Two bedrooms." 'What a waste to have booked a two-bedroom,' Abby thought. But, after checking the reservation, she saw that they had booked in mid-June. There might have been a cancellation. "How was the drive, Mrs. McLean?" she asked, desperately trying to catch her critical eye.

Turning to Abby, she replied, "Oh, it was fine."

"Let me show you the lodge and get ahold of Craig to show you to your cabin. I have two more families to wait on up here, and then I'll join you and show you around a little more."

They left the bags behind the front desk and walked down the hall towards the main room of the lodge. As they were walking, a voice came from behind them. "Mom? Dad?" The entire party stopped.

Abby spoke first. "Hi, honey."

"Hey. Could you take some of these?" Craig stood behind a tower of towels he could barely see over. Abby took a few off the top and gave him a quick kiss on the cheek. Craig looked back at his parents and continued, "You guys can find the cabin road off the parking lot. I gotta get these towels down to the beach for the moms who can't be bothered to go back to their own rooms to get them. I'll meet you there."

"Ok, honey," Linda said forcefully, as though reclaiming the word from Abby.

They all went their own way after Abby gave Craig the extra towels back. He made quick work of the delivery and went to Cabin 8 to meet his parents' truck. Craig felt a sense of both pride and apprehension having his parents at the resort. He used his master key to open the door, then turned on the lights even though there was still a lot of natural light in the main room. Abby had turned the cabin over herself early that morning. "I want everything to be perfect, Craig. If your parents are going to complain, it's not going to be about the cleanliness of the cabin," she had said.

"Here you go," Craig said, walking in to the smell of fresh flowers on the dining table. The cabin looked like it had a fresh coat of varnish on every wood surface. "This is the two-bedroom. You have a small kitchen and nice living room, and there's satellite TV. The bedrooms are in the back with the bathroom between them. I'm guessing you'll be eating at the lodge most of the time."

"Well, isn't this cute," Linda said sarcastically, putting her purse down on the table.

"Linda," Mike snarled. "We're here to relax and spend some time with our kids."

She smirked and walked toward the bedrooms.

"Master is on the right, Mom." She moved in that direction.

Mike turned to Craig. "Don't mind her. This isn't normal for us, Craig. She's used to being pampered. My fault, I guess. She'll get used to it."

Craig wasn't sure how to take the comment. "Here are your keys. I'll park the truck in the lot and meet you back at the lodge in half an hour?"

"Yep. Where's Claire?" Mike asked enthusiastically.

"She's either in the kitchen, in the lodge, or out by the beach doing an art class."

"Sounds good," Mike said as Craig turned to go. "Craig."

"Yeah?"

"Nice beard." Mike laughed.

"Thanks, Dad." Craig rubbed his face and went out the door.

Craig made his way over to the front of the lodge to see if he could catch Abby. She was still fumbling around at the front desk. "Still waiting?"

"Yep. One to go. Big family, over in Cabin 3. Eight to ten people."

"That is a big family. Staying the week?"

"Yeah. Nine days. They're regulars. The grandparents were here for Thanksgiving. You might remember them if you see them."

"Cool." Craig let out a sigh that seemed to deflate him. "My parents are getting settled, and they're going to try to find Claire later. I'm supposed to meet them in a bit. I hope it's not too weird."

Abby smirked, then became serious. "It is too weird, Craig. Too late to think it's not."

Laughing, he responded, "Yeah. You're right. I guess we'll make the best of it."

"This one's on you, bud. I'm going to be too busy to notice.

Other than the fact that my parents, my mother mostly, wants to have them over for lunch at the house tomorrow, I'm out."

"Really?" Craig exclaimed sadly. "Some fun. I better go see if Frank needs anything."

Coming from behind the counter, Abby reached out for a hug. "Want to go fishing tonight or tomorrow?"

"Fishing?" Craig asked suspiciously.

Abby pushed away until just their hands touched. "Maybe," she said, then winked.

Craig kissed her quick and went down the hall. 'She's really in love with me. Damn.' The thought made him break into a jog.

Claire was sitting with a large group of children down by the lake. Paints and canvases rested on table-top easels that Shane had made for her. The kids were painting landscapes, or whatever they could, and Vickie and Claire were constantly called over from one child to the next to see what was being done. The busyness kept Claire centered on the now. Sharing a love for art with the kids was rewarding. When they excitedly showed their parents what they did, it made her happy. However, when a mom would stay and help her kid despite the child's protest, those were challenging times. Her own mother must have gotten all the helicoptering out of the way with Sarah, and her dad was always focused on Craig. Claire was often left alone with her reading or her sketchbook. She could create her own reality, which was exactly what she was doing every day of her life. Whenever she and Craig sat up and talked in their cabin at night, she encouraged him to do the same.

Into the perfect little world of summertime bliss came the vision of a storm. Linda, with her overexposed, fit, little body, was coming to the beach trailed by Mike. Hoping for a few last moments of peace, Claire focused her attention on a child's painting. "I really like how you included the reflection of the sun on the water. You have so much light…"

"Claire. Claire honey!" Linda yelled from a few yards away.

Trying to look surprised instead of completely dead inside, Claire said, "Oh, hi, Mom."

Linda gave her an overly dramatic hug. "It's been so long since I've seen you. How are you?"

Mike gave Claire a quick hug. "Hey there, Claire Bear."

Claire hugged her father hard, inspired by the use of her childhood nickname. "Wow, Dad, you lost weight."

Chuckling, he responded, "Thanks for noticing."

Turning back to her mother, Claire asked, "So, how was the trip? How's the cabin?"

"Oh, fine. Fine, honey. How are you?" Linda replied.

"Good. Busy, but good."

Vickie walked over towards the small gathering. "Claire, are these your parents?"

"Yes. This is Linda and Mike McLean."

Pleasantries were exchanged, and Claire was called away by a student. She overheard bits and pieces of the conversation.

"They've been such a big help."

"This is such a lovely area."

"Dinner begins at five and goes until six thirty or seven."

They were all smiles, and then Vickie called for Claire. "I'm going to show your mother around for a bit. You good to clean up?"

"Sure, Vickie. I got it."

The two of them walked off towards the Whitworths' house.

Mike moseyed over toward the kids and sat down by a young boy. "I'm Ms. Claire's dad. That's a wonderful picture you got there." The boy looked up curiously. Mike continued, "Is that a boat?"

"Yeah. That's a speeeeed boat," the boy said excitedly.

Claire stared incredulously at her dad for a moment, and he winked back at her.

A little later, Mike helped Claire clean up. She showed him around the lodge, and then they went to meet Frank.

In the kitchen, Mike shook Frank's hand. "It's nice to meet you. Craig's said a great deal about you. Thanks for being so kind to my children."

Claire couldn't quite understand what brought this change in her father.

Stumbling a bit, Frank replied, "Oh, yes. Good to meet you. It's been a pleasure working with your daughter. She's a very talented young lady."

"Thank you. I'm discovering that."

Frank smiled pensively, then shot a wide-eyed look towards Claire before turning back to Mike. "Can I interest you in a little lunch? The dining room is closed right now, but I could throw something together."

"No thanks," Mike said, patting his belly. "I was hoping my girl could show me around the place a bit more."

"Let's try to find Craig, Dad. I have a photo tour in twenty minutes, and then I have to be back for dinner service."

"Sounds good. They sure are keeping you busy around here, aren't they?"

Claire nodded. They left the kitchen and found Craig at the bar, talking with a few guests who were watching ESPN. The bar wasn't technically open, but Craig served them anyway. They were deep in conversation about the recent Brewers games and Packers training camp opening in a few weeks. Noticing his family coming towards him, Craig said, "Hey guys, can I get you anything?"

"Glass of ice water?" Mike asked.

"Claire?"

"Can you get me a bottled water? I gotta get out to prep for the tour."

"Got it." Craig threw Claire a bottle, and as she turned to leave, she said, "See you later!" Then, she rushed out the door.

Mike sat down at the bar with his ice water. Craig asked, "So how's the diet, Dad?"

"Not bad. Lost twenty-five pounds so far. Trying to take it easy and relax more. Not getting so stressed out, you know."

"Being here should help. We try to stay chill. At least the guests do." Craig turned to the remaining guests at the bar and called out, "Can I get anyone anything before I close down the bar for a while? Going to show my dad around."

People finished their drinks, taking the hint.

"John will be back at four to open things up."

After cleaning up the bar area, Craig and his father stepped out onto the deck. "Welcome to Wood Lake."

They walked the grounds, and Craig showed his dad the place as thoroughly as Abby had shown him the first time he came. He even recounted a few of the stories Abby had told him. Mike listened and asked questions, patting Craig on the back from time to time.

When they came to the base of the stairs at the back of the Whitworths' house, they saw Vickie and Linda on the large deck overlooking the lake, enjoying glasses of wine. "So, that's about it, Dad. During the mornings, I go to the high school to help with the football team, and then I spend my afternoons up on the roofs of the cabins."

"They're working you hard this summer then, huh?"

"Yeah, but I like the work. It's better than just working out and playing on my Xbox all day."

"I guess."

Craig nervously looked behind himself, trying to get out of the moment so he could get back to work. "Tonight, there's a big meal and a campfire afterward. Abby leads the evening photo tour, and I run the fire."

"Wow," Mike said, looking out over the lake, then taking one step up towards the deck. "Let's go join your mother and Mrs. Whitworth."

Craig checked the time. "Actually, I should be getting back to work. I'll be sure to catch up with you and Mom later."

Mike nodded. "Ok, kid. See you later."

After the photo tour and fire, Craig and Abby found time to get away for a little boat ride. They went to the middle of the lake and let the boat drift as the stars began to show themselves in the thousands. Craig was still amazed at the number and clarity of them. He was lost in the sight when Abby asked, "How's it having your parents here?"

Chuckling nervously, he replied, "I don't know. I can't speak for Claire, but my dad seems different somehow."

"What do you mean?"

"I can't really say. He seems nicer, more interested. It's weird."

"Do you think it's his heart thing?"

"It could be. Mom's still snarky as ever, but she did have a nice chat with your mom this afternoon."

"That's what my mom said at dinner. She actually came into the kitchen to tell me. Don't know what they talked about, but whatever."

"Yeah. You got me. I have no idea."

"Did Mike meet John yet?" Abby asked, using first names for emphasis.

The mock formalism elicited a smile from Craig. "I do not believe they've become acquainted," he responded. Abby punched his arm. "It's too bad your dad couldn't make it in for dinner. I guess they'll meet at lunch tomorrow."

"I guess so."

Craig sprawled out on the cushions, and Abby lay on his chest. "What am I going to do with you, McLean?"

"Where'd that name come from?"

"I don't know. I kinda like it."

McLean was the only name Craig had ever gone by in high school. It was his alter ego, the one that allowed him to block out everything and play. He wasn't sure if he could find McLean again when he went back. He wasn't sure he wanted to. Pensively, he said, "I don't know."

"Well then." Abby took a deep breath. "Now, I like it even more."

Craig laughed nervously.

Abby, Craig, and Claire reported to lunch prep right after breakfast service was over. "If none of you are going to be around for lunch, then you'll be here to set up." Frank's orders were clear. They set up the buffet and cooked all the food in advance. There was nothing left but to fill in the backup when things ran out. Claire packed up what they needed for lunch at the Whitworth house, and they marched out of the lodge with their heads hung low.

As Mike and Linda walked through the deck door of the house, John greeted them, and everyone sat down at the table to eat.

"You've gotta nice place here," Mike said loudly. The Whitworths were quiet people in their own home, but Mike didn't have a mute button.

"Thank you," Vickie said.

John nodded in agreement. "We work very hard at it." He began to pass the food around, and Craig, Abby, Claire, and Taylor followed the well-worn routine quietly.

"Well, it shows. Really, nice place," Mike repeated. A plate of vegetables was pushed his way by Craig, along with a look meant to quiet him down.

After everyone had food and had begun eating, Linda chimed in, "We can't wait to take some of the tours tomorrow."

"Yes," Mike interjected. "I'd like to go fishing for a bit too." He took a bite of his veggies and grimaced as he choked them down.

"I'll take you tomorrow, Dad."

"I could take him as well," John said. He had hardly taken a bite of his food.

Craig turned to John. "I got it. You have a lot to do."

"You know where to go, Craig?" Mike asked.

Craig finished chewing and put his fork next to his plate. "Sure thing." He put his hand on Abby's leg. "Abby and I go fishing all the time."

Claire coughed. Craig stared in her direction, then winked. Claire grinned and said, "Maybe you could go for a photo tour this afternoon, Mom."

"That would be lovely. I'd like to go to town as well. It looked so cute when we drove through yesterday." Linda looked around the table, smiling.

"We have some lovely little shops. I can take you if you'd like," Vickie said.

"Well, it's settled then," John announced. "Does anyone want wine?"

Everyone nodded in affirmation, and John used the excuse to go to the kitchen for a moment of peace.

Taylor seemed intent on getting out as well. She quickly finished her meal and asked if she could go help Frank. "Sure, honey," Vickie said. "Thank you."

The rest of lunch went without incident, and as Craig, Abby, and Claire were about to leave to get on with their tasks for the resort, to their surprise, Mike and Linda stayed behind.

"It's really early, kid," Mike said as he gingerly got into the boat the next morning.

Craig heard him, but didn't acknowledge the comment as he prepared Abby's boat.

"Where are we going?"

"Out to a good hole on the west side. Abby and I usually have luck there in the morning." Craig started the boat and pulled out from the dock. "Hold on," he said, then gunned it. The front of the boat rose out of the water before finding its balance as it skipped across the lake.

Within minutes, they reached the spot. Craig set the anchor and pulled out two rods. He had already prepared the lures and gave one of the rods to his father. "You need to aim for the weed bed over there and pull the lure along the front of it. The fish are in there. They just need to be brought out for a little morning snack." Craig cast his line right on the spot and began to reel it in slowly.

"You're learning a bunch of stuff so far this summer, huh?" Mike stated.

"Yeah, it's cool. It seems like every day there's something new. I like it."

Mike tried to cast out but only made it halfway to the weed bed. When his line cleared, Craig dropped another perfect cast and watched the water closely. He steered his line right along the edge. With a few bubbles visible near his cast, there was a clear sense that the line was being watched. Craig waited until he felt the hit. He snapped the rod up, setting the hook. After hauling in the fish, Craig removed the hook and threw the fish in the cooler. The hesitation of the early summer had been replaced by precision and confidence.

"Try again, Dad. Get your wrist into it and cast it way out."

Mike stood, then launched the lure right where he needed it. He reeled it in slowly and got a hit, but he pulled it up too quickly and lost the fish. After that, he seemed content to just watch Craig. He put his rod away and sat down on the driver's side of the boat. "So, what are you doing again at the high school?"

Mid-cast, Craig responded, "I'm coaching. I get the kids from ninth to twelfth grade in the weight room and run them through patterns afterwards. I actually get a good lift in as well."

"Are you having fun with that?"

Knowing that his dad would approve, Craig said, "Yeah, it's pretty fun. But I have a lot of work to do around here, so I can't spend too much time there."

Mike looked out over the lake and then ran his hand through the water. "About that. They have you up on a roof?"

"Yup. I'm redoing the single-story cabins. I'm actually having fun with it. Like I said, I'm learning a lot. It's like there's a rhythm to each day, but something new as well, you know?"

Nodding, Mike simply said, "Good."

"How's your diet and exercise?" Craig was desperate to change the subject. His father seemed content to move on, so the rest of the fishing trip was filled with Mike talking. Craig was happy for that.

"Hey, Mom!" Claire yelled from the porch. "We're already running late. Vickie is waiting back at her house to drive to town. There are things to do here later this afternoon." Claire paced back and forth. Her mother was always running late. This trait may have been the reason why she and Craig were never late for anything.

When her mother finally emerged, she was wearing shorts that were too short, a spaghetti strap shirt, and a high ponytail. Claire decided not to say anything. It wouldn't be worth the wasted breath. "Let's go, honey. I'm so excited to see the town," Linda said with too much exuberance. Again, Claire let it go.

As she climbed into the back seat of Vickie's truck, Claire said, "We have to be sure to stop at the bait shop for Abby and John. They had a few things they wanted us to pick up."

"No problem," said Vickie. "John mentioned something about that to me this morning over breakfast."

"The bait shop?" Linda asked, looking back at Claire and then sideways at Vickie.

"Yes. The bait shop." Vickie wore a prim smile that made Claire roll her eyes in the rearview mirror. "You can wait in the truck."

The town was a bustle of activity. Vickie parked on a residential street just off the downtown grid, a place no one but a local could find. Being local was something Vickie would never admit to, but after fifteen years in Eagle River, it was the reality. The three of them started towards the main street festival. During the holiday weekends, one or two streets were closed to traffic and tents were set up to accommodate local artists selling their work to visitors. At first, Claire thought of it like the farmers markets and small street festivals she had attended in Chicago. However, the first time she sat with Shane in the tent he and his mother shared, she found it to be so much more. People with tremendous talent were all over the place. She was amazed at the diversity of the art and how welcoming everyone was in discussing process and technique. The community was warm and inviting in a way that breathed life into the town. Gone was the boredom and casual disinterest that seemed so prevalent in larger cities.

They came upon the festival, and Linda went into cooing

mode. Everything was "just so cute," and Claire was sick of it thirty seconds into the proceedings. If Linda had her way, she'd walk out of the festival with four bags of stuff that she would leave in the basement until she forgot where she purchased it. Claire had too much respect for the town and its people to let her simply waste their time. She directed her mother to some of the more authentic stands with people who did art for a living and could use the business. These were the people Shane had the greatest connection with when they had been here the week before.

Vickie had flown the coop for a little while with the promise of meeting Linda and Claire at Shane's booth. Claire was left alone with her mother, who flitted from vendor to vendor. "If I buy too much, I don't know where I would put it."

"Then don't buy too much," Claire said plainly.

"I just don't know."

"What don't you know, Mom?"

"I just don't know what to buy."

"Then don't buy anything. Let's go sit for a while. I know a good place," Claire said, walking away from the tents.

"Ok, dear. Let's do that," Linda said as if it were her idea.

They strolled over to a bench just off the main strip of the festival. It faced the river, where the hustle was less overwhelming. Claire smiled as she looked over the peaceful scene. "So, what do you and Dad think of the resort so far?"

Without so much as a breath, Linda responded, "It's so lovely. Just cute."

"Really? Cute?"

"Well, I don't know what you want me to say, Claire. I never really know what you want me to say."

"I don't know, Mom. I guess…this place has really had an effect on me. I didn't think it would, but it has. I don't think I'll really understand it until I go back."

"To Chicago?"

"Yes."

Linda briefly shook her head. "You and Craig."

Annoyed to the point of bursting, Claire managed to compose herself to simply ask, "What?"

"You two have always seen the world a bit differently from your dad and me, and Sarah. We just take it as it comes. A day at a time. You two are always thinking about stuff. Thinking and thinking."

"Is that a bad thing?"

"No, but don't expect me to understand it. I'm too old for all that." She smiled at Claire. "But we love you."

"I know that." Claire took a deep breath as she watched the river flow by. "Do you want to meet Shane? He has a booth at the other end of the strip."

"Oh, Shane is it? Is that your guy? Is he handsome?"

Claire laughed. "Yes, Mom. He's pretty handsome."

"Well then, let's go."

CHAPTER 13

"Hey, sleepy," Abby said as she lay down beside Craig. She pushed his hair out of his eyes and kissed his nose. "Wake up."

"What time is it?" Craig asked, then snuck in a kiss on Abby's lips. He pulled her to his chest. "Not time to get up. Time to sleep."

Abby squirmed her way out of his embrace and pushed him onto his back. She ran her fingers on his chest as she sat up. "But we have to get up and go."

"Where do we have to go? Breakfast service doesn't start until six thirty."

"I know, but it's the Fourth of July, and we need to prep for lunch and dinner and get rounds done in between." She was not interested in going, but obligation trumped desire on this day more than any other. She laid her head down on Craig's chest briefly and gave him a squeeze before getting up.

"Ok." Craig got up suddenly and lifted Abby from the floor, then set her down again. He smiled, got dressed, and they walked hand in hand to the lodge.

Frank put Craig on grill duty, but his dad took over quickly so Craig could get back to running around wherever Abby told him to go. "My dad is actually very good with the grill," he told John while running an errand down the cabin road. "It's one of his few virtues." John laughed.

Abby stayed mostly between the front desk and dining room directing traffic. Requests for towels or cleaning came in, and people were sent out. Meghan showed up to open the water for swimming. Claire was stuck in the kitchen. Abby could feel her dad pulling away from the holiday, spending more time at the bar and less trying to organize and be sure everyone was on task. The people who worked for them knew what to do, but she was now the director. Craig was easy, but Frank was more intimidating. What was she supposed to tell him? He was the one giving the orders in the kitchen. Abby approached hesitantly. "So, when do we plan on serving lunch?"

"I think we'll be ready around one and we'll serve at quarter after. Most everyone will be back from the parade by then. That sound good?" Frank rattled it all off without looking up from his make table. "I guess it depends on how Mr. McLean is doing with the grill."

"He's all good," Claire said loudly. "Grilling is what the man does. If we were home, he'd be in the same spot."

"All the same, he should move on to burgers soon. I think all the brats and sausages are out. Did you get the burgers seasoned yet, Claire?" Frank asked.

"Just finished!" she yelled. She and Frank were already in mid-dinner rush mode.

"I'll take them," Abby said, trying to insert herself. She went to get a cart to roll them out to the deck.

When Abby got out to the deck, Craig's dad was surrounded by a group of men around the grill. He was pontificating about the Brewers' chances coming out of the All-Star break. A robust "argument" had broken out, and Abby was unsure how to move in. "Mr. McLean? Mr. McLean." There was no answer. "Mike!"

she said sharply. The crowd went silent. "Sorry. Mr. McLean."

"Yes, Abby," he responded, startled. "What can I do for you?"

She smiled awkwardly and said, "It's time to move on to burgers. Are you done with the sausages?"

"Oh yes," he said, clearing the grill and placing the meat in a bin before covering it with tinfoil. "Here you go." He lifted two full bins of sausages onto the lower shelf of the cart, then grabbed the burgers. "These look great. Do I grill them all the same?"

"That would be perfect."

"How about I char some of them for folks who like them well done?" He looked up at the guys who were gathered around.

"Great. I gotta get these in," Abby said, totally ignoring Mike's question.

"No problem."

As she walked away, Abby could hear Mike saying, "That's my son's girlfriend. Her folks own this place. Great girl." She smiled to herself.

The lunch went perfectly. All the food was served on time, and Abby thanked everyone for coming. A sense of accomplishment came over her as both Craig and her dad congratulated her on a job well done. A day without any problems, so far. Everything was clicking so well, she even remembered to thank Mike for grilling. He stood up to accept the applause. "A typical Mike move" according to Craig. As the lunch wrapped up, Abby noticed Craig talking to Tim Granger, a Phy Ed teacher from the high school and the football coach. He had been at other celebrations when she was younger, always complimenting the food, but he had not been at the resort for quite a while. Craig's dad was also hanging around, so Abby thought about pressing her way into the conversation, but if Craig had something to tell her, she was confident he would just come out and say it. Instead, she waved at him and went on her way.

The fact that Abby waved made Craig nervous. He felt almost compelled to explain Coach Granger's presence, but decided to stay engaged in the conversation.

"Craig's been a big help this summer," Coach said. "He has a knack with the kids and really knows his stuff."

"That a boy," Mike said, smiling widely.

"Good to hear, Tim," John said from behind the bar, staring straight at Craig. Craig felt a pang of guilt knowing that at least one cabin would likely be left undone. Expectations weighed heavier than any compliment could lift. He didn't know how to tell anyone about his new plan over the next few weeks.

Mike and Coach continued to talk while John went off to make some drinks. Craig felt the pull of Abby's eyes from the kitchen and said, "I gotta get back to work."

"We'll be seeing you out at school later this week?" Coach Granger asked.

"Perhaps. I'll try to stop by."

"Good deal."

"They look like two peas in a pod," Abby said as Craig walked into the kitchen.

"Yep. They sure do." He tried to catch Abby's eyes, but

she was looking past him. He turned to see Coach Granger walking out onto the deck. Facing Abby again, he asked, "Have anything for me to do?"

Finally, their eyes met. "I think the bonfire needs to be built, and you can help the DJ get his stuff set up on the deck when he gets here. We're going to have music and a singing contest for the kids tonight before the fireworks."

"Fun. I'll get right on it. Anything else?"

"Not that I can think of."

"Alright." Craig moved to give Abby a little kiss, but she averted her face and his lips caught her on the cheek. "See you later."

"Yes." Abby smiled and raised her eyebrows.

After getting the wood for the bonfire and helping with the music setup, Craig walked down the cabin road and saw that a few cabins were missing wood, especially the lake cabins. Despite the fact that it was summer, people used a lot of wood, mostly for the private firepits by the three-bedroom cabins so guests could sit out by the lake well into the night. Craig decided to go chop some wood and get it delivered for the nighttime festivities.

He had cut a few logs when his father showed up. "What are you doing?"

"Just getting caught up on the wood. Crazy how much people use in the summer." Craig lined another log and set the wedge. With one shot, he blew it up. Rarely was a log not split on the first try anymore.

"Isn't this what you were doing the first time you came

up here?" Mike asked. He walked around, picking up the split wood and putting it in the trailer. "Mind if I give one a try?"

"Sure." Craig set a log and tapped in the wedge. He handed Mike the hammer.

Mike eyed the wedge, raised the hammer, and hit the spike with a thunderous strike. Wood scattered everywhere as he stood back to admire his work.

"Lucky hit," Craig chuckled. "Try another one." He set up another log.

"Sure thing," Mike said as he flexed his still impressively large arms. He raised the hammer and drove the spike so hard it stuck into the stump after annihilating the log. "Still got it."

"Where'd you learn how to do that?"

"Pounding tires. We had to pound the crap out of them with sledgehammers back in school. Thousands of reps." He nodded to Craig, ready for another log.

"Really?" Craig said sarcastically.

Mike chopped another dozen logs, and they went to do their deliveries. When they got to the end of the cabin road, Craig noticed Abby setting up tents in a clearing in the forest. He left his dad to return the four-wheeler and walked over to her.

Running up to him, Abby said, "Oh, thank God you're here." They made their way through the woods beyond Frank's cabin. "I totally forgot to set up camp." Her eyes were wide and her hands shook trying to get the tent pole in. She was in panic mode.

"Camp?" Craig took the pole from her sweaty hands and fed it through the holes of the tent. "What camp?"

Exasperated, Abby replied, "Every year we set up a campground for the kids to sleep under the stars. We stay out with the kids and let the parents have a night off. I completely forgot until one of the regulars asked me about it. Now, we have to get the tents up and all the other shit."

Craig came up behind Abby and rubbed her shoulders. "Don't worry." He kissed her neck. "We'll get it done. I'll work through supper." He released her and began on another tent.

Abby took a much-needed deep breath. "Why are you so good to me?"

"You know," Craig replied, not looking up.

"I do."

They got the first two tents set up, and then Abby left to check on dinner prep. Craig finished the last three tents and still had time to grab a snack before the nighttime activities. The bonfire went well, songs were sung, and s'mores were made.

After the fireworks came the time to camp out. Craig stayed up with Abby. Most of the kids, despite their best-laid plans, didn't make it to midnight. Abby and Craig slept in a tent together, but both were too exhausted to even kiss each other goodnight.

In the morning, a small child pulled on Craig and Abby's tent. Craig woke up and unzipped the door.

"Mr. Craig, I don't know where my cabin is, and I need to go potty."

"Ok. What's your name?"

"Jake. Jake Sullivan."

"The Sullivans are in Cabin 3," Abby stated quietly as she started to get up.

"Ok. Thanks," Craig replied. "I'll get him."

Abby straightened up and watched Craig walk away with

the child. He was holding his hand and turned towards him, listening. The sight made Abby feel warm all over. She lay back down and snuggled up with the sleeping bag. Craig's smell lingered.

The Fourth - Abby

Plan and Panic
Plan and Panic
That is the only rhythm
I know anymore
Food to make
Food to serve
Dishes to clean
When I talk
In front of the guests
I leave my body
It is some other me
Who thanks
Who mentions all
Those who made
Everything possible
"That went well"
"That was great"
"Well done, Abby"
Kind words spoken
But at what cost
Today, the cost was
All of me

CHAPTER 14

After the Fourth of July, the next week ticked by. The rhythm of these weeks was familiar, and Abby found herself back in the office trying to sort through the mess. Despite getting the mock website almost ready for launch, the whole filing system needed to be updated and the resolution of Frank's pay still needed confrontation. She simply couldn't believe that he was not being paid. Projections based on reservations and a modest expense report had the resort in the black by Labor Day, even with the roofing project. It was going to be a good year, and that made Abby feel better. Still, she wanted to explain to Craig how the resort wasn't really a moneymaker, but she couldn't figure out how.

Meanwhile, Craig was busier than ever. He had his morning workouts and his roofs: one more cabin down, three to go. The problem for Craig was, if he decided to go back to Whitewater for camp, there would still be one cabin to go. He asked Coach Granger to run him through his tests: 40-yard dash, pacer, shuttle run, and lifts. There was almost no change from the year before. In fact, he was a little faster on the shuttle run because it didn't hurt every time he made a cut, like it had previously. Rested and ready, Craig asked Granger to make the call. He knew he should discuss it with Abby, but without knowing for sure if he could come back, he didn't want to speculate.

After such a busy start to the week, Craig and Abby hadn't had much time to connect and talk. However, there they sat at Butch's on Wednesday night in mid-July with almost nothing to say. They could recap the work week, or gossip about Claire and Shane, or debate whether Meghan's relationship would last, but neither of them had the guts to speak the truth. So instead, they ate, smiled at each other from time to time, and remained secretively silent. The weight of the air between them smelled of more than pineapple and pepperoni. When they were done, neither of them had said much of anything, and Craig dropped Abby off at her house before walking back to his cabin.

Craig met Claire in the living room of their cabin. He had few occasions to speak with her outside of small conversations they had in passing or right before they went to sleep, but the evening was early, and Claire wasn't out with Shane. He sat down and kicked his feet up on the coffee table. "I'm so tired."

"Me too. This place will kick your ass if you don't get in the swing of it. But I love the sense of space. It's like having a new frame on the picture you thought you had."

"No kidding. So, you like it so far?"

Claire thought for a moment. "It's pretty awesome. Just what I needed before going back to school. There's so much to do and so much to see. I've hardly given school a second thought."

"That's cool. I've barely given school any thought either." Craig knew he was lying. He'd been thinking about going back to school and football for most of the summer.

"You and Abby good?"

Nodding, Craig replied, "Yeah. I think we are. Really good. We had lots of time to talk and relax on that camping trip a few weeks ago. I've never felt as close to anyone as I do to her. It's like I can tell her everything and she just listens and accepts." Craig saw Claire smiling. "What about you and this Shane guy?"

Claire crossed her legs, trying to get comfortable on the couch. "I don't know. He's nice. I think it's just a summer thing though." Her cheeks reddened.

Craig chuckled quietly. "Yeah, right. A summer thing. You're not getting off that easy."

"What?" Claire said, shooting a mocking look at him.

"You like the guy."

"I do. What of it?"

"Nothing. What's he like?"

"He's just so different, in a good way," Claire said, twirling her hair around her finger. "Lots of stories about traveling around the country. He's been so many places. I don't know. I feel like I know him, but then I don't."

Confused, Craig asked, "How so?"

"Well, for instance, he's got this scar on his wrist, and I asked him about it. All he said was he had an accident. Wouldn't tell me what type or when. He'll talk about Colorado or Florida or any type of art I want, but some of the personal stuff is a mystery."

"That's weird."

Claire nodded. "I met his mom a few weeks ago. She's a potter. Works at Walmart in Minocqua and picks up shifts as a cleaner at a resort closer to town. She seems nice. Told me to say hi to Frank. Not sure how she knows him though."

"It's a small town. Not like Chicago," Craig interjected.

"True." Since she hadn't been there that long, it hadn't occurred to Claire how small the town really was. "How are things at the school, or football practice, or whatever you're doing?"

"I'm having a good time with it. Getting in really good shape."

"Why? You going to play again or something?" Claire looked at Craig closely. His nostrils were flaring.

"No," he said a little too sharply. He couldn't tell her. She would keep his secret if he did, but he couldn't do it.

Holding her hands up in surrender, Claire replied, "Ok. Just asking."

"Sorry. No. I'm just trying to help the boys. It's kinda gratifying in a way."

Claire stretched her arms above her head and yawned loudly. She knew she wasn't going to get it out of him. "Well, I'm going to turn in. It's not often we get an early night around here, what with Frank making me close the kitchen most nights."

"How's he doing?"

"What do you mean?"

Craig thought for a moment. "Abby's mentioned that she was worried about him. I was just wondering if you noticed anything."

Getting up, Claire replied, "He seems normal to me. I guess I don't really have a baseline. The guy's old. He's worked all his life. He can't keep this up forever." She began to walk around the room, pacing. "I think this place just really gets to you, you know?"

"Yeah. The first time I came here, I felt like I came home.

It's not like where we grew up. It has a weight. Not a bad one, more like a gravity."

"I know what you mean. Every time I think about going back, I kinda get sick to my stomach. Home, that is."

Craig nodded. "Me too. There's just a sense of the real here, the authentic."

"I know I could never do what Sarah did. Go back to stay."

"I think Sarah understands the irony of her choice, but she likes comfort. Being back in the neighborhood makes her comfortable. I can appreciate that. We all do it in some way."

"I guess we do." Claire walked towards the bedroom. "Goodnight, Craig."

"'Night, Claire." Craig went to his bed and lay down. He texted Abby, *Love you. Goodnight.*

A moment later, she responded, *Love you too, Craig. 'Night.*

Craig was asleep in seconds.

In the third week of July, the sky decided to open for the first time all summer. With tar paper replacement necessary on all the cabins, there would be no work done until things dried out. "We've done good work, Craig," John said while they sat at the bar on Monday night. A few guests were milling around, but the lodge was calm. "You only have three cabins left and the whole summer to finish. Might have to think of another project."

Craig tapped his fingertips nervously on the bar top. "Thank you, sir. Yes, I think it's going well. I hope I can get back to work soon."

"I'm sure you will. We've been lucky so far. It's been a good summer. You've done well here." John gave him a quick pat on the shoulder, then walked away to help another guest.

"I hope so," Craig said to himself. He knew he would have to break it to Abby if Coach agreed to let him come back. Telling her was one thing, but telling John was a whole different deal. He felt the same as the summer before, when he thought about telling his dad he wanted to quit football. He didn't know how he'd do it.

Later that night, while writing in his journal, he got a text from Coach Brewer, the coach of the Whitewater football team. *Call me tomorrow.*

Craig's Journal

What am I going to do? There is no way to get everything done. If I go back to football, then I will run out of time. God, I'm stupid. Abby's going to kill me. I don't even know what John will say. And Frank? Shit. This so dumb. Why do I even want to play? I guess I have something to prove to myself. Nothing gives me that feeling. I mean, what could be better than burning someone for a touchdown? I know I can do it. I know I can play. Abby doesn't know that side of me. What if she doesn't like him? I don't know. I hope this all doesn't go to shit. I guess I'll work like a dog until I leave. That's all I can do. How can I have two loves? I know that's how Abby's going to see it. I'm screwed.

On Tuesday, the rain did not let up much. 'Another wasted day,' Craig thought to himself. Since many of the outdoor activities were canceled, Craig floated a plan to get a big set of tournaments going, from ping pong to pool to cards for the adults and Uno for the kids. John and Frank thought it was a great idea, and Claire piggybacked with some creative ideas in the game loft. Craig helped Claire bring tables up and got some poster board to set up brackets, then planned to go to the office to make some flyers. There seemed to be enough guests to make a go of it at breakfast. Besides, what else was there to do?

When he walked into the office to use the copy machine, Abby was working on updating expenses and payroll. She was not in the mood to deal with anyone, but somehow, Craig's enthusiasm raised her up.

"Hey, babe," he said. "Whatcha doing?"

"Nothing much," Abby responded cheerfully. "Just trying to get payroll done. Paying the bills."

"Be sure to stick a big, fat bonus in there for me." Craig chuckled.

Abby rolled her eyes. "What are you up to?"

"I'm making flyers for some tournaments we're having in the game room this afternoon."

"That sounds fun. I wish I could help."

"Why can't you?"

"I gotta get the bills paid and get checks cut for Meghan and the boys for Friday."

"Just Meghan and the boys? What about Frank?"

It was none of his business really, but Abby was still caught off guard. "Frank? Yeah, Frank too." She looked at her computer and leaned in.

Craig could tell she was agitated, so he went about making his copies, then said, "You know…" Abby turned towards him.

"You're in here half the day, every day, and I don't really know what you're doing."

"Well, that's because you never ask." Abby smiled.

"Well, now I'm asking. You never talk about what's going on. Is everything ok?" Craig kept all his attention on Abby. "You always seem a little off when you get done in here."

Abby pressed her lips. 'Should I tell him? Is now the time?'

She paused so long, gripped by indecision, that Craig could only mutter, "Cool. Well, see ya."

"Yeah. Bye." The moment passed, to the relief of Abby.

Just before lunch, Craig went out to make his call. Sitting on the bench under the covered porch of his cabin, listening to the raindrops, he let the phone ring. Coach Brewer picked up. "Hello?"

"Hi, Coach. It's Craig McLean."

"Hey, Craig. How are you?" he asked brightly, to the surprise of Craig.

"Fine, Coach," Craig stammered. "How…how are you?"

"I'm good. Got your email and talked with Coach Granger. So, you want to come back to play football?"

"Yes, sir. I think so."

"Well, Craig, I can't have you thinking so. You gotta know."

"I do, sir. I know."

"What brings this on?"

The memory of playing with the boys at the Pewaukee field came back to him strongly. "I just got back into it this spring, and now this summer. You know how I said I didn't love the game last year?"

"Yes, I recall."

"Well, I was wrong. I do love the game. I think I didn't love the pressure of expectations. Being my father's son."

"Has that changed?"

"I believe it has. I can tell you that if you give me a chance, I will give you the entire season."

"You can make that commitment? I don't want any surprises come mid-season."

"I can."

"Coach Granger says you're in shape. Will says he thinks you're better than last year." There was a pause.

Craig should have known Coach would have talked with Will. "Yes. I think coaching, even though it's only been for a few weeks, has given me a lot of perspective."

"That's good to hear. Well, do you still have the playbook from last year?"

"I do."

"Not much has changed. The base offense is still the same. You think you can handle it and be down here the weekend after next? I'll give you a tryout. Nothing official, of course, but I'd still like to see how you do."

"Thank you, sir."

"Now, Craig?"

"Yes, sir?"

"You know, if you make the team, the guys are going to give you a lot of crap. You will need to prove yourself in a way that is next level. You understand that, right?"

"I do."

"Good. We'll see you next weekend."

"Thank you," Craig said, then hung up. Emotions rushed

over him. He was sweating, not from the heat, but from excitement, nerves, and dread. He looked at the lake for strength, but the turbulent surface gave him no answers.

The tournaments went well, and for a time, Craig forgot about the phone call. The guests had fun, and some asked if he could organize the same events for the next day if the rain didn't let up. He gladly agreed, then went to help turn over rooms and cabins for weekend visitors who were coming on Wednesday for four- or five-day stints.

Meanwhile, Abby got the payroll and her expense report done. Things were looking good. The remainder of the year was expected to be profitable, especially if her dad worked on getting snowmobile reservations in the winter. Abby still felt uneasy about not filing a check for Frank and was determined to ask her dad about it soon, but she was unsure about how to bring it up.

Abby and Craig had a rare dinner at her parents' house, then went out for an evening boat ride. Abby brought poles along since they hadn't fished for a while, and with the hard rain of the day, the fish were probably on the move. When they got to a good hole, they both cast their lines and slowly reeled them in. Craig caught the first fish and brought it in with no help, tossing it in the cooler. Abby smiled. She remembered how skittish he was around the fish only a few weeks before. She cast her line out leisurely, not really aiming for a hole. When the line came in, she just pulled it in all the way and set the rod aside. "You know what you were asking about this morning? In the office?"

"Yeah," Craig replied, half-listening as he cast out another line. He kept replaying the call with Coach in his head and just stared out at the lake water.

"Craig!" Abby barked.

Shocked by force of her voice, he turned to look at Abby and carefully asked, "Yes?"

"You want to know what I do in the office every morning?" She was still speaking louder than she needed to.

"Yes," he said, sitting down and pulling in his line. Abby sat before him, the moonlight shining in her eyes.

Now that she had Craig's full attention, a calmness spread over her face and a half smile crossed her lips. "I'm doing the books. I'm trying to create a website. I'm trying to learn the business of the business." She blurted it all out. It felt so good to tell someone. Her mom was sick of hearing her complain, and she was scared to talk with her dad.

A little cautiously, Craig asked, "So, how's that going?"

"It's fine. I mean…" She sighed. "It's just a lot. My dad keeps records of everything, even stuff from years ago, and my mom sorts through it when she can. It seems like I've spent the whole summer just catching up."

Craig waited quietly, but being met with nothing, inquired, "You seem to want to tell me something. Is the resort doing ok?" He leaned over and propped his head up with his hands, his eyes focused on her.

Abby shrugged and said, "This year it is. We've had a good beginning to the summer, and we'll turn a profit this year. Not every year has been that way."

"Really?" For some reason, Craig thought the place was doing great. It was always busy when he was up here.

"I guess it's mostly a lifestyle." Abby was parroting her mother. "I mean, we can always pay our bills, and we have almost no debt. The assets alone are worth a bunch, but it seems most years we break even somewhere between Labor Day and Thanksgiving. This year is better. My dad organized a lot of spring hunts, and the early spring snow made for good snowmobile business. We're booked straight through Labor Day."

"Well, that's good."

"Surprising is more like it."

"Why's that?"

"With two cabins lost most weeks, we're still doing well."

A twinge of pain shot across Craig's chest. "That's good."

"Yeah. But there's a bunch of weird stuff going on that I want to ask my dad about."

"Like what?"

"I don't know." Abby was suddenly very aware that she was going too deep. But it was Craig. "Some stuff about how we bought the place and how Frank fits into the whole thing."

"Don't you know that stuff?"

"I thought I did. I just don't know anymore." Abby stayed silent after that, and Craig didn't press.

They moved on to simpler subjects, then made their way back home. With the promise of a dry rest of the week, Craig hoped to get up on a roof and get the tear-off done at least. Even if he worked quickly, with only two weeks to go until training camp started in August, he would still be one cabin short if something couldn't be worked out. He could come back on weekends, but that was not going to cut it. He needed to say something.

CHAPTER 15

"Hey, Abby," Claire said as she reached the cabin she shared with Craig. Abby was sitting outside on the porch swing, enjoying the evening after dinner service. No bonfire tonight, just a chance to reflect and rest before another weekend.

Abby moved over to give Claire room to sit down. "Hi. How are you? I feel like I haven't gotten a chance to really visit with you since summer began."

Claire turned to face Abby. "I know, right? Things got really busy around here. I've just fallen into a rhythm with art lessons, tours, helping in the kitchen. You know?"

"It's been a busy summer. How are the tours?" Abby was still a bit jealous of the fact that Claire had taken over that part of her job.

"They're nice. I have the routine down pretty well. I just wish I knew more about the history of the place. Outside of what you told me, I don't really know that much."

Abby thought for a moment. "You know, I don't really know that much either. I know it opened in the late '60s or early '70s, in the heyday of these kinds of places, but beyond that…" She shrugged.

"Weird."

"It is, isn't it?"

Claire looked out at the lake peeking through the lakeshore

cabins. "Other than that, it's been a relaxing summer. Just what I needed."

"Good. I'm glad. My mom has been happy to have you. Dad too."

"Vickie and John are great. I've learned a lot from watching them. They're special."

"Thanks. I like them too." Abby chuckled.

Claire got up and stretched. "I'm going to go get cleaned up, probably take a shower."

"Ok."

"You can come in and wait for Craig if you want. I assume that's who you're waiting for."

"Yes. Thanks." Abby followed Claire in and sat down on Craig's bed. He made his bed for the most part every morning, a trait Abby appreciated. Books covered the nightstand, and a large pile of papers sat on the ground next to the bed. The top booklet said "2017 Whitewater Playbook." Abby picked it up and paged through it. 'Why would Craig have this?' she thought. On some of the pages were notes written in Craig's handwriting. She didn't really understand what any of it meant, but he had obviously been studying it. She put the booklet back down on the floor, then sat back against the wall and waited. The shower came on just as Craig came in. He looked tired and sweaty.

"Hey," he said. "What's up?"

"Nothing," Abby replied. "You?"

"Got the roof done from last week." He went to get a towel to wipe his face. "Still have two to go. I wish the guest wasn't here next week. Then, I'd be all done."

She made room for him to sit down on the bed next to her. "Good for you, Craig."

He moved the playbook over with his foot and gave her a quick kiss. "I gotta take a shower."

Abby laughed. "Yeah, you stink."

"How was your day?" Craig was nervous. He had to tell her soon.

Abby took a moment to compose her thoughts. She didn't turn to face Craig, but said, "What's the book for?"

"What book?" Craig asked, looking to the nightstand at his collection.

"The playbook. The one on the floor next to you."

A rush ran through Craig's chest. He couldn't lie to her. "That's the playbook for this season at Whitewater."

"Why do you have it?" Abby asked, trying to remain calm.

Craig shifted to face her, dangling one leg off the bed and leaning on his hand. "I'm going to try out for the team this year." The statement flushed his system down to his toes. He had finally said it.

Abby said nothing. Her face grew taut, and a single tear fell from her eye. "When?"

"Next weekend," Craig said without emotion.

Abby was ready to burst. "Next weekend!"

"Yeah. I need to try out this year, cause last year…you know."

"So, you'll be gone for the weekend?"

"Yeah, but I'll be back Sunday…Saturday night, late?"

"But if you make the team?" Abby said sharply.

She had connected the dots. "If I make the team, I have to report for camp the middle of the first week of August."

"If you make the team, you'll be gone all of August?"

"Mostly. I can come up for the weekends."

"What about the cabins?"

"I think I can get them done." He wasn't entirely sure.

"You think?" Abby got up and began to walk around the very small front room. She didn't know how to get out of the moment. "You think!" she yelled.

Craig took a breath and sat back against the wall. "I guess it all depends on the guests. I'll get one more started next week. That leaves me with one for the last half week. Or I can get work done on the weekends."

"But what if you can't?" Abby felt more tears flowing down her face. She hated crying. She reached for a towel that draped over the chair housing Craig's bag. "You made a promise."

Craig stared silently.

This pissed Abby off even more. "Why? Why would you go back?"

"I missed it."

"You missed what? People ragging you? People knocking your head in? All the boys you can't stand? What?" Abby could hear Claire rummaging around the bedroom.

"I missed all of it," Craig plainly replied.

Even more enraged by his calmness, she spewed, "What is all of it?"

"The competition, the boys. I'm good at it. I miss being good at something. Really good at something. You know?"

"Yes. I know what it's like to be really good at something." Abby paused, then continued, "So do you."

Confused, Craig shook his head slowly. "What?"

"We're good at us. Did you ever think about that? You and I are good at being us. Together. I didn't think you needed more. I guess I was wrong." She walked towards the door.

"Abby," Craig called, getting up from the bed.

"No!" she yelled, then walked out the door.

After Abby left, Craig sat back down on the bed. He knew she wasn't going to be happy, but she hadn't even let him explain. But really, how do you explain a feeling, an urge? The call he felt to go back to football was overwhelming. There was no explaining.

Claire emerged from her room, combing her hair. "What the hell was that all about?"

Craig sighed. "Abby found my playbook, and I told her I was going back to play football. I leave next week if I make the team. I'll only be able to come back over the weekends."

"Well, shit." Claire stared at him, crossing her arms.

"What?"

"What the fuck are you thinking?"

"What do you mean?"

"Going back to football? The return of the golden boy." She smirked. "When you put something to bed, Craig, you put it to bed."

"It's not like that. I need to play. I left something out there, and I need to go find it. It's like…it's like my art form. I'm still looking for that perfect piece, that perfect game. I'm looking for the stillness in the chaos."

"What? Don't try to be clever," Claire snorted. "You'll never find it. Believe me."

"But I have to try."

"That's not it." Claire sat down next to Craig and continued calmly, "You don't get it. You'll never find it on that field, cause you found it here, with Abby. She's your perfect piece. Being with her is your art form. You're better at that than anything else I've ever seen you do. She's your stillness." She sighed. "But, if you need to get football out of your system, I guess that's what you need to do."

Not really knowing how to respond, Craig nodded.

Later that evening, he got a text from Abby. *You're telling my dad.* That was all that came that night.

The next morning, Craig got up early, hoping to catch Abby as she went out to fish, but when he got down to the dock, her boat was already gone. There was no practice this Friday, so he decided to go for a run to clear his head. He chose a path close to the lake, cutting through yards and trails when he couldn't be right on the shore. The rhythm of his breath and pounding of his feet brought his body a sense of peace, but his head was buzzing. Despite his attempts to bring his mind back to the task at hand, he kept picturing Abby yelling, "No!" Both she and Claire said he should concentrate on the relationship, but he thought that was all good. After a while, he found that he was running harder and harder as he moved onto an open road. The road came to a dead end, and he realized he had reached the mouth of the river that fed into the lake. Abby's favorite fishing hole was just to the east of where the river came in. He made his way through the woods and brush to the shore. Just as he'd expected, Abby was there, sitting in her boat with a line in the water. She wasn't reeling the line. Instead, it was limp in the water, and the rod was lying on the side of the boat. Abby was staring off into space. Without thinking, Craig waved and yelled, "Hey!"

Abby thought she heard something. She looked up,

searching the shoreline. Who would yell at her at six in the morning? Seeing Craig surprised her. She timidly waved back. She was still angry with him.

Craig was smiling. He felt a sense of accomplishment in having found her. "Can I get a ride?"

"You realize you're like halfway around the lake. You ran probably five miles." Abby couldn't believe he was standing there on the shore. 'What the fuck is with this guy?' she thought.

"Really? I didn't know," Craig said, walking a few steps closer to the water. "Soooo, whatcha say?"

Abby reeled in her line. She took a deep breath, then sighed. "Fine."

The motor started, and the boat slowly moved towards Craig. As she pulled up, she said, "I'm still really pissed at you."

"I figured," Craig responded, throwing his shoes in the boat and wading out. He climbed in, stepping over to kiss Abby. She kissed him back and then pushed him down into the passenger seat.

"Why can't I hate you?" She glanced out across the lake, then turned back, staring squarely at him.

"I don't know. I'm kinda cute." Craig put on his cheesiest smile. "But I keep fucking up."

She smiled. "Yeah. You do. And you're not that cute. You're a big, sweaty mess is what you are."

"Sorry. I'm really screwing this whole thing up, aren't I?"

"Yeah. You are." The boat idled across the lake. "You need to talk to my dad. I don't know what he's going to do."

Craig bit his lip, then said, "Yeah, that's going to be a tough one. Any ideas?"

"Nope. That's on you. And you can't charm him."

"I guess not."

Abby gunned the boat, almost knocking Craig out of his seat. She laughed as he regained himself. When they got to the dock, Craig tied the boat while Abby cleaned up the deck. "I'd go talk to him now. If you wait until things get too busy, that won't be good. That's my only hint."

"Thanks."

Abby walked past Craig and ran her fingers down his back. She whispered in his ear, "I'm still mad at you. Maybe you'll be able to explain this to me in a way I can understand someday." She smiled sarcastically, then danced away.

Craig went over to the woodpile and noticed that the uncut log supply was way down. "We're going to have to go cut a few trees next week and haul them over to cut up," a voice said. It was John, walking down the driveway from his house. "Time to start thinking about getting the supply up for fall when I lose all of the help."

Startled, Craig replied, "That seems like a good plan." He set up a log to chop, and John turned to go into the woods. "Can I talk to you for a second?" Craig asked without looking up.

John stopped and turned around. "Sure, Craig." He seemed overly cheery for it being so early in the morning.

"So…I'm just going to say this," Craig started, then took a deep breath. "I'm going back to Whitewater to play football."

After pausing for an uncomfortable amount of time, John replied, "Ok. Why are you telling me this?"

Craig felt lightheaded, but he continued, "I have to leave next Friday for a tryout, and then if I make the team, I'll only be back for weekends for the rest of the summer."

John studied him, a calm expression on his face. "Well, that's going to be an issue, isn't it?"

"I know that."

"No. I don't think you know that, Craig. We run this place with a razor-thin margin both in terms of money and time. I have to get things done when they need to be done and on budget."

"I know that, sir," Craig said more forcefully.

"I don't think you do. I have projects that I need to get done. Projects that include you. This is just a distraction."

"I don't follow, sir."

"I know you don't. How are you going to get the cabins done? That was your project."

"I'll get one done next week. Then there will be just one left."

"And that one is booked every weekend until the middle of September."

"It is?" Craig's eyes grew wide as his plan began to crumble.

"Yes. And the wood project. Getting ready for the fall and winter is important. It's basically me and Frank for the fall, and he's not chopping anything."

Craig started to panic. "Claire and I could move to that last cabin, and I can finish it on the weekends."

John shook his head. His face was red and hard around the eyes. Despite his apparent anger, Craig was amazed at how composed he was. There was a deliberateness to every word as though he had preplanned the entire conversation. "I'm not sure that would work. I'm not sure I want it to work."

Craig was confused. "What do you mean?"

"You took on a responsibility, and you are not fulfilling what you said you would do."

"I know that, sir. I am very sorry. But…"

"And football," John cut him off. "Why football?"

"I just need to go back."

"Need to go back?" His face was unmoved, without emotion. Craig was almost afraid. "Yes. I need to go back. There's something out there I need to find. Does that make sense?"

"It does, and it doesn't. I found what I was looking for when I came here. Both Abby and I hoped you would find it too. I'm not sure what you're going to find on a football field. Seems a bit selfish."

Craig hardened. "But that's how I feel. That's what I need right now."

John started to walk away again. Then, he stopped without looking back. "You know, Craig, the only things worth doing in life are those things you do with and for others. Everything else is bullshit."

"That's what football is to me, sir. Doing something with and for others," Craig said sharply.

John spun on his heel, and his eyes met Craig's. "As for the time you have left with us, get this week's cabin done. If you're not working on next week's cabin, I want you chopping. Don't even think about touching the last cabin. That should get you ready for football." He walked off into the woods.

Craig chopped the log he had placed minutes before. Then, he chopped another and another. The rhythm he set began to hurt. In the pain, he hoped to find a moment of salvation.

CHAPTER 16

Early in the day at the library in town, Claire had set about finding answers.

"Can I help you?" a voice from behind Claire asked as she sat by a computer.

"Maybe?" she responded. "I'm looking for information about Wood Lake Resort."

"I know the place. What kind of information are you looking for?"

"How it started. Who the owners were. Anything really."

"Well, we can look at ownership records, and I'll see if there are any articles from the local paper about the resort. There might be something about when it opened. The paper used to cover stories like that. Come with me." The librarian smiled at Claire and beckoned her to follow.

Claire got up and went with her, a spark of hope in her eyes.

Abby walked from her house to the lodge carrying a few receipts from her mom's "emergency" shopping trips over the weekend. Despite her father's and Frank's best efforts, something was always missing and either she or her mother had to go to town to get this or that. However, for the most part, the weekend was good. All the cabins were filled up, and the week ahead promised to be busy as well. It was like the summers she remembered as a child, busy with both new and familiar faces. Abby didn't know how long it would last, but she was doing her best to enjoy every minute she had at home.

Through the trees, she first heard, then saw Craig chopping. His rhythm seemed faster than normal. A pile of cut logs that her father had delivered over the weekend sat off to the side. The chopped pile was growing quickly. Despite the early hour, Craig was already shirtless and his hair was pulled back under a bandana. Sometimes, Abby forgot how good-looking he was. His body rippled with strength. He was chiseled from top to bottom, and even though he was still sporting a beard, when he was focused, his jaw was straight and strong. When his eyes were narrowed on his target, Abby almost felt like leaving him be. He'd been working like a dog every day since he told her dad his plan. But she walked up to him anyway. "Hey, babe. Looking good this morning." She smiled.

"Am I?" Craig chuckled. His laugh flexed his eight pack of abs.

Abby stretched out her hand to touch him, but pulled back when she saw sweat drip down his chest. "How's it going?"

"I don't know. I'm trying to do whatever I can. I just feel bad about letting your father down." Craig set the hammer down and used his bandana to wipe his face. He pushed his hair back and gave Abby a quick kiss, careful not to touch her with his sweaty hands. "I mean, he went and bought all this wood."

"I'm sure he traded for it, but you're right, you're letting him down," Abby spoke plainly.

Hurt, but understanding the consequences, Craig said, "I'll come back on the weekends to help when it gets busy."

"I know, but that's really not the point. My dad is a man of action, you know?"

"I'm learning that."

Abby felt bad for Craig, but she pressed on. "Don't expect me to take your side with all of this. I still don't know why you're doing it."

"I know. I'll try to help you understand."

"Maybe I don't need to. Maybe it's for me to question and for you to understand." She leaned over to pick up some of the cut pieces and put them in the trailer. "I need to get going."

Craig leaned down to grab another log. "Ok. Love you."

"I love you too." With that, she went into the woods.

This girl, who had come as a challenge to his life, continued to astound him. She was lovely in every way, and Craig suspected she knew it. He watched as she swayed away.

In the office, Abby began her tasks, running debits and credits from the weekend, preparing cash deposits for the bank, and running the receipts for her mother. Just as she was finding her groove for the morning, her father came in and sat down. "Quite a summer so far. How're we doing?"

"What?" Abby responded, distracted and a bit annoyed.

John looked at his daughter crossly and waited until she turned her attention to him. "How are we doing? How are the books looking?"

Remembering who she was talking with, Abby softened. "Good, I think. I don't know. I think we'll break even by Labor Day. Is that good?"

"If we're turning a profit by Labor Day, that's a good year."

"Ok. Then, things are good." Abby expected her father to leave the office right away since he had spent next to no time in there all summer.

Instead, he continued, "With the finances, yes. I'm still angry about Craig leaving. Claire is going to move into the spare bedroom in the basement to open up the cabin for the next few weeks. We'll offer two-night rentals on that one to get the business."

"Sounds good. I'll get that posted on the new site for this weekend."

"How's the new site going?"

"Good. I got it up last week. Sent out an invitation to all our current clients through email and Facebook. Already got a few reservations for weekends in the fall."

"That's great." John nodded his head approvingly. He started to get up.

"Dad, did you trade for that wood, or do you have a receipt?"

John sat back down. "Traded some hunting time on the land this fall. That reminds me, could you throw a couple hundred more at Ted for the last cabin? He'll have to get that one."

"But can't Craig do it on a weekend?"

Calmly, John replied, "No. He needs to learn to finish things he's started. I already talked to Ted."

Abby knew her father was being more than fair, but it sounded like he was more interested in teaching a lesson than getting the work done.

"You understand why I'm doing this, right Abby?"

"Yes. Of course."

John stared at the floor. "He needs to fail."

"I know. I'm not entirely sure why he's doing this, but…"

She paused. "I have to respect your point of view and support him at the same time. Does that make sense?"

"It does. I know your mother feels the same way about this place."

"I really love him," she blurted out. She looked at her father for a response, but he didn't look up.

"I know. That's pretty clear. He's a good kid. Don't tell him I said that."

Abby smiled. "Hey, Dad. Can I ask you about something else?"

John raised his head. "What?"

"It's about Frank. He doesn't show up on the payroll. I've found some retirement payments, but he doesn't show up anywhere else."

John looked past Abby, towards a picture of the lake hung on the wall, and scratched his head. "I thought you'd ask about that sooner or later."

"Well…tell me then."

John took a deep breath. "So, when I bought this place, Frank was already here. He'd been on this resort for thirty… forty years or so. And when I bought it…" He paused and rubbed his beard. "I bought it from him. He and a friend started it up and…long story short, Frank ended up owning it, and I bought it from him."

"Frank owned the resort?"

"Yes. Don't talk to him about it. He doesn't like to talk about it."

"Ok. But why don't we pay him?"

John shifted in his chair. "It's like this. When we sat down to discuss terms, he said he wanted to retain the rights to the land past his place, where his cabin is and beyond. If we made his insurance payments and retirement payments, we didn't need to pay him or Rita cause they had enough. I tried to protest, but he was having none of it, and Rita agreed. They'd eat in the lodge and draw cash from their savings. He doesn't need much. We figured his expenses, after Rita died, and it came to less than five thousand a year. It's not much."

Bordering on tears, Abby asked, "Really?"

"Really. The man could retire a king with the assets he's built up, but I don't know what he'll do with the money. Like I said, he doesn't like to talk about it. Never, I mean never, bring it up."

"Ok, Dad."

John gave Abby a small smile. "Now, is there anything else?"

"Not now. Thanks."

"Alright then. I gotta get back to work. Get the accounts settled and try to have some fun with Craig this week. If he asks, I'm still mad at him." John winked at her and went out the door.

"Thanks," Abby called after him. She knew her dad and Frank were special people, but Frank was a guardian angel she never knew her family had. He was the reason the whole resort was a go. If they paid him, they might never make a profit. She sat back in her chair and smiled.

John's anger finally relented, and over the next two days, Craig worked on the second-to-last cabin roof. Craig had become an expert at the process now and felt his mind wander from time to time as he worked. The pieces he threw off the roof landed in a pile almost as though he stacked them from the ground up. As for the new tar paper and shingles, the patterns were the same, and he no longer really needed to measure. The nails flowed from his pocket to an exact placement, and it only took one shot from the hammer to drive them in. Given the rhythm he fell into, he spent a lot of time looking at the cabin that he would not have a chance to get to. A pang of guilt rose up every time he walked past, like last year when he would go by the football stadium at school. He knew he could get it done if John let him, but he was beginning to understand why he wasn't letting him finish. He had to face the fact that he failed.

To take his mind off the unfinished cabin, Craig tried to memorize routes and coverages. It was something he prided himself on in high school. Knowing the playbook as well as the quarterback was important in a balanced offense. As a speed receiver, he could be motioned into the backfield, be used on end arounds, or run a myriad of different routes depending on how the defense lined up. Some of the best plays he could remember running were when the quarterback just locked eyes with him before the snap and they both knew the adjustment. He wanted to be that well prepared this Saturday. If Coach Brewer called a play during his tryout, he wanted to be able to see it working out in his brain as he went to line up.

In the midst of his visualization on the roof, Frank walked down the cabin road and called, "Hey, Craig!"

"Yeah, Frank?" Craig replied, taking out his earbuds.

"Come to the kitchen when you're done and cleaned up. I want to talk to you."

"Ok." Craig went back to finishing the joints and seams on

the last side. Picking up a skill like roofing was a positive in his mind. There were other things he knew John could teach him, but this one set of lessons was valuable enough. Even if he never roofed another cabin or house, the ability to work physically through an entire day was a revelation. To live on the resort was to work all through the day. It was your life, at least in part, and Craig enjoyed the labor.

When he got to the kitchen around an hour later, dinner service was winding down for the visitors who were staying through the midweek. Frank had two plates set up for Craig and himself. Sitting down at a corner table, Craig said, "Thanks for dinner."

"Well, I figured you could use a good, big meal after working all day up on that roof."

"It's not so bad," Craig said as he dug into a plate of seasoned steak, mashed potatoes, and a salad. Frank knew it was his favorite meal. Chewing, he said, "This is really good."

"I'm glad." Frank took a bite himself. After chewing slowly, he broke the silence. "So, you're leaving us tomorrow?"

"Yeah. I gotta get home and get my stuff for the tryout on Saturday. I don't want to drive all the way Friday and then have to get up to go the next day."

Frank stared at him. "Probably a good idea...football, huh?"

"Yeah. Football." Craig barely looked up.

"You didn't get to have your last game. Isn't that right?"

Craig paused to chew. "What do you mean?"

"That's what this is all about. You didn't get to have your last game. When you finished your last high school game, you thought there'd be more."

"I guess that might be part of it," Craig said, taking another bite.

"Part of it? That's the whole deal. You just want to get back out there."

Craig had gone over this talk again and again in his head since the week before, and it was well-rehearsed. "You got the second part right. I do want to get back out there, but not because I need one more game. It goes deeper."

"Deeper? It's football."

"Yeah, Frank. It's football. It's the purest expression of physicality and teamwork there is. There's so much imagination. It challenges every part of who you are. It's an artform. That's the way I see it. I'm chasing that perfect play, so I guess you're right in one sense. But there's more to it."

Frank sat silently as Craig continued to attack his meal. Then, he let out a chuckle. "I guess I get it, but then again, it kinda sounds like a little bullshit to me."

"Yeah. Maybe it does, but I'm going with it."

"Have you explained this all to Abby?"

"Not really. She says she's fine with not fully understanding it. I don't know if she is, but that's what she says."

"She's a special girl. So damn smart about a lot of things. I'd hold onto her."

"I intend to, sir."

"I hope so. I really do." He took another bite and stared out the window. "You know, I'm not going to be around here forever. Things are going to change faster than you think."

"Really?" Craig said, smiling. "I thought you were always going to be here."

"Seriously though, Craig, Abby wants to take this place

over in a couple of years. Now, I've seen how a change of generations goes, badly, most of the time. You need to have a game plan, a vision for how to revitalize the place. I'll be here to help, but the real work will be on the two of you."

"Is that so?" Craig had no idea where Frank was going with this, but he was more than willing to indulge him in whatever he wanted to say.

"Yes. I know that girl of yours better than you do. If you intend to hold onto her, then you intend to hold onto this place. You're staying right here, cause she ain't going anywhere. It's a package deal."

"I know that, sir. I have no delusions."

"But she doesn't want to change, and things have to change. New generations mean building a new client base. New ideas. You need to innovate. People aren't just going to come here cause John's daughter owns the place. It'll all dry up if you're not careful."

"We'll come up with a plan." Craig didn't know what else to say.

"I hope you do. I sure hope you do."

They ate the rest of their meal in silence until Frank asked, "What kinda offense do they run down there at Whitewater?"

With that, the mood was lifted, and they were on to brighter topics and stories of the summer.

Part of the reason for Craig's dinner with Frank was to buy Abby some time. She wanted to get the whole cabin turned over before he got back. She packed up his stuff and even brought new bed linens for the morning. It was Craig's last night at the resort save for a few weekend nights when he would be sleeping on the couch in the family room at her parents' house. Everything needed to be perfect. She was the one planning the "big date" tonight. Claire had already moved to the room in the basement.

When Craig got to his cabin, he thought it was weird that Abby hadn't come to the lodge but figured that she was probably at home or working around the resort. Instead, when he went in, he found his things neatly packed, sitting by the wall. The bed was made, and the extra dresser was already gone. On the bed was a note saying, "Meet me by your car. Stay casual." Craig smiled to himself.

He changed clothes and went to meet Abby. She was wearing a sundress and sandals and was leaning against his car. He had not seen her in a dress since school let out. With her hair down out of the summertime pony, she looked beautiful. Jogging to catch up to her, he said, "What's up?"

"Nothing. I thought we'd go get some ice cream and have a little date."

"That sounds nice," Craig said. He walked over to let her in the passenger side. As he went back over to the driver's door, Craig realized that, aside from a few trips to get pizza, they had not really been out all summer. Things he was used to doing with friends, going to the beach, going to concerts, and just going out to eat or for ice cream, were things he had not missed. With Abby and the resort, he hadn't had time to miss them.

Once both of them got into the car, Craig started driving off the resort. Abby turned to face him and said, "We're going to the Country Store. They have candy and ice cream, and I thought you could get some candy for your parents and Sarah. You're going home tomorrow, right?"

"Yeah. I'll be home tomorrow night and Friday."

"Are you nervous?"

Craig let out a long breath. "Yes."

"What are you nervous about? You're in shape, right?"

"Yes, I'm in shape. That's not really the issue. I can play the game."

Abby moved her hand to Craig's thigh and squeezed it. "Turn right here. It's up a ways, on Wall Street, downtown."

Craig caught a quick glance of Abby and smiled.

Looking out the window, Abby continued, "If it's not the fitness, then what is it?"

"It's the other guys."

Very calmly, trying to mask her frustration with the whole situation, Abby said, "But isn't that one of the reasons you want to go back?"

"It is. But I left them last year, and I know they won't trust me."

"Then prove it to them on the field. If you go kick some ass, they'll have nothing to say."

Craig almost felt like stopping the car. Instead, he looked sideways at Abby. She never spoke like this.

Sensing his confusion, Abby continued, "You know I don't get all this football crap. I don't know why you want to go back. I never really played sports, and I don't get them. But, if you're going to do it, you're going to do it well. You hear me? I'm not coming to watch you play just to have fun with your boys. I want to see the Craig everyone's been talking about. If you're going to be him, you're going to be the best version of him."

Craig reached up to wipe a tear from his face, then scratched his nose in an attempt to cover up what he was doing. "Why are you so good to me?"

With no hesitation, Abby responded, "Because I love you. I love you more than I have ever loved anyone. You get me? I want to see you do this and do it well."

"I love you too."

"I know."

Claire stood on the porch of Frank's cabin, wondering if she should knock. She had pumped herself up to talk with Frank, to ask him all of her questions, but she assumed she could do it on familiar ground, in the kitchen. However, Frank had taken off early, leaving her to close down as he had done so many times this summer. Tonight, he hadn't been just tired, he was completely off. Instead of his normal, upbeat style, he barked and shuffled and paced. Claire suspected there was a problem as soon as she came in from the afternoon tour. She was beginning to see the concerns Abby had told her about earlier in the summer.

She knocked on his door. "Who's there?" Frank called from the front room.

Claire could hear him coming towards the door. "It's me. Claire."

The door opened. Frank looked disheveled. His hair was a mess, and his shirt was halfway unbuttoned. "Hello, Claire. What can I do for you tonight?" He stepped back.

"Can I come in and talk with you? I just wanted to know if you're doing ok."

"Well, that's awful kind of you to worry about an old man, but I'm fine, just a little tired."

"Ok," Claire responded. "But you're also full of shit. So, let me in, and we can talk."

Frank smiled and opened the screen door. "Alright, come in. Sorry about the mess."

Claire looked around and saw nothing out of place. Frank's house, though weathered and homey, was impeccably clean. She noticed a tumbler on the end table next to the easy chair. Frank walked over to it and downed the contents of the glass, then poured it full again from a bottle he had on the small table near the kitchen. He sat down. "Please, sit. What can I do for you?"

Claire sat on the loveseat after looking at the pictures on the wall. Some were Abby's pictures, but the one that captured her attention was of a young Frank and his wife, Rita. "I just really want to know what was up with you tonight. You're off, and now you're drinking."

"I have a nightcap most nights, dear. There's a lot you don't know."

"I'm sure there is, but that's why I'm here. You're upset about something. What's the deal?"

Frank sat tight-lipped. He took a deep breath and said, "I'm pissed about Craig leaving. It makes me sad. Everyone leaves here. Nobody stays." He stared off towards the front door.

"The Whitworths have stayed. Abby is staying. Craig will come back."

"Will he?" He took another sip of his drink and looked directly at Claire. "He's being pulled. I see it. He has two loves. You can't have two loves and live here. It has to be singular."

"You had two loves at one time. You had Rita."

"That was different."

"How? How was it different?"

Frank took another small swig and puckered his lips. "Rita and I were different. Rita was this place."

Confused, Claire tried another tactic. "Tell me about her, Frank. What was she like?"

Frank closed his eyes as though trying to call his memories to the surface. "You see, I knew Rita before I knew her. I grew up here. She did too. I knew only the woods and the lakes and fishing and hunting. I was part of this place. Even when I played football or sat in a class, I looked off the field or out the window to the woods. I just wanted to get out there and walk until no one else was around. I wanted to row out to the middle of the lake and drop a line in and wait for a fish to rise."

Claire leaned in, inching to the front of the couch.

Frank looked at her with red eyes. "When I met Rita, it was like meeting all the things I loved, but in a person. She was the personification of this place. All the things I loved, she did too. We could walk through the forest, and she could point out every tree, every bird. It was like the woods and the lake were talking to me. It was like I could have a conversation with all the things I had spent my life pursuing. She was everything and…" He paused. "And, she didn't want to leave. She never wanted to leave here. Sure, there were places we wanted to go and visit, but she never wanted to leave. Not like the rest of you."

Claire let the moment sit in silence. She had no words.

"I miss her so much. Abby reminds me of her. She draws people to this place. She drew you and Craig. But don't you do the same to her. Don't you draw her away. This place needs her as much as she needs it."

They had crossed into deep territory. Claire was scared to move forward but pushed on anyway. "I don't want to draw her away. I don't think I ever could."

"I don't know. I've seen it before. People go away for a time, and they come back changed."

"How so?"

"I don't know how. I just know."

Peering around the cabin at the collection of Abby's photos, Claire said, "There is an allure to this place and to the people. I have to say, I don't really want to leave. I have lots of reasons to stay. You are chief among them. You and John, Vickie, Shane…"

"Shane ain't staying here. God knows his dad didn't when times got tough. He skipped out like the rest of you. Shane too. This place dries up for him, and he goes. Only comes back when he can profit from it."

"What are you talking about? You don't know him."

"What? You do? He comes in and charms your pants off for a few weeks and you…you think you know him."

Angered by the implication, Claire shot back, "Now that's too far."

"Claire, you don't know. Everybody leaves. They always do. The Whitworths, they will leave too. Vickie already has plans to go back to Chicago when they give the place over to Abby. She won't last."

"Abby? She'll last if you help her. She is this place."

"I intend to help her. But, in the end, it will just be me and Rita. Or the memory of her. Everyone goes. And now you have to go too." He got up, went to the door, and looked at Claire as he opened it. "I'll see you in the morning."

Claire got up, turning around to glance at the picture of Frank and Rita one more time. She thought about who Frank must have been. There was such joy in his eyes. Rita, too, with her straight, closed-mouth seriousness, had a strength clearly on display. Claire wished she could have met her.

Walking to the door, she gave Frank a hug, holding on until he hugged her back. "I love you, Frank."

"Love you too, kid. See you tomorrow." The door closed quickly behind her.

Claire walked out into the evening, past her cabin. The night had calmed, and no one was out. The light at the bar was on, but that was the only one. She walked to the end of the dock and found Abby sitting on the bench. "Hey, Abby. Whatcha doing?"

"I'm waiting for Craig to come back."

Confused, Claire asked, "What? Where did he go?"

"I'm waiting for him to come back to me," Abby repeated. She was looking out over the water, lost in her own thoughts.

"He's not gone yet. He leaves in the morning."

"Yes, he is. I'm hoping he'll come back to me." Her words held no life. "I couldn't stay with him tonight. It was too hard. I don't want him to go back to football, but I can't tell him that. Not tonight."

Claire looked at her closely, waiting for more. As Abby faced her, she could tell she had been crying. There was nothing to say. She reached for Abby and held her head on her shoulder as Abby quietly wept.

He's Leaving - Abby

Craig has a new love
An old one has been reborn
One we toiled to get rid of
We let go
Of the pressure and pain
But he's invited it back
Into our lives
He says not to be concerned
But it is all that concerns me
The secret he kept
Hidden from the world
Creeps painfully
Worming its way back
Into a world of obligation
Where responsibility reigns
Over individual desire
Selfish and selfless
I cannot hate
I can only love

CHAPTER 17

Letter to Craig from Abby:

Hey babe,

Although I can't say I fully understand why you're doing this, I want you to know that I'm here for you. It will take me awhile to get it, but I get you, and I support you. I know you care a lot about playing again, otherwise you would not have left. You know when you told me a home is the people you are around who love you? Well, I guess you have to find your people again. Just make sure you are doing this for the right reasons. If you do that, you will be fine. I believe in you. I know that you can do whatever you set your mind to. I'm so glad you set your mind on me. I am proud to be yours, and I will be proud to sit in the stands and watch you this fall. Love you. Can't wait for the weekends. Do your best. Stay present.

Abby

Craig put the letter in the center console of his car. "Stay present." He would need to do that a lot over the next few days and weeks. As he pulled out of the parking lot, a weight suddenly descended on his shoulders. It was a weight he could not lift with a few deep breaths.

In the gridded section near downtown Eagle River, Craig found Will's house.

"Thanks for picking me up, Craig," Will said as he got himself situated in the passenger seat. "I really appreciate it."

"No problem. Where are you staying anyway?"

"I'm going to my girlfriend's house in Germantown. You know where that is, right?"

Craig nodded.

"She's going to bring me to camp, and then I'm staying with Steve and Joe."

Craig interjected, "I remember them."

"Yeah. They stayed in Whitewater for the summer and have a place already. I'm moving in at the beginning of August."

"That's cool."

"Who are you rooming with?" Will asked.

Craig waited at a stoplight in town. Looking around, he realized he hadn't really been able to explore the town at all during his stay. "Brent again. We get along. Even with me not playing last year, he was still cool. He's excited that I'm playing again…if I make the team."

"I wouldn't worry about making the team. I've seen you work. You'll still be one of our best receivers."

"Thanks, Will."

Silence gripped the car as they moved to the main highway. Will looked out the window and occasionally read a text, while Craig was left to his own thoughts. As the trees floated by, he thought of Abby. She was strong and wise beyond her years. He was leaving her at the height of the summer, but the grace she had shown him over the last week, angry, but not willing to let it spoil their time, was comforting. He had to face the fact that he had not shown her the same courtesy. He had been selfish in the midst of a place that seemed to exude selflessness. The whole family, Taylor included, lived to serve others. Frank, especially, breathed service with every breath. He was the soul. Frank and John lived with a conviction, a purpose. There was a right way and a wrong way to live life. Craig could not escape a growing sense that he was on the wrong side. Yet, at the same time, he was drawn south. The force that was pulling him had a life all its own. For the first time, he was doing football just for himself, free from any expectations other than what he created for himself.

When they got just south of Wausau, Will said, "Hey, you want to stop for a bite to eat?"

"Sure," Craig replied. "I usually stop in Stevens Point if that's alright?"

"Yeah. That works." Will turned towards the window, then said, "So, you and Abby are pretty serious, huh?"

Puzzled by the line of conversation, Craig responded, "Yes. We really are."

"That's cool. She's great. Her family has done really well."

"How's that?"

"Well, they're not native, so to speak. They're Illinois transplants, but you'd never know. I think I had Mrs. Whitworth as a teacher one of her first years. My mom probably has a picture of the two of us."

"Really?"

"Yeah. So…if you stick with her, are you going to move back to their place? I know she's really into the resort."

Surprised, Craig replied, "You do?"

"Oh yeah." Will nodded his head. "Everyone knows. Lots of kids can't wait to get out of the area. Move to Duluth, Green Bay, Madison, the Twin Cities. She's never been like that. Always wanted to stay up north."

"Yeah, that's been clear since day one. She's never really wavered. How about you?"

"What?" Will asked, turning toward Craig.

"Do you want to stay or go?"

"I'm not sure. I'll go wherever. Jamie's a city girl, but she loves coming up to visit. I guess we'll see where we get jobs, you know?"

"So, you guys are tight?"

"I think so. We've been together two years."

Craig switched on his blinker to get off the highway. "Awesome."

After dropping Will off in Germantown, Craig headed towards home. Although he still largely thought of his parents as pains in the ass, he hoped they'd be there. He wanted to talk with his dad about his hectic schedule and getting some new football gear, and he also wanted to get his mom's impression of the resort. Claire had filled him in on what she said while they were up there over the Fourth of July, but he wanted to hear it from the source.

As he pulled into the driveway, Craig saw his dad loading a cooler into the truck. "Hey, Craig," Mike said before Craig had even stepped out of the car.

Craig got out and went to see if there was anything he could help with. "Hi, Dad. What's going on?"

"Going to the Brewers game. Tailgating with Barb and Jim and a few other friends from the neighborhood."

"Oh, really?"

"Yep. Sorry. We had the tickets before we knew you were coming. Not that many games we can all go to anymore. Mostly just Jim and I go, but your mother wants to go along this time."

"Ok," Craig said sarcastically. He guessed there was no real reason they should celebrate his return. He was only home for two nights, then he'd be heading back up north. "Have fun."

"Thanks. We'll catch up tomorrow."

"Sure thing."

"Hi, Craig," his mother said, walking outside dressed like a teenager, with a shirt and shorts too tight for a woman of her age.

'Jesus Christ,' Craig thought to himself, rolling his eyes and giving her a hug.

"What are you going to do tonight, honey?"

"I'm not sure. Maybe I'll go see Sarah and Brad or go out with some friends."

"Well, don't be out too late."

Smirking, Craig said, "You either."

"Oh, Craig."

"Let's go, Linda!" Mike yelled as he got into the truck.

"See you kids later." Craig waved, then went to get his stuff out of the car.

Empty of people, the house seemed larger and more unnecessary than it had before. Craig walked upstairs to his room, which was almost as big as the front room of the cabin where he had spent the last two months, and put his bags on his bed. Turning to his desk, Craig saw an orange Nike box with a note. "Try these on. If they don't fit, we can find another pair tomorrow - Dad." Craig opened the box. In it was the newest model of his favorite cleats. He picked them up, feeling each cleat and running his fingers along the stitches. The new-shoe smell brought him back to the excitement he had always felt when he got a new pair as a kid. Craig loved getting new shoes until it became a chore. He looked down at the boots he had worn all summer, seeing that the leather was worn and scuffed. There were scrap marks from a few close calls with the nail gun. Craig had decided to go back to the hammer after almost nailing his hand to the roof once. Looking at the floor behind him, Craig noticed that grains of shingles had made their way to Hartland. He took off the boots and rummaged through his dresser drawers to find some football socks so he could try on his new shoes. When he finally slid the shoes on, he was amazed by the fit. One should never use new shoes without breaking them in first, but these felt like they were made for his foot. No stiffness or hot spots. The feeling made him smile.

Coming out of the shower, Craig felt himself transformed. Without really seeking it, he felt the resort wash off him, and putting on a Hartland football shirt, a little looser than he remembered, completed the change. The beard he would keep. Abby liked running her fingers through it, and it gave him a woodsy feel. The hair, however, had to go. He took out his clipper, something he had not touched since his junior year of high school, and began to cut. Taking the hair down to a quarter inch, Craig thought he looked pretty badass. Badass was the attitude he had to bring on Saturday. He had to find McLean, the player he used to be, over the next two days. What would Abby think of him?

The time to decide had arrived: try to go out with friends or contact Sarah. Craig chose to text Sarah. She quickly replied that she would come over in about a half hour with some Chinese takeout. They had painters working this week, so their whole place was a mess. While waiting, Craig texted Abby, but she didn't respond.

Sarah walked through the door right at the time she said she would. "Hey, kid. Nice beard," she said, grabbing his chin and tugging it. "Brad's out with clients, so I'm glad you texted."

"Me too," Craig said, sitting at the kitchen bar. "How've you been?"

"I'm all good." Sarah found plates and forks. "Should we eat downstairs?"

"Sure." Craig grabbed the bag. He intended on eating the whole combination platter he ordered, so he didn't really need a plate.

They went down to the family room and sat at the bar, Sarah with a beer and Craig with a bottle of water.

"So, what's up?" Sarah started in. "How's my little brother?"

Craig chuckled and said, "Fine. Things are good."

"Really?" Sarah's eyes narrowed.

"Yes. Why?" Craig looked at her sideways. She was sounding almost motherly.

"Well, for starters, you're here, not up north. And what's this shit about you playing football again?"

Nodding, he replied, "You're right. I'm here, and I'm playing football again. At least I'm going to try."

"Don't be stupid with me, Craig. You'll make the team. My question is why are you doing it?"

"I just feel like I need to."

"That's a load of shit. You were so done with it last year. All that fall-out-of-love crap."

Craig cut her off. "I guess I figured you, of all people, would understand."

"Oh, I get it, but that means I turn on the Big Ten tourney and sit down with some popcorn. I don't want to play volleyball again. Hell, I don't even want to play bar league. Afraid I might start yelling at my friends or break some drunk kid's nose."

Craig laughed, but then regained himself. "Let me try to explain."

"Ok. Shoot."

"Ever since Dad gave up on the idea, when he accepted that I wasn't playing, I felt like I could make my own decision about it. I never felt like that before. It always seemed like I was giving into him or defying him in some way. Does that make any sense?"

"Sort of." Sarah looked down at her food and took a bite.

"Now, I can clearly see that I miss it. I miss the competition. I miss the excitement. I miss the focus. Getting lost in it, really. I guess I was wrong last year when I said I didn't love it. I just hated doing it for Dad."

"I get it." Sarah took another bite and chewed slowly. Finally, she said, "But I still think you're full of shit. What does Abby think?"

With his mouth full of food, Craig responded, "She's pissed, but she'll support me. She's worried I'm going to get hurt."

"Are you worried?"

"Not really. I could just as easily get hurt playing soccer or volleyball."

"I guess. She's really ok with it?"

"I think so." If he was honest with himself, he didn't really know. "She was more pissed that I couldn't finish my work at the resort."

"What did they have you doing up there anyway?" Sarah turned her stool towards Craig.

"Roofing mostly. But I helped out wherever I could. There's so much to do. It's kinda nuts. You never really know what goes on behind the scenes at a place until you get in it and start to work."

"What about Claire? She went to do art stuff, and they got her doing tours and working in the kitchen?"

Craig answered, "Yeah. Well, she likes Frank. She works in the kitchen cause she loves it. No one really made her do it. She's a really good cook."

"Oh yeah. I've had some of her stuff when I went to visit her in Chicago. We never went out. She always cooked for me, and it was so good."

"Well, she and Frank are great together. They have a shorthand, and she's pushing him beyond his comfort zone."

"Frank's the main cook, right?"

"Yeah. He's the best."

"Claire mentioned him a bunch the last few times we talked. Sounds like it would be hard not to like the guy."

"It's just so different. It's like a whole other world up there."

Smiling, Sarah said, "Cool. I'm glad you two are having a good time."

After they finished eating, Sarah asked, "Do you want to go for a walk or something?"

Relieved, Craig replied, "Yes. Let's go." After driving all day, he just wanted to stretch his legs.

They didn't set off in any particular direction. All the roads looped around, and a person could get a pretty serious walk in without hitting the same street twice. A block or two down, Sarah asked, "So, Claire and this Shane guy are pretty serious, huh?"

Craig stopped. "Seems like it. How do you know about Shane?"

Chuckling, Sarah responded, "Claire and I talk all the time, Craig."

"Really?"

"We're sisters. We talk. Especially about boys."

Nodding, Craig began walking again. "I guess you probably know more about him than I do."

"I don't know. What's the guy like?"

"He's alright. Artist. Did a bunch of signs with woodcuts that Claire hung on all the cabins. He really seems to be into Claire. I don't know much beyond that. He's kind of a drifter. It's a bit of a mystery."

"That's what she said. He talks about all the places he's been, but not much about his family. It's weird. I guess it's just a fling. She'll be back in Chicago in a month."

"Yeah. Grad school. I'm so excited for her."

"Me too. So, what's up with you and Abby? You'll be coming up on a year soon. Pretty serious."

Craig's face broke into a smile, and he started to blush.

"Aw, my little brother's in love."

"Yeah. I think I am."

Later, when he tried to call Abby, there was no answer. She didn't call back. He left a message and went to sleep.

The next afternoon, after talking with his mother, who went on and on about the resort and Vickie and how she wanted to go back soon, Craig found himself playing catch with his dad in the backyard. In the past, playing catch was a chore, but today, it felt curiously childish. There was a little banter, but mostly, they just threw the ball back and forth. After a while, Mike began to test him by throwing the ball to different sides, high and low. Craig stood stationary because that was the drill. He was fully aware of what his father was doing. Soon, to test his quickness, balls came one or two steps off of where Craig was standing. Every time, Craig caught the ball and tucked it away.

"You want to run a few routes?" Mike asked.

Smiling, Craig replied, "No thanks. I should save my energy for tomorrow."

"Suit yourself. Want to get a drink?"

"Sure."

They went to the family room, where Craig got a tall glass of water while his father poured a sparkling water from the fridge. "This stuff tastes like ass, but it's better for me than beer, I guess. Just can't drink straight water."

"I'm glad you're trying to take care of yourself."

"Thanks. Not sure if it's really worth it, but your mom seems happy about it. At least she lets me have a few beers at the games."

Craig started to head towards the stairs. "That's very generous of her. I'm going to go upstairs and pack for tomorrow. It's going to be a long day."

"You going back up to Eagle River after the tryout?" Mike called out.

Stopping at the bottom of the stairs, Craig replied, "Yes. I have things to do, and camp doesn't start until Wednesday, so I have a few days to get it done."

"Well, ok. You seem pretty locked into that girl. And her folks, John and Vickie, they're good people."

"I know, Dad. Oh, by the way, thanks for the shoes."

"Well, ok," he repeated. Craig didn't know what else to say, so he let it go.

Abby finally Facetimed after seven. "Hey, babe," she said when he clicked on.

"Hey. How are you?" Craig asked, sitting back on his bed.

"I'm good. Really busy. All of a sudden, we got all booked up with big parties of extended families. We are just packed."

"Really?"

"Yeah. Good thing you and Claire moved. The place was snatched up on the first day. And Cabin 8 was taken for a whole week."

"Wow. Wonder why?"

"There's a fishing tournament and some other stuff in town this weekend I guess."

"Well, good deal."

"Yeah. It looks like this is going to be a good summer. Once I got the website and email list together, we started advertising these events and booked more rooms throughout the rest of the year."

"That sounds like it was a good idea." Craig was just happy

to hear Abby talk. She seemed to have her spirit back. He felt she had been muted recently by his decision to leave.

"So, sorry I missed your call last night. What did you end up doing?"

"I hung out with Sarah. It was fun."

"That's nice. How is she?" Abby was searching for any sign of distress. She could tell something was off about Craig. He seemed distracted and not fully engaged.

"Good. Adjusting and starting to get the house together."

"That's good. How are YOU doing?"

Craig's face grew serious. "What do you mean?"

"How are you feeling about tomorrow?"

"I'm nervous." If he had to admit it, Abby was the right person to hear the truth.

"You are?"

"Yes. I'm just hoping I don't fuck it up."

"Why's that? What are you worried about?"

"I just…I don't know. I kinda fucked things up at the resort, so I hope it's worth it."

Abby sat silent for a moment, staring at Craig. "You'll be great. Don't worry about things here. You do your thing. Be great."

"Thanks. I'll try."

"There is no try." Abby laughed.

"I know. Just get it done, right?"

"Right. Call me when you're done. You're coming up here after, right?"

"That's the plan. I might be kinda late, but I'll be there."

"Good. We'll get right to work on Sunday. Maybe we can go fishing." Abby winked.

Craig cracked a smile. "Fishing?"

"Yeah. Like, to catch fish and all."

"I like the 'and all' better."

"Really?" Abby said sarcastically.

"I love you."

"I know. I love you too."

"I'll call you as soon as I'm done."

"You'll be great."

"Thanks, babe."

After they hung up, Abby sat on her bed for a while. There was a campfire and general prep for Saturday still to do, but she wished she could give Craig a hug. He had left the resort determined, but now, he seemed so vulnerable. She loved that there was no longer bullshit between them. They said what needed to be said, for the most part. That was more than most people could say.

CHAPTER 18

"Craig!" Coach Brewer called out. He was an intimidating guy. Taller, with an angular face, Coach was no one to bullshit with. Craig knew he had been around the game a long time. He knew his stuff.

Breathing heavily from the warm-up, Craig replied, "Yes, sir."

"You know everyone here, right?"

Craig looked around to see familiar faces, all but one scowling at him. They were all local players, who, like him, had driven down for the day from towns in and around the Milwaukee area. All, save for Will, who had not told Craig that he was coming. "Yes."

"Good. Now boys, we're here to run through a whole gamut of plays. Some are oldies, but others are from the playbook I sent out last week. Think of this as a jump-start on camp. Also, we are trying this guy out, so don't go easy on him. Got it?"

"Yes, Coach!" they all yelled in unison.

"So first, the jet sweep package."

The defensive players took their positions, and Craig joined the offense in the huddle. Plays were called, and Craig closed his eyes and saw them instantly in his mind. It was one of his gifts. He forced his mind to see every play and himself executing it perfectly. He hit his holes and went to the right

245

place after every snap of the ball. All the angles and cuts were performed just as they had been drawn up.

When they moved to pass plays, he looked over the defensive backs and safeties, finding holes in the zone and making quick moves to shake them. About seventy-five percent of balls thrown in his direction he caught. He blocked when called on and ran decoy when needed. For that whole thirty-minute section of team practice, Craig was purely in the moment. No thought entered his head other than what was coming next.

With the live part of practice done, Coach Brewer called him over. "We're going to do the drills, shuttle, forty, and then Luke's going to stick around and throw some more routes. Got it?"

"Yes, sir."

"Good. Go get a drink and take ten. We have a few things to talk over." Coach turned to go discuss something with the other coaches standing on the sidelines.

Craig went to his bag and dug out a bottle of water.

No one talked to Craig while he drank his water. No one even made eye contact. There was an air of discomfort that Craig didn't feel like addressing, at least not yet. Will had gone inside to cool down. With the only friendly face gone, Craig refocused on the task at hand. He had a job to do. Back on the field, he had to execute the drills perfectly and run as fast as he could. Rather than taking the whole break, he began to jog the sidelines to keep his legs loose.

The shuttle went well, and his 40-yard dash was faster than the one he ran in Eagle River. He almost danced away from every drill, feeling the power he had not felt since the taper of his last track season. An assistant coach laughed at his antics. Coach Brewer simply wrote down the times and distances.

Now it was time to connect with Luke. The most important relationship on the offense was the line; anyone who knew anything about football understood that. However, the next most important relationship was the quarterback and his receivers. The receivers needed to be where they were supposed to be at the time they were supposed to be there. Luke had to know that he could trust Craig. That would take time.

"Fifteen-yard dig route from the slot. Both sides, five times each. Go," Coach said from the backfield.

Luke made the call for the play. Craig lined up and ran a perfect route, right to the spot. Luke skied the ball, and Craig went up to get it, turning awkwardly in the air and landing in a heap. He rolled and bounced up, jogging back and tossing the ball to Luke.

"Keep it down, Luke!" one of the assistants yelled.

"Sure thing, Coach!" Luke yelled back, staring at Craig.

The next ball was thrown at Craig's knees. He still caught it but ended up on his back again. The next ball was behind him, and the sly smile on Luke's face showed that each throw was intentional. Craig caught every ball, but as he moved to the left slot, he turned to Luke and said, "Thought you threw a better ball than that. Keep this up and you'll be sitting on the bench watching me play on Saturdays." He flicked the ball back and added, "Put it on my chest."

Luke nodded and lined up for the next play.

Every throw from then on hit Craig right in the numbers. Throw after throw, catch after catch, no dropped passes. When he was done, Craig went over to Luke and smacked him on the back, saying, "Good job."

"You too, Craig," Luke replied and walked off towards the

locker room. Craig watched him walk away. He knew all he could do was keep catching balls. With every ball he caught, the more the trust would build.

Craig jogged over to the sidelines and took off his helmet and pads.

Coach Brewer walked up next to him. "Do you think you can give it every day like you gave it today?" he asked.

"Yes, sir."

"Cause you'll need to. These boys aren't going to let you get away with any shit. You've got to be perfect."

"I don't know about perfect, sir, but I'll give it all I've got."

"Ok. I believe in second chances, but if the boys wail on you a bit, I'm not going to get involved. You have to earn their trust. I'll call your number, but you better run, catch, and block better than anyone else out there. You got me?"

"Yes, Coach."

"Now, I suppose you're going to go right back up north to that girl of yours every weekend, right?"

"Probably."

"Be sure to get a workout in and study your film. You seem to have the playbook just about memorized."

"Anything you want me to look out for on the film?"

"Weaknesses, as always. How we can exploit them."

"You got it, sir."

"Craig, you know that during the season, team comes first."

"I know that. That's the main reason I'm coming back. The team."

"Good deal. Welcome back."

"Thank you." As Coach strolled away, Craig picked up the rest of his stuff and walked off to the locker room.

Outside of a pat on the back from Will, who was already showered and dressed, none of Craig's teammates said a thing. They were all showered, and Craig was thankful for the time alone. He leaned his head against the wall beneath the showerhead and let out several deep breaths. The moment was over. His focus could wane. He knew he was coming out of character, a role he had not played in a long time. Glad as he was that he could call McLean back from the ashes, he was even more excited to be done. The transition between characters would get easier. It was just that the Craig he had become over the last twelve months was worth coming back to now. When he was younger, he lived in McLean mode all day, every day. He never had to come out. Now, he just wanted to get back to Craig, to the resort, and most of all, back to Abby.

"Hello?" Abby said in a serious tone, like she was answering the phone at the front desk.

"Hey, Abby." Craig was sitting in his car with the door open and his feet flat on the ground. He was exhausted.

"Who's this?"

"What do you mean? It's me."

"Craig?"

"Yeah, Craig. Who else would it be?"

"I just wanted to make sure I was talking to Craig, not McLean."

'How did she know?' he thought. Calmly, he said, "It's me, Craig."

"Oh, great. How's it going?" Her voice had returned to being low and soft, but cheerful.

"It's ok. I made the team." There was a pause. "Abby?"

Abby's heart sank at the acknowledgement of the inevitable,

but she had to be supportive. "Good for you. Was there ever any doubt?"

"I don't think so. They just wanted to run me through my paces. Be sure I was serious."

"Are you?"

Confused again, Craig responded, "Yes, of course. Why wouldn't I be?"

"Good. Cause you're going to see this thing through all the way." Her sharp voice cut through the phone.

"Yes. I will."

"So, how was it?"

"It was good. I did what I came to do."

"How did the others treat you?" This was the question Abby was most interested in. If Craig was going to go back, she didn't want to hear about "the boys" and how badly he was being treated.

"I guess casual indifference is the best phrase for that. Luke kept throwing me shit balls, but we straightened that out."

"What do you mean 'shit balls'?"

Craig tried to figure out how to explain it to her. "He threw too high or too low or behind me to get me out of rhythm. I guess all I can do to get him to stop is catch everything. If I block and catch and run my plays, they'll come around."

"Are you sure?"

"I think so. Luke eventually came around, and he's the leader of the team."

"Well, good. So, you're coming up here today?"

"Yeah. I'm already packed, and I'll be on my way shortly. Just going to grab a bite to eat."

Abby's voice brightened. "Great. We'll have things all

ready to go. You're on the couch in the basement."

"That's alright."

"You going to get here in time to go fishing?"

"Are we going to try to catch anything or just fish?"

Playfully, Abby replied, "I haven't decided yet. We'll see what kind of mood I'm in."

Too tired to play her game, but happy to hear her in good spirits, Craig said, "Ok. I'll see you at eight or eight thirty."

"Great. The bonfire will probably be getting started. We're running low on wood." Immediately after she spoke, she regretted saying it.

Wounded, Craig sighed. "I guess I know what I'll be doing for the next few days."

"You bet. See you soon. Love you. Drive safe."

"Love you too."

When Craig finally got on the road, he put on the riding mix Abby made for him the very first time he came to the resort. It calmed his mind, and he began to get lost in yet another moment of anticipation, one with no pressure or expectations. All that lay before him were endless miles of trees and farmland, the latter giving way to the former the further north he went.

After hanging up with Craig, Abby went into full prep mode. She worked through her to-do list: towels, laundry, cash counts, receipts, and finally, food prep. She still missed working with Frank, even though it was great that Claire and Craig had picked up the slack. But now, with Craig gone, she returned to the kitchen part-time. The conversations were easy and familiar. Frank barked orders the girls had already begun to execute. There was a comfort in chopping and prepping.

Claire had taken over the finish prep of every plate as it went out, and gone were many of the utilitarian plates of the past. The new plates were served with an artistic flair of spices and garnishes, giving a new flavor to the resort. Both John and Abby had heard compliments about the changes from clients who had been coming for years. Frank allowed Claire to shine, encouraging her to bring new life to the classics he had always made. Still, Abby, and now Claire, continued to worry about Frank. It seemed as if time had suddenly snuck up on him, robbing him of a future that was on the cusp of beginning anew.

Being a Saturday evening, the kitchen was a buzz. In between dishes, Claire came up to Abby and asked, "Could I meet up with you later? Maybe before Craig comes back?"

"Sure. What's up?"

"It will take time to explain. Maybe we can just go for a walk?"

"Ok. I need to be back by eight though."

"I know you do. I won't get in the way." Claire smiled at her.

"Thanks. Talk to you later."

When Claire and Abby finally had time to meet, there was no time for a walk, so instead, they just sat on the deck outside Abby's home. Craig was coming soon, and Claire wanted to share what she had found out about Shane. There was so much to say that the conversation only ended because Craig arrived. Abby wanted to enjoy what was left of the evening, and Claire wanted to get to town. Another secret for both of them to keep, at least for a while.

CHAPTER 19

"That was fun last night," Craig whispered to Abby as he passed behind her during cleanup after dinner on Sunday night.

"Yeah, it was. Should we go out again tonight?"

Frank, who had the ears of an owl, chimed in, "Make sure you catch some damn fish this time, why don't 'cha?" He chuckled as he went into the freezer.

Abby looked at Craig, then at Claire, who was now in on the joke, and began to snicker, embarrassed.

"Are you going out with Shane tonight?" Abby asked in an attempt to deflect any more outside commentary.

"Yeah, I think so. That's the plan."

Abby walked over to Claire and whispered, "Have you told him yet?"

"Told him what?" Craig chimed in.

"Nothing," the girls said in unison.

"I'll tell you later," Abby assured Craig.

Claire shot her a look that leveled her. "What?" Abby continued. "He's going to find out soon enough."

"I know," Claire replied. "It's just that…I mean…Shane's mom knows, obviously, but I don't know if he does."

Frank came out of the freezer, and the conversation broke off abruptly.

Later, on the boat, Abby reeled in her line. "What's up? You've been really quiet."

Craig reached his hands high above his head, leaning back in his chair, and yawned. "I'm beat. I think I chopped half the forest today. I tried to get enough wood to last all of August, then started a pile next to the shed so there's backup."

"Wow. My strong guy."

"Hey," Craig said, throwing a life jacket at her.

Abby cast another line in the water and got a hit. She reeled it in slowly while Craig got the net. They had returned quickly to working as a team, like they hadn't missed a single day. A sense of calm had washed over Abby when Craig made it back Saturday night. Without him, despite the overabundance of work, she felt a part of her was missing. Without a kiss goodnight or a hug in passing, there was no surprise in the day. The surprises of chance meetings had become part of her routine. Without them, Abby felt the day was incomplete. She knew they only had a limited amount of time before Craig went back to camp, so they had to make the best of it.

By the fourth fish she caught, she thought they had enough, especially if she went out again in the morning. Turning to Craig, she started in, "So, about that thing in the kitchen."

Craig perked up. "Yeah. That was weird."

"Claire found some stuff out when she went to the library the other day." Abby wasn't sure how to get into what she learned.

"Why was she at the library?" With the internet and all, Craig wondered why anyone would go to a library anymore.

"A few weeks ago, on one of her tours, someone asked about the history of the resort. She couldn't answer, so she asked my dad and Frank, but they didn't really tell her much. I've never really said much outside of when it was founded and my dad owning it. The guests never really asked for more than that. Claire wanted to know more."

"Sounds like her."

"Yeah. So, she found some things out." Abby paused, looking over at the woods, then continued, "She found out who started the place and how the ownership came down to my dad. It's an interesting history."

Craig could tell she was being coy, and it was not like her. She was normally so straightforward, especially with him. He put on a mocking smile and said sarcastically, "What did she find out?"

Abby rolled her eyes and took a deep breath. "So, it seems that Frank and his friend started this place. Frank's name is on the original deed, but his friend put up most of the money. They built this place with their own hands."

"What?"

"There's more. So, Frank's name dropped off the deed sometime in the '80s, and his friend kept the ownership until he died in the mid '90s. Then, he gave the resort to his son. I'm not sure what happened, but a couple of years later, Frank was listed as the owner, and then my dad bought it from him."

Craig shifted in his seat. "That's weird."

"That's not everything. Turns out the son, the guy Frank bought the place from, he's Shane's dad."

"Really?"

"Yeah. Shane might have been three or four when they

sold the place. I don't know if he knows."

"So, Shane's grandpa and Frank were friends."

"There was a newspaper article about them. 'Friends Open New Resort on Wood Lake.' I never knew any of this."

Craig shrugged his shoulders. "Why would you?"

"I don't know. All I know is that Frank doesn't like Shane at the place, but I don't know why. His dad is gone. He's been gone for years."

"I guess you'll just have to ask your dad…or Frank."

"I know, but how? My dad told me not to ask Frank about these things. He said I would upset him." Abby's eyes were welling up.

"I don't know. Claire might do it for you, knowing her."

"That's entirely possible." Abby laughed as a tear fell. She couldn't tell if she was happy, sad, or just frustrated with all this new information. She reeled in her long, limp line. "Let's go in."

Monday morning found Craig up early to go for a run and do his "at home" strength routine that included plyos and bodyweight exercises. The nice thing about life in the woods was that fallen trees and strong branches were all the tools he needed to do jumping exercises and pull-ups. Craig had picked out his favorite running routes along the lake and was able to get a good workout done in about an hour.

As he walked back onto the resort grounds, he saw Ted's truck. Looking around the area, he located Ted up on the roof of the last cabin to be done. He was doing the tear-off. Craig climbed the ladder.

"Hey, Craig. How are you?" Ted asked, putting down his hammer. "How's football?"

"Good, thanks. Practice doesn't start until Wednesday, but I made the team."

"Yeah, Abby told me. Good for you."

"You doing the last cabin?"

Ted fished a crowbar off his toolbelt and moved over a few feet. "Yeah, John called me up. Said it needed to be done, so here I am."

"Can I help?"

"Nope. I've got it. You have lots of other things to get done. Monday's a busy day 'round here."

"You sure?"

"I am. This is my project now. You had your chance, Craig. You made your choices, and now others have to live with the consequences. You gotta own it." He started to pull nails. "You run along now. Enjoy your time with Abby. Wednesday will come sooner than you think."

Confused and defeated, Craig made his way down the ladder. "Thanks for all your help this summer, Ted. It was good getting to know you."

"You too. Good luck."

"Thank you, sir."

Craig didn't know what to do next. Ted was right, Mondays were busy, so he could always fall into cabin turnover mode and help the boys with their work. Over in the lodge, Craig was sure he could find Abby. She would know what to do. In fact, she probably had a list a mile long.

Claire glanced up from her conversation with Frank to see Craig walk through the main room and down the hall. She waved.

"What is it that you really want to know?" Frank asked, not getting up from his stool. His resigned stare still held a touch of anger.

Claire finally felt comfortable enough to push further. She basically knew everything anyway. While chopping the vegetables for that night, she said, "I just want to know what happened. I know you started this place with your friend. I know you owned it for a while and now you don't. I know you hate Shane. What gives, Frank? You know I love you, but what gives?"

Frank looked up, his eyes red around the edges and his lips pressed tight. "I'm quite fond of you, Claire, and your brother. You're good kids. You've done right by the Whitworths. They're good people, the best. I don't want to hurt anyone."

"Frank, you can't hurt anyone."

"Why do you want to know all of this?"

"Because I want you to unburden yourself of it. Because I really care for Shane even though I've only known him a little while. He doesn't have a clue."

"He doesn't?" Frank almost barked out.

Claire calmly replied, "No. Should he?"

"I guess he was only three or four when he left this place."

"Wait, he WAS here then?" This confirmed what she already knew.

Frank sat silent for an uncomfortably long time. "I'll tell you, but then we're done with this. We have work to do."

"We always have work to do. That's what I love about this place."

"Me too."

Frank rolled his upper lip under his teeth and bit hard. "When I was young, Robert and I were great friends. We hung out, played football together, but he was different. He went off to college. Me, I just picked up odd jobs at places and eventually settled into a job at Rick's Place. That's where I met Rita. I mean, I'd known her, but I really met her there, if you know what I'm saying. Like I told you earlier." He smiled softly and continued, "So, as I was saying, Bob went to college, but then he came home. No one around here really understood why. He had a business degree, and there were more jobs south or in the Twin Cities. Things were really taking off in those parts back then. But he had a dream, a vision, you know? He started selling real estate and did well getting Chicago folks up here. Anyway, he had this dream of starting up his own place, so he bought this land, cheap, all of it down almost a half mile past my cabin or more, and we built this place. The trees were cleared, and we used them to build all this. It was just my cabin and the lake cabins to begin with, but then the other cabins and the lodge came along. The house came later. We did most of the labor. If we didn't know how to do something, we brought in people and learned how to do it ourselves. Once we really got running, Rita came over. Bob kept trying to give us a share, but we didn't want to be owners, we just worked to live. When Rita and I found out we couldn't have kids, Bob's kids became ours. His son BJ and his daughter Carla, they ran around here like they owned the place. It was great. He never spoiled the kids. They worked too. We got everything paid off by the mid '80s, and Bob was living on easy street. He made improvements with the profits and expanded the offerings. He put a bunch of money into marketing, and we got a solid crowd, all seasons. Things were good."

"What happened then? If things were good, why keep all this a secret?"

"In the early '90s, '91 or '92, Bob got sick. Carla was away at school, BJ had just started, and Bob got cancer. Rita and I took over day-to-day management. Old Josie, Bob's wife, she moved him down to a hospital in Milwaukee where he died. I wasn't there. Didn't even get to say goodbye. Josie brought him back and buried him up here, but she couldn't take it. She didn't want to run the place, even though me and Rita were doing most of the running. So, she left and went to live with Carla in the Twin Cities. She died only a year or two ago, I think. But before she left, she signed everything over to BJ. That, aside from Bob's dying, is when the whole thing went to shit. So, BJ. That would be Shane's dad."

"I figured," Claire interjected.

"Anyway, he got his girl pregnant when she was eighteen or nineteen and he was twenty-two. Shane was born in '94 or '95."

"'95."

"Ok. '95. BJ never took to taking care of this place. Like I said, me and Rita had pretty much taken over the day-to-day, but BJ had all these new ideas. He bought a couple of speedboats and tons of other toys and had this plan to be a hunting guide and whatever else. He used the equity of the place like a piggy bank. Bought himself a house over on another lake. The kid was just too young. I tried to warn him, but if you give a kid a half million in assets when he is used to living poor, what's he going to do? He didn't know what Abby knows. He was never a part of the place like she is."

Warmed by the shared knowledge of Abby's place in this world, she pressed forward. "What happened then?"

"Well, the bank came calling, and he had to get rid of all the toys, lost the house, everything. The resort was going to go into foreclosure after only four years. So, Rita and I arranged to buy the place. We couldn't afford the whole price, but we'd saved quite a bit. We really didn't spend much. We got a loan and bought it, always intending to sell it to a family if the right one came along. We struggled for a bit. Had to shut down the lodge one summer and two winters just to save money. It was three, maybe four or five years before the Whitworths came along. We wanted a family to take it over. One who wanted to live on the place like it should be lived on." Frank bit his lip again, breathing deeply.

"What happened to BJ and Shane and his mother?"

"That's a whole 'nother story, but to sum it up, we kicked them off the place. BJ tried real estate for a while, but failed, and then he left. Shane and his mom worked, but she struggled a bit, and Shane got himself a job out at Rick's Place, his son owns it now, but Shane stole a bunch of money and ran off."

"With the money?"

"Well, actually, he gave the money to his mom. No one ever gave her any trouble about it cause she needed the help, but he just left. Now, he comes into town every once in a while and then is off again. I don't trust him. He's just like his dad."

Frank looked deflated. Claire knew not to press further, so instead, she said, "Thank you, Frank. You're a good man. I'll keep him away from here."

"I don't know. I guess it's fine if he shows up. The sins of the father don't fall on the son. If you trust him, bring him over. I trust you. I mean, his legacy is tied to this place. He should know the man his grandfather was."

Claire helped Frank to his feet and gave him a hug. "Thank you. I appreciate it. Love you."

"Love you too, kid."

"We probably have work to do, huh?"

"Yes. Don't we always?"

CHAPTER 20

"The first day was ok. We're not in pads, and it's non-contact, but that didn't stop people from getting a lick in on me," Craig said, twisting his sore neck slowly while looking at Abby through the screen on his phone.

"What do you mean?" Abby asked, a hint of panic in her voice.

In an attempt to calm her, Craig said plainly, "I go out to a route or walk through a blocking pattern, and I'm getting an extra shove. It's silly, but I guess I deserve it."

Abby's face grew taut. "Do you really believe that?"

"It doesn't really matter if I believe it. It's just the culture of it all. This is a sport based on trust and results. I have to use one to get the other."

"I see." Abby didn't really understand any of it, but in an attempt to get off the subject, she said, "Things are ramping up here for another weekend. People trying to get little vacations in before school starts. It's coming quick."

"It is. There just seems to be so much to do both here and there and no time to get it done."

"Ted finished the last cabin." The statement was met with silence. Abby didn't intend the comment to hurt Craig. She wanted to lift a burden, but quickly realized she didn't.

Eventually, Craig responded, "That's good. I think I'll get

up there Friday night, might be Saturday early morning by the time I make it."

"Ok. Whatcha doing the rest of the day?"

"Probably studying film. Hanging out. Might go for a walk."

"Without me?" Abby tried to be cheerful to raise Craig's spirits, but she was worried.

"Without anyone," Craig said quickly. "I miss you."

"I miss you too. We'll see each other for a bit this weekend. I'll fill you in on anything Claire learned from Frank."

"Lots of juicy details?" Craig chuckled despite his mood.

Abby smiled at the attempt. "Not exactly, but she got him to talk. More than I have over the years."

"She has a gift for it."

"That's the truth. I think I'm going to get going. Lots to do as usual."

Understanding completely, Craig said, "Now that's the real truth."

Abby giggled. "Love you."

"Love you too."

When Abby hung up the phone, she sat still for a moment. There was no sense in any of it. Craig was sad, and it was only the first day. His stubborn determination would see him through, but she hoped he would find the beauty he was looking for. She didn't want to spend the football season picking up the pieces.

Craig was alone. He had been over the film clips he was given dozens of times, so there was nothing left to see. Deciding that he could play the clips over in his head, he went out for a walk. Campus was alive with summer green, but it was also dead, devoid of people entirely. The first signs of life Craig encountered were on Old Highway 12. Cars zoomed by as he crossed into the neighborhood south of campus. His feet found their way through the grid to Main Street, then down to the lake. He sat under the tree he and Abby had sat under on their first date. Here, he had explained to her why he had left football, running slow motion into the same tree he now sat against.

Out on the lake were two boats. The waves they created lapped against the shore with a consistent rhythm. When Craig closed his eyes, he saw Abby wading into the lake with her sandals in her hand, pushing her long, dark hair back behind her ears, fruitlessly, as not to get the ends wet when she bent over. The vision of her fully engaged in nature, almost part of the water herself, had not fully penetrated him at the time. There was a simple beauty to it. This water held new meaning now, and Craig knew the strength he could draw from it. A calmness fell over him, and without any self-consciousness, he fell in and out of sleep, eventually giving in completely.

"Hey," Craig heard vaguely. He opened his eyes and heard again, "Hey." An older man was standing next to him with a small dog on a leash. "You ok, son?" he asked.

"Yeah, why?" Craig blinked a few times.

"Well, it's eight o'clock, and I thought maybe you should know that. You were pretty out."

Craig looked at his watch: 8:06. "Wow. Thanks, sir." Craig got up and smiled as the man walked away. He had been sleeping for almost two hours. While he walked back towards his dorm, he ran his hand down the retaining wall where he had found one of the leaves he had given to Abby after the dinner with his parents. 'I Choose Her,' he had written on it. He wondered if his parents were really coming around. In the moment, he could imagine a life without them, but a life without Abby was incomprehensible.

Just before reaching campus, he realized he had not thought about football since he left his room. Every thought had been of Abby and the resort. Commitments lay ahead of him, but he knew where his mind would go the moment he let it wander. Outside of the dorm, he noticed some bark chips on the grass around a new tree. He knelt down and picked them up, placing them back in the carefully manicured circle. The irony hit him as he admired his work. He walked into the dorm and went to his room to write Abby a letter. He knew if he sent it the next day, she probably wouldn't get it until after the weekend, but he didn't care.

Abby,

I never thanked you for the note you left in the front seat before I went to my tryout. I've taken it out and read it a few times. I really feel like playing again is the right thing. It's hard. The practices are fine, but none of the guys really talk to me. I get silence all the time, and I eat alone most of the time. Part of the reason I came back was for the guys, but they don't really seem to want me here. The coaches say I just need to work hard and play well, and they'll come around. I guess they're right, but for now, it's a pain.

Your support means everything to me. Just thinking about you up in the stands makes me happy. I couldn't wait to talk to you tonight. I get the feeling that is what I will look forward to most days. I just don't want this to be a bust. I don't want to let your dad down, or you, or Frank, for nothing. Let's not keep secrets anymore. Let's just tell the truth. If we have something to say, let's just say it.

Love you,
Craig

It was early Thursday when Claire brought Shane and his mother to the resort. She would have waited to allow the story Frank told her to sink in longer, but she only had a few weeks left before she needed to be back in Chicago to make yet another transition. A new apartment, same old roommate, but also a new perspective and reams of photos to comb through. She was looking forward to it, yet sad to leave.

This morning, she was coming back to the resort from Shane's mom's house. After moving into the Whitworths', which she appreciated, she found herself staying with Shane more often. He was fun, and his mother, being so much younger than her own, seemed to bridge a generation gap that she yearned to understand. Shane and his mother shared a friendly relationship, which was so different from Linda and her. The rules there were simple: don't be dumb, and treat others well. Besides that, Shane came and went as he pleased. "He brings me stories. Isn't that right, honey?" Janie said one evening.

Embarrassed, Shane answered, "Yes, Mom. I bring you stories."

"That's all I ever want from him. His stories."

Claire loved his stories too. Shane was an intensely engaging guy. Claire could argue with him and joke around. She smiled constantly around him, but it was his stories she loved most. The travels she longed for, he had done. She could go with him through his imagination. The details filled themselves in through his vivid descriptions.

Now, Claire wanted to take him back to where it all began. It had taken an evening's worth of convincing to get his mom on board with coming along. Janie was able to confirm every word of Frank's story and added context to the content, mostly coloring her former husband in an even darker light. Shane had no idea. He had grown up in the storm of his parents' marriage and spent much of his time with his maternal grandparents. He thought of looking up his father and grandma when he went through the Cities, but old memories were sometimes better left buried.

This memory was more for Shane's mother. Claire could see her shaking when they pulled into the parking lot. "I haven't been back here for almost twenty years. The day we left was the last time. I haven't even thought of coming back. Are you sure Frank will be ok?"

"If I'm with you, Frank will be fine."

They parked in the lot, close to the lodge, and got out. Shane pulled out the last wood burn sign he had made for the occasion. Claire held Janie's hand, which was cold to the touch, as they walked around the lodge, towards the lake. Janie's head spun around. "Things sure have changed."

"I wouldn't know, but I'd love to," Claire responded. "Let's go see Frank."

"Ok," Janie said, gripping the rail up to the deck to steady herself.

Claire led them into the lodge, nodding to John, who was behind the bar, then yelled, "Frank!"

"Yeah?"

"I got some people for you to meet."

"I suppose you do. Hope they're worth you missing breakfast service for." A chuckle followed as Frank emerged from the kitchen, wiping his hands on a towel before flinging it over his shoulder. With a smile breaking through, Frank said, "Janie. It's been a while."

"Hello, Frank." She stepped toward him. When they were close enough, she said weakly, "I'm sorry."

Frank gave her a hug, responding quietly, "It's ok, dear. It wasn't you. I know." Turning to Shane, he continued, "So, I've seen you around every now and again, but last time you were really here, you were this high," Frank said, gesturing to his belt buckle. "But I did watch you play football a fair bit. Actually, I never missed a home game. Peewee through your junior year. Or at least until you got hurt."

Shane looked at his mother and then at John. Both of them nodded, confirming what Frank had just said. Shane touched the scar on his wrist.

Claire was happy with Frank's kindness. She expected nothing less from him. He had kept one last secret for the meeting.

Frank continued, "Claire, why don't you let Janie show you around? See if you can find Abby. Shane, you're coming with me. Claire tells me you're quite a cook. Ever done anything with bass?"

"Yes, sir," Shane replied, staring wide-eyed at Claire, who nodded knowingly.

"Well, maybe you could show this old guy a thing or two."

"Ok," Shane said. "Sure thing. Also…" He revealed the sign he was carrying. It said, "Frank's Place." "I made this for you."

Frank nodded. "Thank you, Shane. I know just where to put it."

When they got outside, Janie started in, "I'm not sure why I never told him about this place. I guess Shane never really asked about the past. His dad was such an asshole to Frank."

They walked down by the lake and sat out on the dock. Janie gazed over the whole lake. "This used to be ours, and we shit it away. We were so young."

Claire, trying to be a calming force, said, "I'm sure there were good times."

"There were. Quiet times when we were all about the place and not about getting things. Shane used to play in the water all the time, and I would take him for boat rides."

"That must be a nice memory." Claire couldn't think of what else to say. Sometimes, it was enough to organize the event and leave the details to speak for themselves. Instead of speaking, she reached for Janie's hand and was met with a tight grip.

Later that night, after dinner service closed, John opened with, "That was a good thing you did today, Claire, not only for Janie and Shane, but Frank too." He leaned over the bar.

Claire had gone the day feeling unsure. "You think?"

"I do. You've had an impact on this place. Everyone does, but you and your brother have done a lot."

"Thank you, John."

"No, thank you. We're going to miss you."

"I think I might miss this place more. I always thought the city was the only place I ever wanted to be."

"I asked your brother when he first came up here, 'What do they have down there that we don't have here?' I meant that. Now, Vickie could give you a list of things Chicago has that we don't. Heck, she still wants to move back there when we retire."

Claire had been warned by both Abby and Craig that John had a tendency to open up later in the night. This seemed to be one of those times. Without fear, she pressed on. "Where did you live before, when you were down there?"

"I lived on campus. Northwestern. Vickie lived on the west side, near O'Hare. Nice walkable neighborhood. Beautiful old homes. She lived there most of her life."

"I know the area. You're right about the homes, so much more charming...not like where I grew up."

John smiled. "When we got married, we lived in a small apartment on the north side. Abby told me about your family's home. Seems nice, in its own way."

"Not really. Fake nice."

"Sometimes, you need a little fake. Reality is all a matter of perception. What is most real to you can be nothing to someone else. I think today proved that." He moved off to fill a guest's beer. The moment closed.

Not ready to sleep, and still thinking about what John said, Claire went out for a walk. At the end of the cabin road, she saw someone coming out of Frank's cabin. Hoping it was Frank, she stepped forward. It was Abby. Claire waited for her to move closer. "Hey, Abby."

Seeing Claire clearly after a few steps, she responded. "Oh hey, Claire. What's up?"

"I was just out walking."

"Yeah. Heavy day, huh? Thanks for bringing Shane and Janie. I think it did Frank some good."

"Really? Your dad said the same thing."

"He's right. Just came from talking with Frank. He's excited. Tired, but excited."

"Excited?"

"Yeah. I couldn't really tell about what, but there's a little difference. He's been so off all summer. It was good to see him being more like his old self."

"Was he talking about Shane?"

"A little. Janie too. He never really had a problem with either of them. In fact, I think he thought of Shane like family."

"Maybe that's why he acted so angry around him. No one brings out anger like family."

Abby laughed. "That's for sure. Can I walk with you?" It was a moonlit night, and with another weekend coming, Abby also wanted to clear her head.

"Sure." They walked to the lodge and past the dock. The

shimmering water reflected the moon and made it even brighter, so every step was witnessed and sure. Eventually, they came to the deck outside Abby's home.

They sat, not saying anything until finally, Abby started, "I'm worried about Craig." Claire turned towards her, saying nothing. Abby slowly continued, "That's actually what I went to talk to Frank about. After the day he had, it's selfish, I know, but he played football and Craig called yesterday and seemed upset and I just don't know…"

Claire, having lived through the past and present of a sports family, could fully understand what Abby was struggling with. Although, always on the outside, Claire had sat with both her sister and her brother in times of struggle and celebration. She tried to explain. "Sports run deep in a person. You can't spend the hours, days, years doing something and just let it go."

"But he could get hurt, and his teammates…it sounds like they hate him."

"They don't hate him. They're jealous of him and annoyed with him. He can take a year off and come back. They don't trust him, Abby." Claire put her arm around her. "Craig has to work this out. It's a challenge he laid out for himself, and he needs to work it through. We all long to be in control of something. He feels he can control this."

"I know you never played sports, but do you feel the same about your art?"

"Sometimes. I guess I do find myself going to it when I get overwhelmed, but I also like that I can lose control with it. The best work I do is when a piece takes me over and I just go with it, you know? It's like I'm along for the ride, observing the piece as it dictates itself to me."

"I'm not sure I know what that's like."

"Sure you do, Abby. I've seen you."

"What? When?"

"Here. At this place. This is your work of art, as well as your father's. The rhythms of this place dictate to you what comes next. Sure, you can plan it out, but mostly, it takes hold of you and you go along with it. This place is a canvas that never gets fully filled in."

"You think?"

"Yes, I do. I also see it when you're with Craig. Nothing is planned. You go with the flow, and it's beautiful. Your relationship is a work of art too. Everyone around you can see it."

Embarrassed, Abby said, "Really?"

"Oh yeah. You got what we all want. Hold onto it, ok?" Claire got up to go.

Reaching out and grabbing her arm, Abby said, "Claire."

"Yes?"

"Thank you."

"Thank you, Abby, for inviting me here."

Lost In Place - Abby

Craig said he gets lost
In the moment
While he plays football.
I say I don't understand,
But maybe I do.
Here,
At home,
In the woods,
Out on the water,
I find myself adrift
In a current of the moment.
All I can feel,
All I can know
Is the now.
The feelings,
The memories,
The anticipation,
Of seeing him again.
A smile rising
With the morning sun,
Lighting my world.
I have found Craig
In this place
And so many other places.
I have found myself.

CHAPTER 21

By the time Labor Day weekend was almost upon them, a new routine had settled in with the old, and life became a work of art each day. Abby had a handle on the books, finally, and didn't even miss Craig the weekend he couldn't make it back to the resort. The summer was drawing to a close, and Abby felt the weight of several goodbyes beginning to swell, but she worked it away most days. She and Claire continued to talk each night, going deeper into all they could find, Chicago, art school, Craig, college, the resort, but mostly, Frank. The change in Frank had held. He could be found walking the grounds regularly and sometimes even went fishing before breakfast like he used to. Shane and Janie too became more frequent guests, with Shane helping in the kitchen while Janie talked to Vickie about coming on as cleaner. Vickie was more than open to the idea, especially when the boys went back to school.

Claire had a conversation with Shane about staying on at the resort part-time. Frank couldn't keep up the schedule after she left, and he would need help on weekends in the fall and winter. She expressed to Shane that it might be time to grow up a bit. Surprisingly, he agreed, but only if they could go on a few trips together. Traveling with a partner was a prospect that neither could deny. He promised to make Chicago his first trip.

For Craig, the weeks had gone well too. He practiced as

hard as he could, and despite being ridden to the ground more times than he could count, he got up and went on with his business. Coach was starting to call more plays his way, and he figured that as long as he kept catching balls, the boys would start to treat him better.

It was working for the most part, until one day in the film room. The team was going over tape for their first opponent. Craig was used to the drill. Look for weaknesses and tendencies at every position. If there was anything to exploit, even for one play, it was worth mentioning. After all the coaches finished talking, there was usually time for the athletes to share any insights. Craig had been viewing the plays selected for all the offensive positions, not just the ones he was assigned. He found that if he looked at all the film, he could see the play develop in multiple ways. He could detect the checkdowns even if they weren't called. It was in this frame of mind that he raised his hand.

Startled, his coach said, "Craig? Do you have something to share?"

"Yes, sir. If you back the last play up and zoom in on the middle linebacker, you'll see he cheats to the strong side on play-action. If we run a tight end or double tight end to the right and play-action that way, we can run a slant from the backside into the middle of the zone. If we hit it quick, the receiver will be free until the safety catches up."

"Ok?" the coach said as he backed up the film.

"See," Craig continued. "His feet are already tipped, and he'll step up as soon as he sees the running back move forward. If we run from the slot on the weak side, we can run right by."

They watched the play a couple of times and then observed

a few other plays. The linebacker moved every time, just as Craig said.

"Anything else you're seeing, Craig?"

He hesitated for a moment. "Yes," he said carefully.

"Well?" Coach asked.

"The right-side corner, the one who lines up on the weaker receiver." Craig was acutely aware that everyone was watching him. "He falls in if you throw a slant or hook on the first few balls. He tries to cover the inside more, and if you can get a step, the sideline is free. He can't catch up."

Again, they watched a few plays, and he was spot on. "Good catch."

Craig felt very satisfied but bit his upper lip hard as not to smile. "Thank you."

When they finished and everyone got up to go, Coach pulled Craig aside. "You keep speaking up when you see things. You have a good eye. Even if we get a few plays out of it, it's all good."

"Thanks again, sir." Craig made his way out.

When he got to his mailbox before going to his dorm room, he found a letter from Abby.

Craig,

Thanks for the letter the other week. I could tell you were struggling on the phone. I don't want you to be sad, and I agree on the secrets. I feel like I know you so well, yet at other times I sense you are not letting me in fully. I don't want to keep anything from you. There's no reason to do that.

Thanks for the great weekend. It was so nice to just be with you. When you are gone, it feels like a part of me is missing. Don't get me wrong, I don't want to leave here, but back at school, we can be closer. I can spend nights with you, and we can be together. That's what I want most of all.

See you soon. Love you.

Abby

The weekend before Labor Day, Craig was able to make it up to the resort on Friday. The team had been released at noon and was told to report at eight o'clock Monday morning for a normal week. The real rhythm of the season would begin with the first game on the Saturday of Labor Day weekend. Craig was sad about not being at the resort for the full holiday weekend, but he would make it up after the game, at least on Sunday.

When Craig got downstairs in the Whitworths' home, he was met with dueling packers and no place to put his stuff. Having taken most of his clothes back to school after the last time he was at the resort, all Craig had was a duffel. However, both Claire and Abby had laid out their entire wardrobes, Claire to pack and Abby to sort.

"Wow. You two are beginning to look more like Sarah every day what with the clothes and all."

"Oh shut up, Craig," Claire snapped playfully and went back to folding.

He picked up a skirt with a tag from Abby's pile. "I see someone went shopping." There were several new pieces scattered on the floor, mostly skirts and flowing shirts. Abby smiled.

"Linda took us shopping," Claire said, standing up with

one hand on her hip and flashing a credit card.

"So she did." Craig laughed. "Does anyone work around here, or are we just doing this for now?"

Abby punched his arm. "Why don't you join Frank in the kitchen? We just need to clean up here, and then we'll be along."

Claire nodded in agreement. "I gotta get packed to leave tomorrow so I can be in Chicago late on Sunday. Mom wants me to stop home for the night."

"Ok," Craig replied, kissing Abby quickly. "Fishing tonight?"

"Perhaps." She smiled. "Run along. Frank is probably going nuts without us."

He jogged up the stairs.

Two male voices were talking in the kitchen, and without the girls, Craig couldn't figure out who might be in there. John was settled behind the bar, so it wasn't him. To Craig's surprise, as he walked in, Shane stood at a table showing Frank something about prepping a fish.

"Hello," Craig said loudly, trying to grab someone's attention.

Frank looked up first. "Hi, Craig. How's it going?"

"Pretty well," Craig replied.

"This is Shane. Claire's boyfriend."

"We're just friends," Shane interjected.

Frank chuckled. "Yeah, right."

"Nice to meet you, Shane," Craig walked up to shake his hand, but Shane held up a wave instead, his hands messy from the fish.

Frank asked, "So what can I help you with, Craig?"

"The girls sent me here to help with dinner."

"So they did. We got things going pretty well in here, but you could get the dishes out and get the buffet set up."

Craig set to the task, and soon enough, dinner service had started, and he fell into the routine of getting new dishes, refilling beverages, fetching drinks, and doing whatever else he could find. John put him in charge of the bonfire, which he did without a problem. The wood reserves he built up were holding and would last several more weeks. All the fresh wood was gone, so there was no chopping to be done this weekend.

By ten, everything had wrapped up and only the regulars were in the bar area. Vickie, who had come to greet Craig, lingered for a while because a few guests she knew from over the years were up for the weekend.

Claire left right after dinner to hang out with Shane, and with things winding down, Abby and Craig decided to go for a walk. They strolled towards his and Claire's old cabin out of habit.

After all the small talk, Craig asked, "Is everything ok?" A mixture of concern and frustration spread through his mind if he was being honest with himself. He wanted Abby all to himself, but her eyes were watery, and her voice was soft and distant. Something was wrong, and she wouldn't be in the mood to fool around anyway. They went down the cabin road, into the woods, to the log that looked out over the lake. Outside of a few quick glances, there was no interaction. The moon shone as only a sliver and the darkness of the moment crept even further. In the silence, Craig could hear the crickets and an occasional frog. The lapping of the waves came in regular intervals. He held Abby's hand, waiting for her to speak first.

Abby, too, was waiting. She really wasn't sure how to begin. It was more of a feeling that drove her to want to walk rather than anything specific. In fact, there were too many things she wanted to say, too many feelings hitting her all at once. She didn't want to go back to school, but then she did. She wanted to tell Craig that she was still angry about football, but she saw brief, fleeting moments of excitement in him that made her so happy. There were still feelings of hesitation about Shane and Janie, but then, she was so happy for Frank. And then, there was the feeling she could not escape. She was so excited to see Craig, hear from him, touch him. The first move would have to be hers. Craig respected and loved her too much to push their relationship faster. But she was paralyzed by the fear of what it could mean. On the one hand, it was a simple physical act, an expression of feelings really. Then again, there was something sacred in sharing yourself totally with another. It was something Abby longed to do with only one person in her life. That person, she believed more strongly than ever, was Craig.

Craig stroked the back of Abby's hand with intent, willing her to speak. Some of what may have been troubling her he could predict, but he was often wrong, so he continued to sit.

Finally, she spoke. "So, how was football this week? I mean, I got your letter. You haven't really said if the boys are being nicer."

"It's alright. Mostly, they just leave me alone. I've had more good moments than bad. Wish they would stop riding me all the way to the ground."

"What's that? They hit you?"

"We're supposed to hit, but they're just supposed to wrap

me up on contact days. Every once in a while, someone takes me all the way down. The coaches just look the other way. But it should be done now. We have a game next week."

"How are you feeling about that?"

Craig shrugged. "Fine. I'll probably be nervous as it gets closer, but I know what I'm supposed to do. It's all about getting ready for game speed." He looked down at his feet. "Wish we didn't have to play next weekend."

"Yeah. Me too. It's really busy next weekend, but Shane and his mom said they would be here, so that'll help."

"Yeah, about that…"

Abby turned, facing Craig. "What?"

"How'd that all come about?"

"Claire did it, mostly."

"I know that, but…"

"Frank wasn't really that mad. He and Shane have a lot in common, which is really nice for him. I think everyone feels bad for Janie. She kinda got the shaft in a lot of ways."

"I guess. I mean, from what you told me, that seems to be the case," Craig said.

Abby nodded her head absentmindedly. "So, we're trying to help them out, and they are doing the same."

"I think Claire is happy about it."

"I think she is too."

They sat quietly for a few minutes, unwilling to move forward. Now, nothing else lay between them but the big hills that seemed too steep to climb until, "So, how are you feeling about going back to school? I mean, I'm almost already back." Craig spoke quickly, nervously.

"I don't want to," Abby admitted. "I really don't. I'm sorry."

"Sorry about what?" He turned to her, grasping her other hand.

Abby took her time. She felt like she was losing control. "The only thing I'm looking forward to back at school is being alone with you, like I said in the letter."

There she was, his girl. She had come right out and said it. "I'm looking forward to that too," Craig replied.

Then, it spilled out all at once. "I've learned more in the office this summer than they could ever teach me in school. I know there's stuff I don't know, and the resort has to change and adapt. But I feel like I can do that. At least, the technical side of it. I've already streamlined the process, and the new website is working well."

"I'm sure you can. But some of us can only know what we don't know, and I don't know much." Abby laughed at Craig's little joke, and he continued, "I kinda want to get back. Mostly, so we can be alone."

Abby nuzzled in. "Really?"

"Yes."

The lake shimmered in the moonlight. Almost apart from the conversation, as though she was speaking to the air, or herself, Abby asked, "Craig?"

"Yes?" he replied.

"Do you want to sleep with me?"

Craig took one very deliberate breath and replied confidently, "Yes."

CHAPTER 22

Game day was here. As Craig had expected, the boys laid off the hitting, but most, Will and Luke being notable exceptions, continued to treat him with casual indifference. Brent was friendly, but he shied away from defending him when things got tense. Today was going to be all business. They had all been through this before. A win was expected, and Craig felt prepared. He had not seen game speed in over twenty months, but the sensations he felt were the same. Football was different than most sports. The tension, nervous energy really, before a game could cut in fifty different ways. Each player had his own way of getting into character. That was really what it was all about, putting on your game face. Some players were quiet, some loud. Some acted like it was no big deal, a lie, while others spent too much time actually putting on their game face with eye black and face paint.

Craig was one of the quiet ones. He waited for someone to call him by name before the transition could be complete. It was the name change that finished the deal. Today, it was Will. "You ready for this, McLean?" he asked in passing. Craig turned and nodded, saying nothing.

McLean. That was who he was and would be for the next three hours. Soon enough, Coach said his words and they took the field.

Craig was sent out to take the opening kickoff and caught it on the one-yard line. Without thinking, he took the ball up the right side, high-stepping an attempted low tackle. Landing unsteadily and unable to cut, he got taken out at the twenty-seven yard line by two players. The hit startled him for just a second, but he bounced up and ran to the sideline. Coach Brewer patted him on the helmet. "Good start, Craig."

Craig was out for two plays, then came back in, blocking on a first down on the forty-three. He hit his man, a cornerback, but got turned and couldn't come off to pick up the strong safety, and the run only went for three yards. The next play was another run up the middle for two yards, setting up a 3rd and 5. Craig ran into the huddle, and Luke called the play to the middle with Craig in the slot opposite a two tight end set. This was the play installed to take advantage of the middle linebacker. "You got this, McLean?" Luke yelled.

"Put it up there, and I'll get it!"

"Yeah you will. Ready, set, break!" The entire team clapped and ran to the line.

The world slowed down as Craig approached the line. He stared down the coverage man across from him. Five steps out. One left and in. The play ran in his head.

The ball was snapped. Craig ran hard and stepped once to his left, turning the cornerback and then went straight right, looking up, and he felt the impact of the ball as his hands guided it in. He turned upfield and was met by the safety coming over from his right. Still running, Craig tried to stiff-arm the safety, but was slowed up enough that the corner, the guy he had left behind, caught him by the shoe, and he went down. Twenty yards and a first down. Craig got up, pointing to the endzone, and heard the crowd cheer. He felt a rush from his chest to his toes, broken only by the ref asking, "Can I have the ball, son?"

Craig tossed him the ball and returned to the huddle. There was no time for congratulations. The Warhawks had them on the run. Three runs and a pass to the tight end for a touchdown, and they had the lead. The rest of the half was competitive, but eventually, Whitewater pulled away in the third quarter. Craig caught three more balls and got a block that freed the running back for a touchdown. It was a good game for both him and the team.

When he got back to the locker room and the postgame speeches were done, Craig texted Abby. *We won. CYL. Out to eat with the parents :(*

There was no reply, even after he finished showering.

"Where do you want to eat, Craig?" Mike said loudly.

Craig was still recovering from the smack his dad had given him on the back. "Somewhere quick? I gotta get on the road."

"Going to Eagle River for the weekend?" his mom asked.

"Yeah. I'll be there for tomorrow, and then Abby and I are coming back Monday. School starts Tuesday."

Mike chimed in, again too loudly, "Back to the grind, huh?"

"Would you rather not go?" Linda asked.

"No, let's go. Just fast food. I don't want to get to the resort too late."

They went to Culvers, where Mike rehashed the entire game while Craig and Linda sat in silence. Craig needed to find a way out of these dinners in the future, otherwise his father was going to backslide into old habits. After the quick bite, they moved over to the gas station next door, where Craig gassed up and got a large coffee. They said their goodbyes and went their separate ways.

Abby received Craig's text, but was in the middle of the Saturday afternoon photo tour with one more to do in the evening. She hoped Craig would be on the road by four so they could still fit in a boat ride after he arrived. A missed call came in around 4:10, so she assumed he was on his way. After getting the people back to shore, she rushed up to the lodge for the beginning of dinner service and to help prep; they were having steaks tonight with a trout option and grilled food on Sunday night. Abby decided to snack for the time being and would eat with Craig when he got there. She wanted to surprise him.

Dinner service was great. Shane was a wiz, having worked in over a dozen restaurants over the years, and a steak dinner for sixty people was not even a challenge. Frank seemed happy and spent more time up front talking to guests from behind the bar. Abby noticed that Shane's mood was always positive, and his quick wit made it easy to see what Claire was so attracted to. There was a smoothness to all his movements, and the plates he sent out were works of art. He even managed to remember Abby's surprise, which she had planned to prepare.

"Don't worry about it, Abby. I'm going to be here tonight prepping for tomorrow and Monday. I'll do them up nice."

"Thank you, Shane."

"Hey, no problem." He kept walking as he talked.

"Have you heard from Claire yet?" Abby asked.

"Oh yeah. All into her new apartment. Mike and Linda are helping her with rent, so she's got the place looking really nice already. She sent me some pics."

"That's good. She sent me some too. Are you planning on visiting her?"

"I think so. Later in September maybe. I know some people in Chicago."

"Can't you just stay with her?"

"Wouldn't want to impose. We're just friends, you know." He winked. "You better get out front to see how things are going. Tell me if you need more of anything."

As she left the kitchen, Abby chuckled to herself about how smoothly things were going. Labor Day weekend was unique. Three huge days followed by near silence. Wouldn't be too long until the next shutdown week. She wished she could just skip school and come home. It had been such a quick summer, but so much had happened. Abby had gotten to know Claire really well, had learned the ins and outs of the resort, and had fallen so in love with Craig that she could barely stand the fact that she still had to wait three hours for him to come.

To pass the time, Abby went to find Sarah and Brad, who had taken advantage of a late cancellation to come up for the weekend. Even though they arrived on Friday night, Abby hadn't had much time to see them other than to say hello and show them to their room in the lodge.

Finding them out on the deck, she asked formally, a mischievous grin on her face, "Is there anything I can get you?"

"Oh shut up, Abby," Sarah responded playfully. "You can get off your feet and visit for a little while."

Abby smiled and sat down. "I could do that?"

"You weren't kidding about how much you work around here."

"Yeah," Abby sighed. "It's a lot, but I love it."

"I can see why," Brad said.

Both the girls looked at him curiously, waiting for more.

"Well, it's lovely. I went fishing with your dad this morning, relaxed out by the water, had a drink in my hand since four, and the food. Holy crap. Those guys in the kitchen are great. That was the best steak I've had north of Chicago."

"Well, there you go. High praise from my subdued man," Sarah chimed in. "When does the evening tour start? I signed up."

"Eight," Abby replied. "Thanks for reminding me. Claire was running that, but this is the first Saturday since she left, so it's up to me tonight. I better go get ready."

"Can I help?" Sarah asked, already getting up.

"Sure. Thank you."

"What are you going to do?" Sarah asked, running her hand down Brad's back.

"Sit here, maybe shoot the breeze with Abby's dad or talk to the guys in the kitchen." Brad raised his glass.

"Ok. Off we go." Sarah followed Abby down towards the shed.

Abby was happy to have a moment alone with Sarah. Even though she felt a strong connection with Claire, Sarah had come to her aid on her first visit to Craig's home, sensing how uncomfortable Linda had made her.

"This place is great, like Brad said. I can't believe you grew up here."

"It's home to me. I have to share it with lots of other people, but it's home."

"That's kind of weird to think. No offense."

"None taken. I guess it is. Certainly different than most people's homes. It took time for Claire and Craig to adjust."

"It sounds like Claire did well. We talked last week. She really loved her time here, and she met a guy too, I hear."

"Shane. Yeah, he's nice. His mom is too."

They reached the shed, and Abby got a gas can to fill. "So, we have to gas up the boat and then get some beers and wine coolers from the bar for the guests. We also need towels to wipe down the boat." Abby paused, looking up at Sarah. "I'm so sorry. I don't mean to boss…I guess I'm just used to giving orders."

Sarah laughed. "It's not a problem. Let me help you with that." She grabbed the gas can from Abby's hand, and they went down to the lake.

Craig came right at ten. Abby could tell by the way he laid his head down on the bar top that he was exhausted. She came up behind him and rubbed his back. "How are you doing?"

"I'm so tired. Sore." He raised his head. "I'm so happy to see you but getting in the car to drive five hours after a game was probably not the best idea."

"I'm sure. You guys won?"

"Yes."

"Were you happy with how you played?"

"Yup. I only missed one catch. Got most of my blocks."

"That's good. Did you get hit a lot?"

Craig knew Abby was concerned about that particular subject. "Not too bad. Took a lick on the opening kickoff, but other than that, nothing major."

The game room was humming, and plenty of people were still at the bar or milling around tables. Despite the buzz that had annoyed Abby since she returned from the sunset tour, now, with Craig there, everything faded away. "I've got some food for you if you're hungry."

Craig smiled. "That would be great."

"Ok. I'll be back in a bit."

"Thank you." Craig watched her go all the way to the kitchen. He nodded his head slowly and exhaled. Even though he was more tired than he had been in a long time, coming to the resort was the right idea. He felt pulled throughout the drive. His focus never wavered, but now, having achieved his goal, his whole body let go. But then…

"Hey, little bro."

"Sarah?" Craig was surprised to see her. With the game and all, he barely registered when Abby told him they were going to be there.

"How are you doing?" she asked as she sat down next to him.

Craig stared at her for a few moments. "Ok," he exhaled out.

"Brad and I came for the weekend. This place is nice. I can totally tell why you love it here."

"Yeah, it's pretty awesome."

"How was your game? You guys won?"

"We did. How'd you know?"

"Brad was looking up stats this afternoon."

"Really? Where is he?"

"He's sleeping." She rolled her eyes.

Craig snorted into a chuckle. "That's rare."

"It is, but we're on vacation. He thinks he's going to get up early in the morning and go fishing."

"We'll see. I'll be up." Craig yawned, knowing his day would begin at six o'clock.

Sarah gave him a little squeeze on the shoulders. "Back to work."

"That's what we do here. It's fun though. I love it."

"You love her," Sarah said, pointing through the window into the kitchen towards Abby.

"I do." Craig smiled. His sister always knew how to cut to the chase.

"That's so awesome, Craig. I'm really happy for you. You want a drink?"

"Actually, I could have a glass of red wine. That would go well with the night."

"Ok." Sarah flagged down John.

"Hey, Craig," John said. "Game go well?" He brought over a full glass of red wine before Sarah even asked. "Can I get you anything?" he asked Sarah.

"I'm fine, thanks," she responded.

Craig took a sip of the wine. "The game went well, sir."

"That's good. So, you're taking Abby with you Monday?"

"That's the plan."

"Well, enjoy tomorrow."

"I'll try."

"Good deal." John moved down the bar.

Sarah playfully punched Craig on his shoulder. "So, tomorrow. I think we might go into town for a while, and supposedly, there's going to be a party once it gets dark."

Craig noticed on the schedule Abby shared with him that there was no bonfire going on Saturday night. "I guess so. It'll be fun. The town is cool. I'm sure there's some street festival going on with shops and local artists. You should ask Shane. He knows all about that stuff." Talking with Sarah was giving Craig some energy. "So, how are you guys? How's the house?"

"We're good. The house is coming along. There's just so much to do."

Abby came back with two plates. "You want to sit at a table?"

"I would like that," Craig said. He got up and grabbed his wine, and they moved towards a table on the far side of the dining room.

"I'm going to go upstairs," Sarah said, taking the hint.

"Thanks, Sarah," Abby said. Her eyes, gleaming in the low light, focused only on Craig as Sarah walked away.

They were together, alone. Both rendered mute in mutual exhaustion. They ate in silence. The steaks Shane made were phenomenal, but Abby was too tired to acknowledge them.

Craig, too, thought the food was amazing. He managed to ask, "Did Shane make this?" He continued chewing.

"I think so."

"It's good."

"I agree."

They finished in silence, and Craig took the dishes to the kitchen. Everything was dark, so he rinsed them and set them to the side to be washed later. The lodge had wound down. Three stragglers held on at the bar, but everyone else was gone.

Craig came back, and before he could speak, Abby said, "Would you…" She paused to take a breath.

Craig started before she could continue. "Do you want to just go to your house and watch a movie or something?"

"Yes," Abby exhaled. "That would be perfect."

Back at Abby's house, they got comfortable on the couch downstairs. Craig spooned Abby and pulled his head in close to hers, burying his face in her hair.

"Are you comfortable?" Abby asked.

Sleepily, Craig replied, "Yes. I'm good." He put his arm over her waist and squeezed. His voice was soft and deep. It was the voice he used when they were alone, in bed or on the boat. He kissed Abby's neck, and she felt the tickle of his whiskers.

"Me too." She pressed play on the movie and turned the volume down.

The next thing Abby felt was someone was putting a blanket over her and Craig. She was about to get up, but a voice said, "It's fine. Stay there, Abby."

Abby whispered, "Thanks, Mom."

The TV was turned off as well as the lamp. Abby fell asleep instantly.

They left after breakfast on Monday. Craig had to be back to campus by three for film and new play walk-through. For Abby, there was no other option but to go with him.

Abby was sad but determined to put a positive spin on the situation. Before they were out of town, she began, "It's going to be great to get back and see Kate and get into a few higher-level classes."

Craig knew she was lying, but he played along. "Yeah, it is." He put his hand on her thigh and patted it lightly. "Everything will be fine." They were quiet after that.

CHAPTER 23

"Abby!" Kate squealed as Abby entered the door. Abby dropped her things off on the bed, then turned to hug her. "Oh, hey, Craig," Kate continued as he came in with three bags dangling from his shoulders.

"Hey," Craig replied, unburdening himself. "I've got to get to film. I'll bring the rest of your things from my room tonight?"

"Oh, yeah," Abby said, hardly noticing. "Or I can come get it. Whatever."

"Alright." Craig gave Abby a quick kiss. "I'll text you when we're done with practice. Between seven and seven thirty."

"Sounds good. Bye."

When Craig shut the door, Kate pulled Abby next to her on the bed. "So, tell me about your summer. How was it having Craig and his sister all summer? Did I hear right? Is Craig playing football again?"

Abby put her hands on Kate's shoulders to steady her. "The summer was awesome. Lots of fun. Yes, Craig's playing again. What about you?"

"Oh, you're not getting off that easy, girl." There she was, the sassy Kate Abby had missed all summer.

"Ok. Where to start. Craig decided to play almost right away this summer, I think, but he didn't tell me until mid-July. They've already played one game."

"How are you feeling about it?"

"I was pissed at first, but I think I'm getting there. He loves it. And I love him."

Kate gave Abby a little nudge. "I know you do."

"No, Kate, I really love him. When he left at the beginning of August, that's when it really hit me. I love the hell out of that boy. I don't know. He's it. There's never going to be another."

"I'm so happy for you." Kate's face broke into a smile so genuine Abby started to giggle.

"So how was your summer?"

"Great!"

Kate went on and on about her trip to Spain and how she was planning to go back for winter break. She met a boy in her church group back home, and they were still texting even though he went to UW-Stevens Point. Abby listened intently. She had missed having her confidant. Claire was great, but she always played the big sister role. Kate was Abby's equal, and they could speak about anything, especially Craig. Kate never judged.

When the week began, the first thing Abby noticed was that her schedule and Craig's did not match up at all. There was almost no point in the day when they could meet besides evenings in the library, and Craig came late the first three nights. However, there were some positives to the schedule. For one, Abby could get her studying done without distraction. But, unless she went back to her room and hung out with Kate, her days were lonely.

On Friday of the first week, during lunch in the Union, Jen sat down across from Abby. "Hi, Abby," she said, a little more subdued than usual but still more chipper than most.

"Hello, Jen," Abby responded, willing to give her a chance. "How was your summer?"

"It was good. And yours?"

"Oh, it was great. Lots of fun. Classes good?"

"They're fine. What about you?"

"I don't know. School is school, you know?"

"Yeah." Abby tried to move the conversation along. "What can I do for you, Jen?"

"Oh yeah. So, some of the girls and I are going to the game tomorrow, and we would love it if you sat with us."

"Some of the girls?"

"Yeah. The girls." Abby raised her eyebrows, and Jen continued. "The girlfriends. Of the guys on the team."

Abby's gaze narrowed and a slight smile came across her face. "Ok. Thank you. I'll think about it. You seeing someone?"

"Yeah. Me and Luke hooked up this summer."

"That's nice." 'The quarterback. Fitting,' Abby thought to herself. "Like I said, I'll think about it."

"I hope so. You and Craig are still cool, I assume."

"We're good. Really good."

"That's great. I'm so happy for you guys." Jen got up to go. "Abby?"

"Yes?"

"I love your dress. Really. It's so cute."

"Thanks, Jen. See you tomorrow."

"Cool. Bye." And she was gone.

Abby looked down at her dress, a sundress she had bought with Claire before she left. All week, Abby had been wearing long skirts or dresses. She was actually more comfortable on the last warm days of summer than she would have been in leggings. Abby felt new and fresh. It was a feeling she wanted to keep.

Craig didn't make it up to the library until almost seven thirty. Unless he was traveling, Abby had made it clear that this was one date she intended to keep. Without hesitation, Craig had agreed.

"I'm sorry I'm late. Luke wanted to run over a few plays for tomorrow."

"That's fine," Abby said candidly. "How was practice?"

"Good." Craig sat down, sensing that she was annoyed. "But enough with that. What are you working on?"

"Intro to Marketing," Abby proudly said.

"That's cool," he replied, casually opening his book bag and searching for his copy of Kafka's stories for Euro Lit.

"Actually." Abby turned towards him. "It is."

This got Craig's attention. He locked into her. "Really?" he asked, sarcastically.

"Really. I know I'm usually a downer about school shit, but this is interesting, and I think it will really help me at the resort. There's a semester-long project, and I think I'm going to ask the professor if I can use the resort website as the basis of mine. Do a little double duty."

"Awesome."

"What are you going to work on?"

"I've got this Euro Lit course I have reading for." Craig chuckled. "Actually, I just have reading for everything. And some work for my Education class."

"Great. Then we both have work to do."

They studied until nine thirty, then went out to their bench. Fridays were no longer a night they could spend together,

Abby assumed, and she wasn't going to push, but she didn't want to end the night just yet.

She held Craig's hand as they both stared straight ahead. "Jen invited me to sit with her tomorrow."

Craig slowly turned his head towards hers. "Well, that's nice."

"Guess she's seeing Luke now?"

"That's what I heard. You gonna do it?"

"Do what?'

"Sit with her."

Abby thought about the question, then squeezed Craig's hand. "I don't know."

"Better than sitting alone."

"I could sit with your parents."

Craig snorted. "Sitting alone would be better than that."

Abby laughed, leaning her head on his shoulder. "This is my favorite place on campus."

"Me too." Craig ran his hand through her hair. "There's no water to look out on, but if you close your eyes…"

"I can see it," Abby said abruptly.

"Yeah. Me too."

The following day, Abby met Jen and some of the other girls before the game. Craig had informed his parents that Abby would be sitting elsewhere, and they were fine as long as everyone could meet up afterwards. This was the second home game of the season, and the Warhawks would be going on the road for the next two weeks. Abby decided to wear one of her new long skirts from Claire and a short, white peasant shirt with a blue pattern. The other girls had on cutoff jean shorts and jerseys. Abby had obviously not gotten the memo.

"That is a really nice outfit, Abby," one of the girls said. Abby hadn't picked up everyone's names yet. "It's cool you're coming with us. Craig's such a nice guy. You two are great together."

"Thanks. He makes me smile," Abby responded, feeling a little better about the situation.

"I love what you did with your hair," another girl said. Abby ran her hand across the top of her head. She had braided her hair from the front on one side, gathered the rest in the back, and pinned it up off her neck. It was going to be a hot day, and the loose clothing and updo was mostly done in the interest of staying cool.

They all made their way into the stadium and found seats in the student section. Abby only went to two games last year, but this year promised to include many more. She was excited to see Craig play, but also nervous. When she took a seat, Jen said, "Abby, stand up. We don't sit."

Abby never liked how comfortable Jen was with giving her orders or advice, but everyone else was standing, so she did the same.

Craig received the opening kickoff and returned it forty yards. Abby watched as he cut left and spun out of one tackle and high-stepped another. The Warhawks were on the forty-five yard line. She didn't know much about football, but she knew from the way Craig's teammates swarmed him that it was a good play. Abby smiled at the effort, and the girl who commented on her hair, Emma, she thought she heard, grabbed her shoulders from the back. "That was awesome!"

The rest of the first half was a grinder that ended in a 14-14 tie. Craig had two catches and a run, but all were short and not very exciting. Abby found herself wanting him to get a big play. She didn't know why, but she wanted everyone to cheer for him again. It made her feel good.

Coming out of the half, the Warhawks got a quick turnover and had a first down at the thirty-five. Craig lined up to the left of the formation, and when the ball was snapped, he immediately got a step on the defender and put his hand up. Sprinting down the sideline, Luke's pass hit Craig in stride, and five steps later, he was in the endzone. Touchdown! The stadium erupted. Craig spiked the ball and ran back up the field towards the sideline. He jumped around and slapped everyone high fives. When he finally stopped celebrating, Abby noticed he had a cocky swagger as he went to get water and talk with a coach.

After a three and out, Craig went to receive the punt, but it was a fair catch. The Warhawks went to work. They started to pass more, and Craig had two first downs. Both times, he got up from the ground, pointed downfield, and flipped the ball onto the ground. The second time, Abby started to get annoyed. When they scored another touchdown, Craig joined his team on the sideline, and in a soft huddle, Craig made a motion with his thumb across his throat. The gesture was met with laughter. Abby just stared at him. The rest of the game turned into a rout of the other team. Craig didn't play at all in the fourth quarter.

Abby filed out with the other girls and said goodbye before going off to find the McLeans. When she finally met up with them, they were talking to other parents. Craig's mom noticed Abby first and broke off her conversation to do introductions.

"Pam, this is Craig's girlfriend, Abby," Linda said, putting her arm around Abby's back.

Abby held out her hand. "It's nice to meet you," she said, playing along.

Pam shook her hand firmly. "It's nice to finally meet you. We're from the neighborhood. Linda told us so much about you."

Abby smiled at Linda and wondered what that conversation was like. "I'm going to wait for Craig over by the locker rooms. Do you want to wait here, or should we meet you somewhere else?"

"We can wait," Linda responded. "We can drive together then."

"Great," Abby said with sarcasm she assumed Linda didn't get. She went over and found a spot on a bench, away from the crowd that was gathering, texted Craig her location, then took in the moment. Although she was happy that Craig had played so well, she was also a bit annoyed with his antics. However, the day was beautiful, and she hoped he was up for walking back from wherever they ate downtown. She wanted to spend time alone with him away from all the fray. She just wanted her Craig back and to be there for him when he came down from the game.

Twenty minutes later, Craig came out. Abby stood up, and he took her in his arms, lifting her from the ground. "Hey, babe," he whispered and kissed her on the cheek before setting her down.

"Hi," Abby replied, smiling. "Great game, Craig."

"Thanks."

"McLean," a voice interrupted. "Nice job out there."

Craig's attention was taken from her as a small, congratulating crowd gathered around them. Everyone was recounting one play or another, and Craig was fully engaged in every exchange. Abby held tightly to his hand, then finally tugged it a bit. "We have to go meet your parents for dinner. I don't want it to take the rest of the day."

"Oh," Craig said, turning his attention back to Abby. "Yeah. We better go," he announced, and they went off to meet his parents.

Abby finally understood what Craig had been talking about for the last year as his dad rehashed every play. Craig nervously bit his lips throughout the analysis, and his gaze was distant as he sat silently, only nodding his head to register his attention. Linda talked with Abby about the resort and how much Sarah and Brad loved their stay. She added that the whole family would be coming back sometime soon and that she couldn't wait for Sarah to have kids so they could run around in the water. Abby, too, nodded and smiled, but said little. She was more interested in the pain Craig must be going through. She put her hand on his thigh. He turned to her and rolled his eyes.

Walking home, both Craig and Abby were quiet until they were off Main Street and headed into the neighborhood. Abby grabbed Craig's hand and swung it gently, slowing their gait. She smiled coyly, and he laughed. "Why are you so perfect?" Craig asked.

"Wow. That's a heavy burden." Abby stopped and sat on a rock wall, peering at Craig out of the corner of her eye.

"No, I mean it. When I need to talk, you listen. When I just need time to think, you give it to me."

"That's just being nice, Craig."

He sat down next to her and leaned in for a kiss. They sat quietly for a time until Abby said, "Your dad is a pill."

"Yes, he is," Craig said, laughing.

She rose to her feet and pulled him up for a quick hug, then they walked on towards campus. "Why do you put up with that shit?"

"I don't know. It's just better to let him get it all out than have him go over everything the whole week long. We used to have 'meetings' during the week. So now, I just let him go, and it's over."

"I guess. It's kinda shitty though."

"It is," Craig replied, defeated.

They walked farther and made it back to the campus. "Can I ask you something?" Abby said.

"Sure."

"Why do you do all that macho shit when you get a first down or the team scores?"

"What do you mean?"

Abby made the cutthroat motion and then stepped forward very dramatically, making the first down motion. It was awkward. "That shit?"

"I don't know." Craig tried to laugh it off. "I guess it just seems right for the moment."

"I don't like it. Could you, like, tone it down a little?" Abby asked, her face scrunched up.

Craig couldn't believe she was calling him out. "What?"

"I don't know. Just like, don't do it. Just hand the ball to the ref and go back to the huddle."

"But…"

"But what? It's not who you are. You're not this McLean character. You're Craig."

Craig took a step back. "Listen, Abby." His words were

sharp. "I gotta do what I gotta do to get through. McLean's my game face."

"Do you like him?"

"I need him."

"During the play maybe, but afterwards, drop the bullshit." She looked at the ground. "If you want me to keep coming, drop the bullshit." She was trying to tell him the truth.

Craig paused, then turned and started to walk away slowly. It pissed him off, but he sort of understood it. McLean wasn't who Abby had come to know. But it was who he needed to be.

"Don't walk away from me," Abby said, half-joking.

"Then follow me," Craig playfully said, trying to move on from the moment.

They walked to Craig's dorm. In his room, Craig lay down on his bed and closed his eyes. Abby went to his computer and turned on some music.

"Brent went home after the game," Craig said sleepily.

"I know," Abby replied and slid on top of him, pulling his cover over both of them.

Craig reached his hands up to pull Abby close and realized that she had no clothes on. He opened his eyes.

"Shhh," she said as she removed his shirt. "It's ok."

Craig pulled her in tight and kissed her. He tried to be slow with his movements, but he got excited.

Abby pulled down his shorts. "It's ok," she repeated, and, after a time, they slowly came together for the first time.

It was over quickly. Craig was shaking while Abby lay on top of him. "Are you ok?" he asked.

Relaxed and confident, Abby replied, "I'm fine, Craig. Don't worry."

"But we didn't…"

"I've been on the pill for over two months. It's ok."

"Oh. Ok."

"We can try again later."

"Ok."

After a while, they did try again, and it was more successful for both of them. From then on, this was how their relationship progressed. From time to time, Abby indulged Craig's desires, but, for the most part, she was in control, and he was a more than willing participant.

When they were done, Abby whispered while lying on his chest, "This is only between us, Craig. You understand? I don't want you talking with your boys. 'You're the love I've always known.'"

Knowing the exact song from Sarah Jarosz that she was quoting, he replied, "Never. Just you and me."

"I love you."

"I love you too."

Craig went to the campus post office and dropped off a letter he wrote to Abby the morning after they made love for the first time. He was still in a bit of a haze, but he wanted to gather his thoughts in a way that was more composed. He hoped Abby would go to check her mail on Monday, but if she didn't, he would hint around until she did.

Abby,

I've thought about what you said to me while we were walking back from downtown after the football game. I admit, it took me a while to get my brain back after what we did. Whatever part of my brain I can recover has taken to heart some of what you said. The ideas of who I am when I'm playing and when I'm with you are so very different, but I like them both. I love that you have helped me become the best version of myself whenever I am with you. I like the way I feel when I even think about you.

But, when I'm out on the field, I feel a different kind of focus. Everything happens so fast, but McLean can slow it down. When I'm him, I see things before they happen. I don't know how to explain it. I guess it's like a high I can't let go of that easily in the moment. I get what you're saying about being a dick, but I also really don't even know it's happening. I feel like in "game mode," I am more present than at almost any other time. The only time I am more present is when I am with you. I love you.

Craig

CHAPTER 24

Craig stroked Abby's hair as she tried to study at one of the tables next to the fireplace in the Student Union. From time to time, she stopped to look up at him and smile, then she would go back to her work. After a while, she gave him a caramel apple sucker, his favorite, to keep him from trying to talk to her. Torn, she tried again to study as he thought of something to say. She wanted to be with him again but thought to herself that last night was enough. Even so, he had tried again this morning, but she told him she needed to get work done before class. Now, seeing how much she needed to study, Craig went back to stroking her hair. There was so much going on in the Student Union this morning, some sort of high school creative writing festival. Craig wished he would have discovered writing in high school, but he loved the enthusiasm of the kids. As he was doing more and more work with high school students, he knew education was what he wanted to do. His life was coming into focus and finding its rhythm in the midst of the chaos.

Abby finished her work, then looked up a funny video she had been wanting to share with Craig. It was something Meghan had sent her. She offered Craig one of her earbuds, and they disappeared into their own world. For a time, all distractions ceased to exist. The smell of hotdogs being sold for some club's fundraiser, other students scurrying from one class to another, and even the din of the high school students raving about this or that workshop all faded away. When the video was done, they packed up and walked outside. Craig embraced Abby as she kissed him gently on the lips. They turned to walk off in opposite directions, and Abby looked back while Craig sauntered slowly with his bow-legged gait. Abby giggled to herself, but kept watching him until he was around the corner.

In the middle of a week in late September, Shane went to visit Claire. Despite his protests, she insisted he stay with her and her roommate, who had no problem with the arrangement. Instead of going out, they decided to go to a local market and compete to prepare each other their best dish. They gave themselves ninety minutes and had to share a space, so the competition was both fierce and intimate.

When they finally sat down, Shane had prepared a habanero salmon with garlic green beans, while Claire made a fillet with mixed greens complemented with blue cheese and roasted almond slivers. Shane started, "Well, I think you certainly won on presentation, but after the first bite, I think the winner will be clear." He smirked and stared her down. "That is, if you can handle the flavor."

Claire shook her head. "If it's too hot for me, you lose. You should know your audience and tailor your dish accordingly."

"Not a lot of heat with this one, but since when did a true artist compromise his vision for an audience? Just take a bite."

Claire cut her fish carefully, got a little sauce and a bean on the fork, and put it in her mouth. There was an explosion of flavor. It seemed every taste bud was engaged at the same time. Involuntarily, she shuddered.

"That bad?" Shane asked, still chewing his first bite. "Yours is pretty good. I like what you did with your sauce. Sweet, but with a little kick. And the steak is cooked perfectly. I can almost cut it with my fork."

Claire recovered her senses. "This is so good. I'm going to have to cut it into smaller pieces just so I can enjoy it longer."

They ate their plates in relative silence and then cleaned up, deciding that the competition was a draw. Afterwards, they went to sit out on the small balcony that looked out over the downtown area. Claire felt a calmness in just having Shane there.

"I just love the city," he marveled. "It's so alive."

Claire laughed.

"What? I'm trying to share a moment here," Shane said, trying to be funny.

"But it's so cliché." Mockingly, she repeated, "'It's so alive.' That's such bullshit. It's loud, that's what it is. I haven't been able to sleep since I got back."

"Why?"

"All the noise. I can't even close my window to stop it. It's all the cars humming and honking. And there's too many people. I feel like I might need one of those sleep machines with the nature sounds and all."

"Really? I thought you couldn't wait to get back."

"Yeah. I don't know what's wrong with me. I was so looking forward to being back here, and all I find myself doing is thinking about being up north again. I've already done a project with a lot of the pictures. I feel like all grad school is going to be is an exploration of why I don't want to be here anymore. Time is different here. Too fast. I want to get back to a place where I can feel still."

Shane seemed to be lost in the Chicago skyline. His face suddenly became serious. "I get you. I feel like I'm being pulled back there as well. I mean, it's cool and all not being there for a few days, but I almost feel obligated to get back there."

"What? No more travel?"

"Oh no. I'm going to travel, but not for a while. Frank's been talking to me a lot. He's been encouraging me to live up to my legacy. I didn't know I had one until a few weeks ago. Did you know he went to all my football games?"

"I heard. You were like his son before you left. The man is loyal to those he cares about. And you do have a legacy. It's tied to Wood Lake."

"Yeah, I guess. I wish I knew my grandfather. Seems like he was a remarkable guy."

Claire leaned into Shane's shoulder, and he put his arm around her. "If he was anything like Frank, I bet he was pretty special."

"He even reintroduced me to Rick. You know, the guy I stole the money from. His son runs the place. Frank wants me to make amends. Not sure how."

"Couldn't you do some art for the place?"

"You know, that's a good idea. I could make signs like the ones I did for the resort."

"Good idea." Claire paused for several moments. "Hey, do you want to go on a trip after Christmas?"

Turning his head to catch Claire's eyes, Shane replied, "Sure. Where'd you have in mind?"

"I was thinking New York."

"Kinda pricey, don't you think?"

"Mike and Linda will pay for it," she said, chuckling. "I'll tell them I need to go for a school thing. They'll never know. Have you ever been?"

"Surprisingly, no. But they have some great museums, and we could try to get tickets to a show."

"Let me plan it out," Claire said. "I think I can find a way to get it all done. We just need to get through Christmas and the first week of January up north."

"Wait, you're coming?"

"I was planning on it. Frank could use the help. And, I heard it's beautiful at Wood Lake in the winter. Know anyone I can stay with?"

Shane smiled. "I think I might know someone who has a room."

After reading Craig's letter, Abby took the week to respond. She was trying to strike the right tone. Football and competition were so new to her, but getting a "game face" on was not. It was just like running the big celebrations at the resort. Sometimes, you needed to step outside of yourself to get it done. For her, it was getting easier. She realized Craig was really doing the same thing.

Craig found the letter sitting by his computer one morning after Abby left for her early class.

Craig,

I'm sorry I snapped at you about your "game face." I guess it just shocked me to see you in a different context. I know football runs deep with you, but you know I don't fully understand. Like I said, maybe I don't need to understand. I just have to be ok with whatever and be proud of your success. I will work on that.

As to taking our relationship to the next level, I've dreamed of it since shortly after we started dating last year. I love that you took it slow with me. You made me wait, and that makes it mean so much more. The way you are with me makes me feel special. I know you love me because you show me whenever we're together. Thank you for loving me in that way. You are the person I hoped to meet someday, but now that I have you, I almost can't believe it. I love you too.

P.S I'm going to see Claire next weekend. I know it's the bye week, but maybe you should hang with the boys a bit.

Abby

CHAPTER 25

Abby didn't quite know what to expect as she pulled Craig's car into the visitor space of Claire's apartment complex. Even though traffic was still terrible, she had followed the directions closely and encountered no real problems. She could not understand why anyone would want to live in a place like Chicago. Claire's apartment was near the top floor with nice views of downtown and the lake. Abby had seen pictures, but she was excited to see it in person. When she got to the door, she knocked loudly.

"Abby!" Claire yelled as she opened the door, then hugged her tightly.

Smiling wide and disengaging from the hug, Abby responded, "Claire! Wow! So good to see you." She scanned the room. New furniture, bright colors, and an incredible view, which drew her to the window. The place must have cost a fortune. "This is so nice."

From the other side of the room, Claire called, "Thanks. It works."

Abby laughed. "It's not Wood Lake, but it's ok."

Walking over to Abby and looking out the window, Claire said, "So, how are you? How's school?"

"It's great. Nice to have a different rhythm and get a little privacy." As soon as she said it, Abby could feel herself going flush.

"I get it. I had such a great time up north, but it's time to get back to it, I guess."

"You'll be heading up soon, right? My mom said something about it."

"Oh, yeah. Shane and I talked about me being up there for a few weekends. I've got Fridays off from class, so I can get up there pretty easily."

"Great." Abby milled around the room, waiting for Claire to make the next move. She mentioned she had the day planned out, so Abby was excited, but she had no idea what they would be doing.

After letting Abby soak in the sights of the city, Claire said, "So, I've got some fun things planned. We could go downtown and walk around for a bit. Go to the art museum and maybe the Shedd Aquarium, get some coffee and a bite to eat and hang out down at the lake?"

"That all sounds great. We're not going to drive, are we?"

Claire chuckled. "No, silly. We can take an Uber. There's literally no place to park."

"Ok." This was all going to be new for Abby, but she was open to it. New experiences and new possibilities. That was her goal for the next year. A day with Claire was the best way to start.

After getting a tour of the Art Institute of Chicago, where Claire played the role of guide, it was off to Grant Park and the Shedd Aquarium. Where, at the museum, Claire could tell Abby the history and the use of light and medium, texture and style of every piece of art they encountered, fish were Abby's thing. She was fascinated by the varieties and colors. Everything was so vibrant, and it pulled her in, exhibit after exhibit. After trying to move Abby along, and failing, Claire finally said she was hungry and Abby realized she, too, could eat some food.

They found a hot dog vendor, and Claire insisted that Abby try an authentic street cart Chicago dog. When they got their food, they went to the lakeshore to eat. Stretched out before Abby was an endless plain of possibility. In the middle of the sounds of the city, there was an oasis of peace and hope. She was beginning to see these things now. She was taking the time to appreciate the moments and let them wash over her like the waves on the shore. She could hear the rhythm.

Claire simply let Abby be for a few minutes. She admired the smile on her face and the life in her eyes as she surveyed everything around them.

"I really like it here," Abby said, finally resting her gaze on Claire.

"Yeah. It's nice, isn't it? I like to come here and sketch. There are always so many faces."

"I would guess. I mean the lake. It's just so big. I've seen the lake before, but I've never really looked at it."

"Yeah. It's remarkable. Look at that guy over there with the red hat."

Abby followed Claire's eyes to see a guy with an old coat feeding the birds. He was smiling, seemingly having his own conversation with his feathered friends.

"I could stay here all day and just watch people. There is almost always something new to see." Claire took a breath. "So, how are you doing with Craig playing football?"

Abby thought for a moment. "I'm getting used to it. I still

don't like it that much. I guess I don't like that he lied to me about it all summer." She faked a smile. "He's really good. It's exciting to see him in that moment. I guess I should be proud of him. I tell him I am, but I don't always believe what I am saying."

"He is good. I remember that from high school. Sometimes, you have to fake it a bit for the people you love."

"Yeah. It's cool though, when everyone cheers for him. I like that. And I can tell it brings him up. It's hard to explain."

"I totally get it. I know that moment for him. Of course, it was always coupled with my dad yelling something absurd, but I remember."

"So, yeah. I just want to see him do well."

Claire put her hand on Abby's shoulder and squeezed it before getting up. "You know you can tell Craig the truth. He's a big boy."

Abby looked up. "Yeah. I know. It's just different. I don't want to disappoint him."

Claire nodded. "Let's get going."

"Ok." Abby stood up and took a deep breath as she looked out over Lake Michigan.

They walked around for a while, then went back to Claire's apartment with takeout they had picked up on the way. Sitting on the couch in front of the TV, Abby asked about how things were with Shane and how grad school was going.

"I don't know about school. I'll finish, but I just want to get started with life. I'm done learning things in books. Shane wants to travel more, and he agreed to take me along. I want to see things."

Abby watched Claire intently. She was animated and alive, and her arms were moving with each word. It was as though she was a tour guide for her own life, or what she hoped it could be. When she finished talking about the trip to New York she was planning for after New Year's, she came back down to earth, saying, "I really miss Wood Lake. Does that sound weird? I mean, I wasn't even there for three months."

"It's not weird at all. I miss it every day. Even when I am having the best day, like today, I miss it."

"I know. I miss the silence. I miss joking around with Frank. I don't know if I could build a life around being up there, but I'd like to give it a try."

Abby reached out to give Claire a hug. "If you want to, we can build a life up there. I know I'm ready."

"I know you are."

They gathered pillows from the other furniture, turned on *Lady Bird* on Netflix, and ate their takeout. The movie was about moving on to new places, which touched Abby in the moment, and it was artsy, so Claire liked it too. It was just the day Abby needed to break up the routine.

With Abby in Chicago visiting Claire for the weekend, Craig decided that since it was a bye week, he would cave to the pressure and go to a party where many of his teammates would be. He had lamented to Abby that some of the guys were giving him shit about not hanging out with them. Together, they thought if he went to just one party, it might appease the more militant members.

The evening was still quite warm for a fall night, and Craig could get away with a long-sleeve shirt and shorts. However, reports from up north had temps in the 30s already, with the leaves at peak color. Whitewater was still at least two weeks from peak. Craig observed the trees as he walked the nearly abandoned streets towards the house party several blocks from campus. He could now name them, oak and maple, and recognize that the pine and birch of the northern forests had given way the further south he lived. Running his fingers across the bark of one tree, he caught a grip on one of the ridges. The feeling made him pause to ponder what he was going into. He could not escape the feeling that he was about to jump over a fence into enemy territory. Even though he knew these guys, many of them since childhood, he had a feeling that he was an intruder in their world.

The sounds of the party could be heard before he got to the house. 'It's amazing these things don't get busted,' Craig thought to himself. But in reality, it was better to have students walking a few blocks than driving out to a bar in the boonies and getting too drunk to drive home.

When he went into the house, he was met with a chorus of "McLean!" and slaps on the back. He shook them off and shuffled down into the basement where someone immediately offered him a beer, which he declined. Taking a seat on a couch, he took in the room. Rap music beat constantly, creating a din that stifled Craig as he checked the room for his teammates. He wanted to be sure he was seen. The house was rented by a few guys who weren't even on the team and who Craig was pretty sure were in their sixth or seventh years of school. But, there were girls. Lots of girls. That was really the point of the parties. Everyone could meet someone and hook up. Craig was over it as soon as he sat down.

This was totally his scene a few years back, one where he could master the room. He and Jen were the center of attention. Now, he hoped that, other than registering his attendance, everyone would leave him alone. The longer he sat, the more it felt like the walls were closing in around him. He caught glimpses of friends, but he found it hard to focus. The whole scene was almost dizzying until Jen sat down next to him. She put her hand on his knee and said, "Hey Craig, you ok?"

He blinked several times in an attempt to snap out of his daze. "Hey. No. I'm great," he mumbled out unconvincingly.

"You seem a bit out of it."

"No. Just tired." 'Play the role,' Craig repeated in his mind.

"You look like it. You guys do have a busy schedule in the fall."

"Yeah. It's a bit much."

"Luke's only taking twelve credits. You?"

"Fifteen. Eighteen in the spring."

"Wow. Education, right?"

"Yep. And English."

"That's great."

Finally turning from the room to face her, Craig asked, "So, how are you, Jen?"

She smiled, but not as brightly as Craig was used to seeing. "I'm good. Got in some marketing classes this semester and knocking out the Gen Eds."

"Nice."

"Where's Abby?"

"She's spending the weekend in Chicago, with Claire."

"Oh. That's nice. They're friends? How'd that come about?"

"Claire spent the summer up north at the resort. She was the Artist-in-Residence. I was up there too."

"Oh, that must have been fun."

"It was. Completely different way of life."

Jen peered out on the room and asked, in a distant voice, "Really? How so?"

Craig could tell she was losing interest, which was typical Jen, so he spoke louder to get her attention. "There's so much to do, but at the same time, it's a really relaxed place. Everything is about service. I mean, where we grew up was all about what we had. Up there, it's about what we can do for others. It's cool."

"I'll take your word for it." Jen shifted to look back at Craig. "So, you and Abby are good?"

"Yes. We're great. She centers me, you know?" He felt the awkwardness of the statement almost as soon as it came out of his mouth.

Jen looked at Craig sideways. "I'm not sure what that means, Craig." She stood up, still looking confused. Playfully tugging at his beard, she said, "But I'm happy for you. It's time for a shave, don't you think?"

Craig ran his hand over his face. The room came crashing in on him once again, and he felt even more out of place than before. No one here could understand him. Without thinking, Craig got up to go. On the way up the stairs, Luke bumped into him. "Hey, Craig. Where are you going?"

"I just need some air," he responded by rote.

Outside, Craig sat glued to the front steps. Moving forward, towards campus, was not an option. He couldn't make sense of it. The party was a place he should have felt comfortable, but for some reason, he didn't. It was too loud, too crowded, and held no meaning. There was no responsibility and no sense of service, other than self-service. Just as he was working up the courage to head home, Brent came down the block with his girlfriend. "Hey, Craig," he said. His girlfriend tugged at his arm. "Yeah. I'll meet you inside."

"Ok," she said, letting go and heading for the door.

"Dude, what's up? Why are you out here?"

"I don't know. I just can't." Craig stood up.

"What?"

"I can't do it, man. It's not my scene."

"Come on. It's just the boys."

"That's not it."

"What is it then?"

"I think it's me. I'm just not that guy."

"Are you too good for us now?"

Craig started to walk down the block, and Brent followed. "That's not it at all. It's just different. I feel like I've changed. Don't get me wrong, I love playing. Practice is awesome, and the focus is just what I need. It's just that, when it's over, I need something else." They walked on further, then Craig stopped. "Wait, don't you need to get to the party?"

"No, I'll walk you home. Katie won't even know I'm gone."

"Ok. Thanks."

They walked a few more blocks before Brent started in, "How do you think you've changed? You seem like the same old Craig to me."

"I don't feel like it. There's just so much."

"What are you talking about?"

"You know, in high school, how you just jumped from

assignment to assignment, getting it done but not thinking about it?"

"Yeah. I do that now, for the most part."

"Well, now, I can't do that anymore. I'm always being asked to think about stuff. It's cool, but it's a lot."

"What do you mean?"

Craig kicked at a crack in the sidewalk. "Have you ever thought about why we're here or who we really are?"

Brent laughed. "No. Not really."

"Really? Like isolation. I mean, if we're here, are we really ever with someone or are we always totally alone?"

"You're not alone, Craig. I mean, you might feel out of place at practice or at a party or whatever, but you're never alone."

"It doesn't always feel that way."

"You have Abby, dude. Even when you're not together, she's with you."

Craig stopped walking. They had reached the edge of campus.

Brent continued, "I'm right, dude. She's why you're here. You're not alone."

Craig looked a Brent for a few seconds, then looked at the ground. "Thanks, man."

They parted ways, Craig back to the dorm and Brent to the party. Craig was left to wonder what Abby's day was like in Chicago. Sunday was their day off from football practice. He hoped she would be back early enough for them to go for a walk or out for a picnic or something. He knew he was not alone, but the feeling of being part of something different, something apart from it all, still crept into his mind and set up camp.

CHAPTER 26

"Hey, Craig," Robert, one of the offensive linemen, said as he stood over Craig in the locker room, flanked by a few other linemen. "What's up with you and that girl?"

"What do you mean?" Craig replied from the bench, looking up and trying not to sound annoyed.

Robert moved in closer. "I mean you're always with her. Outside of practice, you never hang out with anyone from the team."

It was like this guy was speaking on behalf of the team. "So? Who cares?" Craig got up and stood face-to-face with the lineman, almost bumping his chest.

As though he was finishing his previous thought and didn't hear Craig at all, Robert continued, "You never eat with us, you left the party early the other night. Heck, you barely even notice when we walk by if you're with her. What gives?"

Craig shook his head and sat back down to put on his socks and shoes. "She's perfect," he said, not looking up.

"Perfect? What do you mean?" A small crowd had gathered by now, and Craig could tell that this was something they had been talking about. He and Abby had become locker-room talk.

"Like I said, she's perfect." Craig got up to gather his bag and clothes from his locker, then turned to face the group.

"She's my equal in every way. She challenges me. She doesn't put up with my bullshit. She is my partner in all of this, and I'm hers." Slinging his backpack over his shoulder, he continued, "Every day with her is better than any day without her. It's that simple. I hope you can find someone who makes you feel like that someday. It's pretty cool." With that, he walked out.

When Craig got up to Abby's room, he asked, "Is Kate around?"

"No, she's at church. She said she'd be back around six. Why?"

Without speaking, Craig kissed Abby hard. They made love without saying a word. For the first time, Craig took the lead.

When they were done, Abby was in a daze. "Wow. What was that about?"

"I love you. That's what that was about. Don't forget it."

"Don't worry, Craig. I won't. I love you too."

"Good. We should probably get moving before Kate gets back."

They got dressed and walked over to the Union for dinner before going to the library to study. If you asked either one of them, they would have said they were the only ones on campus. Every other person simply faded from view. They had found a place all their own, and nothing was going to break it.

A few days later, Craig's new view of the world was challenged in class. He had found that his European Lit class, although being discussion-based and quite fun, included ideas and topics that were meant to shake the core of what it meant to be human. There were only a few teachers at Arrowhead who got into the philosophical ideas of the literature they read, but Craig had never really listened. However, for this class, he had to take note of the discussions because he was meant to reference the comments of others. Today's discussion was about Albert Camus, specifically *The Stranger*. They were to demonstrate their understanding of the concepts of absurdism and existentialism. After reading a few passages, the opening challenge of the teacher was to state whether one could find any meaning in life or if it was a waste of time because finding meaning was essentially impossible. Meaning for one person could be something totally different for another. The pursuit of truth and meaning is therefore absurd and useless. After several comments that parroted either the teacher or the text, Craig decided to chime in. "So, what are we doing here then?"

The blank stares Craig got when he made any statement earlier in the semester had made him shy away from speaking up. He assumed that most of his classmates thought he was some dumb jock who didn't have anything worthwhile to offer, but he knew he did this time.

"What do you mean?" the teacher inquired.

"Well, isn't the search for meaning that ends up in the absurd still a search?" There were a few snickers.

"Silence. Let Craig explore this."

Craig took his cue. "I mean, to believe in nothing is to believe in something. Therefore, the belief in nothing is impossible. This is the same, I think."

"Continue," the professor said. A few people leaned in.

"So, if the search for meaning is ultimately absurd, the

conclusion of the search that leads to this idea is also absurd. Thus, thinking that meaning, or at least the search for meaning, is absurd is, in and of itself, absurd."

"But have you found anything meaningful?" the professor asked.

"I don't know."

"You are already down the rabbit hole, Craig. You can't crap out with an 'I don't know.'"

"Ok. Love. Love has meaning."

The snickers returned.

"Continue," the professor said, forcefully looking around the room.

Craig was trying to be present. 'React, don't think,' he thought to himself. "Love is why I get up in the morning. It is why I do almost anything and everything I do. Love is why I'm having this discussion."

"What do you mean?" The professor closed his book and took a seat. He stared at Craig.

"I don't want to believe that there is no meaning and the whole search is absurd. But at the same time, I'm not searching anymore. I've found my meaning, and I live for it every day."

"Football," someone muttered sarcastically.

"Don't be ridiculous," Craig said, turning from the professor to his classmates. "Laugh if you want, but it's not football. I am in love, and she sustains me. She's all that I need to sustain me. She is my meaning. She is my purpose." Craig stared at the guy who had laughed at him until the guy looked down.

Silence fell over the room for a moment, and then the professor concluded by saying, "Well then, she's a lucky girl. That's all for today."

Immediately after class, Craig went outside and sat on the grass under a tree near the Union. He was shaking. It was not from the fact that he had said anything he didn't believe, but because he had revealed so much of who he was, and it hit him at his core.

Abby found him staring into space. "Are you ok, Craig?"

"Yes," he said, looking up at her without blinking. Everything around faded away. "You are my purpose. You know that right?"

"I know." She smiled and reached to help him up. She hugged him right there in the middle of the green. "Thank you."

The following week, Abby had a presentation about her marketing plan for the resort. She had worked through the weekend and was thankful for the away game to get the time back.

Craig had looked it over when he returned and assured her that she would be fine. "You are probably the only one with an actual project that means anything. The rest are just theoretical."

"I know, but I almost feel like I'm rolling it out to my dad. There's actually something riding on this!"

"Right now, it's just a grade. You have a chance to fix it before you roll it out for real."

"I know, I know." Abby got up from her chair. "Do I look ok?" She had on slacks and a white blouse.

"You look great." Craig smiled. "Go get 'em."

"Thanks, babe. I'll catch up with you tonight." Abby gave Craig a quick kiss.

It was humorous for Craig to see Abby, who had been so confident all summer, falling out of sorts. "Text me how it goes."

"Got it."

She was off, and Craig watched as he always did. She had a nervous, almost scampering gait, not her usual sway.

Abby performed brilliantly. As nervous as she was, she hit all her points and was able to answer questions and even elicited a positive review from the professor, who directed the others in the class to follow her lead. Conversation on the way out of class included a few girls asking if she really lived at the resort. Abby's affirmative answer was met with "That's so cool" and "Wow. That would be really awesome."

Abby looked down the hall, desperately wanting to talk with Craig, but knew he was in class and then had practice. Instead, she went back to her dorm to change out of her dress clothes and hopefully see Kate.

"How'd the presentation go?" Kate asked right as Abby entered the room.

"It was great."

"Really? That's awesome!"

"Thanks. I was really nervous."

"You're fine, Abby. Come on. Have confidence."

"It's weird, you know?"

"No, what?"

"I have so much confidence in some parts of my life, but not others."

"That's not weird. It's normal. You are always confident with Craig."

Abby blushed and laughed quietly to herself, thinking about the last time he was in this room.

"See," Kate said. "You guys are so good together."

"We are. We really are."

Kate smiled and shook her head. "So, take that confidence out to the world. You won't put up with his bullshit, so don't put up with the world's."

Abby thought about that idea for a moment. She was lucky to have so many great people in her life to support her. "You know, you're right."

"Soooo, what is up with you and Craig?"

"What do you mean?"

"You're over there all the time? But then, sometimes you're here at lunch? Should we get a code on the door?"

Abby looked at the floor and kicked a shirt around.

"You guys are sleeping together, aren't you?"

Abby scrunched up her face and didn't answer. She had told Craig it was their secret.

"I knew it."

"We were trying to just keep it to ourselves."

"Well, who else would it be between?"

"Please. I don't want to talk about it. I'm really happy right now."

"Good. I'm happy for you."

"Thanks, Kate."

A week later, Abby got word that her parents and Frank would be coming to see Craig's next game at home. Her dad had something to do in Madison, and her mom just wanted a weekend away. They were going to close down the resort, but Shane and Janie said they would cover, and there were only a handful of guests staying in the lake cabins anyway. Claire would also be up north for the weekend. She mentioned to Abby that she missed the place too much and needed a break from the city.

Abby told Craig, who was stunned at the news. "Wow. Pressure. They're leaving for a weekend in October?" he said.

"Well, they said it was fine. We did have a good summer."

"I suppose. Just seems weird. Frank's coming too?"

"Yeah. That will be fun. He knows football."

"Well, I'll be sure to tell my parents. Maybe they can sit together."

"That would be great. I won't have to sit with the girls then."

"It's not that bad, is it?"

"No. Not that bad. It's actually been kinda fun. I'm just not like those girls."

Craig wrapped his arm around Abby. "No, you're not, and that's why I love you. Frank's coming, huh?" he repeated with a big sigh.

"Supposedly. Don't be nervous."

"Ok."

CHAPTER 27

After a fairly routine week with another win for the Warhawks, Craig began preparing for homecoming. It was the third week of October, and they were having a good season. Craig was now integrated into the team, and his efforts were being noticed not only by the coaching staff, but, more importantly, by his teammates. He was still excited about playing, and per Abby's request, he was acting a little more like he had been there before. Gone were the antics of the first few games. Actually, he was playing better and wasn't nearly as tired when he went in and out. His focus was calmer than when he rode the high of "McLean" all the time. He was able to come to the sideline and focus on the comments of his coaches and teammates.

Whenever he got off the bus from an away game and saw Abby waiting, the world disappeared. No one really gave him any crap again about his focus on her. When they were together, in any context, it was only them. His studies continued to be easy in the most academic of senses, but the new thoughts and ideas he was having excited his mind. He was reevaluating the way he viewed the world. Gone were the narrow, upper-class, suburban assumptions of the world. Craig was being forced to defend positions he had never thought through. It was invigorating.

Abby, too, ran through her life in bliss. Nothing was out of place, and she often caught herself thinking it was all a dream. She was growing in confidence. Craig was great. Her future was bright. Even the other players' girlfriends were people she began to appreciate. 'You do you,' a favorite quote of Claire's, was the phrase she reminded herself of often. Gone were her judgments of these girls and Craig's teammates. Everyone was just trying to do the best they could, and if they were nice and kind, then who cares what they wanted from life. Abby knew who she was and who she wanted to become. The visions of doom that consumed her freshman year and the past summer were pushed back. In their place was a new day. She couldn't wait to wake up to each morning to a future where her dreams could actually come true.

Abby met her parents and Frank outside the stadium before game time. Mike and Linda were going to meet them in the stadium later.

"I'm glad this is an eleven o'clock game," Frank said.

"Me too," John replied.

The exchange struck Abby as a bit weird, but she was already on to giving directions.

"We have to meet the McLeans inside. They are saving us seats, so let's get going."

"Great," her mother said. "I'm looking forward to seeing Linda again."

Abby looked at her sideways and shook her head. They made their way inside the stadium.

The seating arrangements went two by two: Vickie and

Linda, Mike and John, Frank and Abby. This made Abby happy. She was excited to share the game with Frank. She was also happy to be sitting far away from her mother and Linda.

"I haven't been to a football game in years. I can't remember..." Frank trailed off.

"It'll be cool. Craig is really good." Abby could barely contain her excitement.

"So I've heard. John keeps me filled in."

"He does?" Abby looked down at her dad, who flashed a thumbs-up. "What are they even talking about down there?" she asked Frank.

"Your dad had some insurance questions."

"Don't we always deal with Randy?"

"Yeah. Some things have changed."

"What?" Just as Abby spoke, the players began to take the field. The stadium stood up and cheered, and they got ready for the introductions, but Frank was locked in, looking for Craig.

"Is that him?" he said, pointing.

"Yeah, 82. That's him," Abby said.

"Ok. I see him. Will he take the kickoff?" He looked at Abby.

"I assume. He has been."

As Frank turned back to the game, Abby tried listening in on the conversation next to her.

"We just enjoyed our time up there so much. Sarah did too," Linda said.

"Thank you. We were happy to have you. Say, why don't you guys come up for Thanksgiving or Christmas?"

"That would be great."

"We'll reserve a place for you."

Linda nodded. "We don't need a cabin or anything."

"We'll work it out," Vickie said.

Craig slapped his hands together just as the ball was kicked. The kickoff was up, and he had dropped back. He caught the ball at the five yard line and broke left. The wall began to develop, and he accelerated down the sideline. At the forty, Craig cut into the middle, and the rest of the field was open. His hips came under, and his knees raised up. Abby's whole body began to tingle as she rose to her tiptoes. When Craig crossed the goal line, he pumped his fist and raised the ball above his head. He waited for a ref to catch up and handed him the ball. As he jogged back to the sideline, mobbed by his teammates, he looked up to find Abby. It seemed as though he saw her because he nodded, pointing his head. "I'll keep my head in the moment today," Craig had said this morning before he left. It seemed to be working.

"That was awesome," Frank said.

Abby just sat down and smiled. The din of the crowd silenced in her head, and she felt as though it was just her and Craig in the stadium.

The defense took over, and the crowd sat down, except for the student section which never sat. Sitting with her parents was a welcome break. Abby tried to reengage Frank.

"So, how was Madison?"

"Good," Frank replied. "We had some business to get done."

Abby tried to catch his eye, but after waiting a moment, she asked, "Did you get it all done?"

Frank continued to look out in the field. "Almost. Just a few more signatures."

"Really? Who else would need to sign things?"

"You."

Abby shifted in her seat and faced Frank. "What? Why me?"

Frank grabbed Abby's hand and turned to look at her. "Because the forms pertain to you."

"What are you getting at?"

With a bit more concern in his voice, Frank said, "Abby. I need to tell you some things."

The Warhawks finally drew a punt and took over on offense. Abby could barely focus on Craig. He had a first down catch, and the ball started to move quickly down the field. They scored. Again, Abby felt excited in a way she could not fully understand. There was pride in seeing the man she loved doing his thing. Frank just shook his head. "He really is good."

"He is," Abby started in, but then changed the subject back to the matter at hand. "What's going on?"

"So, here's the deal. When I sold the resort to your dad, after the debt was paid, I put the rest in a trust."

"Ok."

"Also, as you know, we have enough land for five to seven lakefront properties beyond my cabin and in the woods back to the road."

"Yes."

"I owned all that."

"You owned? Did you sell it?" Abby felt her heart beating in her neck.

"I placed the land in the trust."

Abby thought, 'Trust, trust, what's a trust?' The vision of walking through the woods with Craig and discussing the land beyond Frank's cabin came into her head. She managed to mutter, "Ok."

Confidently, Frank continued, "I'm signing the trust over to you."

"What?"

"I'm signing the trust over to you. You can access it when you graduate."

"But…" She could barely breathe.

"With the land and money, it's maybe $600,000."

Abby sat silently. 'Six hundred thousand dollars.' What would she do with that kind of money? She couldn't find the words to respond.

"Now, I'm setting some aside for Taylor, but you are going to have enough to get started with the resort when you take over."

"But what about you?" By this time, the tears had begun to flow.

"Don't worry about me, Abby. I have more than enough. I'm good."

Abby sat in stunned silence. She leaned on Frank's shoulder as he put his arm around her. With a little squeeze, he said, "I love you, and your sister. I've always said you were like our children, and I meant it. I've always wanted to take care of you, and now I can."

"But, why now?"

"I'm going to take some time off."

Abby lifted her head. "What?"

"Rita and I always wanted to go to a few places, so I'm going to see the places we planned on seeing. That way I can tell her about them when I see her again."

Tears now streamed down Abby's face. "Who's taking the kitchen?"

"Shane. He's great. That kid is something."

"Shane?"

"Yep. He's been talking to Claire, and I guess she told him to pull his head out of his ass. I love that girl."

Abby nodded. "I love her too."

Nothing more was said. Craig continued to play well. He had three more catches and a couple of runs. It was actually a great game. Abby couldn't wait to get out to talk with him. Her whole life was coming together.

When they finally got out of the stadium, Abby and Frank went to the parking lot to sign the paperwork while everyone else waited for Craig. As they made their way over to the locker room area to wait for Craig with the rest of the family, Abby held Frank's hand, just as she had done as a kid when he showed her the lake and the forest.

They only had to wait a few more minutes, and Abby took the lead in embracing Craig.

"You know," John said. "That was a great game, Craig." He shook Craig's hand firmly.

"It was," Frank added, hugging Craig tightly. "Awesome."

The crowd that had gathered around the entrance to the locker room to greet the players began to dissipate.

John announced, "Mike, Linda, you have a great kid here. Craig, you are more than welcome to come work up by us next summer. You and Claire both. You both were great."

"Thank you, sir." Craig smiled. He was still pretty hyped

from the game and was looking forward to a little quiet time to decompress.

Frank walked over to Abby and whispered, "I'll be home for Thanksgiving and Christmas."

"Ok." It was all she could get out.

People said their goodbyes. No post-game debrief dinner today. Once they were alone, Craig took Abby's hand. "You ok?"

Taking a labored breath, Abby replied, "I guess. I have so much to tell you."

"Really?"

"Yes."

"It's a pretty nice day. You want to go to the bench?"

"Yes." She smiled. "You always seem to know what I need."

"That's cause I love you, Abby." He looked at her with a sense of confidence that felt as though they had reached a new level of intimacy. One that needed no explanation.

"You're the best," she said.

Sarcastically, Craig replied, "I know."

Abby laughed. "You don't know anything, McLean." She grabbed his hand, leading him up the path, almost skipping. "But you will."

Abby realized in that moment that the world was full of secrets, and those secrets would reveal their answers randomly. Yet, even in the midst of all the randomness that surrounded her, a rhythm could be found. The rhythm was made up of the routines and habits with which she lived her days. The routines of her study, the discipline she employed to structure her life, and, of course, the habits of love she shared with Craig. They all resonated within her at once. The habits were how she recharged, to not only face the randomness of the world, but also to harness its beauty. It was the beginning of a life well lived.

Benjamin R. Nysse is foremost a husband and father. When he is not teaching English and Creative Writing at Hamilton High School in Sussex, Wisconsin, he can be found on the sidelines of a track or cross country meet, at a soccer game, or sitting in the audience at a concert or play. This is his second novel.